MW00414984

If Loving You Is Wrong

Book Two of the Forever and Ever Series

E. L. Todd

This is a work of fiction. All the characters and events portrayed in this novel are fictitious or used fictitiously. All rights reserved. No part of this book may be reproduced in any form or by any electronic or mechanical means, including information storage and retrieval systems, without written permission from the publisher or author, except in the case of a reviewer, who may quote brief passages in a review.

Copyright © 2014 by E. L. Todd
All Rights Reserved
ISBN-13: 978-1505445770
ISBN-10: 1505445779

"The course of true love never did run smooth."

William Shakespeare

Chapter One

Cayson

The sun rose and distant rays of light flickered through the curtains. The warmth was appreciated. Snow covered the ground and the earth wouldn't thaw until spring. The joy from the holidays still lingered, but I couldn't care less about it. I already had everything I wanted.

Skye was still asleep. Her lips were relaxed, and the freckle in the corner of her mouth caught my attention, like it usually did. She wore one of my t-shirts and my boxers. We were cuddled under the blanket, keeping warm against the winter chill outside.

I stared at her face, unable to look away. I'd been getting less sleep since we got together. Instead of drifting off, I preferred to stay awake and enjoy every second of her. She was mine—finally. It was hard not to appreciate her, to soak her up every minute we were together.

My hand moved around her waist, feeling her petite frame. She was small in comparison, dwarfed by my large size. It took me a moment to understand this was real, that she was really by my side. We stayed up late talking about nothing in particular. And now I was still here—but not as her friend.

I brushed a loose strand of hair from her face, feeling its softness. Everything about her was perfect. Her thin legs touched mine under the blankets. I was only in my boxers, and I liked feeling our skin touch.

It was hard not to press my lips to hers. I wanted her to wake up, to stare into those beautiful eyes I adored. But I held back, letting her enjoy her slumber. Another hour passed before her eyes fluttered open.

She took a deep breath and released it as a sigh. Her eyes took a moment before they focused on my face. Then a grin spread on her lips, making my heart melt. "Morning." Her voice was hoarse and cracked.

"Morning." I took a deep breath, feeling the happiness flood my body.

Her hand moved to my chin, feeling the thick stubble that formed over the week. I'd been staying at her place every night so I forgot to shave. "You're hairy." The smirk was still on her face.

"Do you want me to shave?" My hand moved slightly up her shirt, feeling the skin of her ribs.

"I'm not sure...I like it."

"You like hairy men?" I teased.

"No. But I like you." She moved the back of her hand along my chin, feeling the resistance.

"I'll leave it then."

"Just don't let it grow into a beard. I don't like those." She cringed slightly.

"Maybe I will anyway."

"Fine. Then I won't shave my legs," she threatened.

It was my turn to cringe. "I win."

She smirked. "I always win."

My fingers trailed along her ribs. "Because I let you."

Fondness shined in her eyes. "I guess chivalry isn't dead after all."

"Not for you, no." I cupped her face then leaned in, the excitement coursing through my veins. Every time I leaned in to kiss her, my heart wanted to give out. My lips longed for hers, needing a taste. I pressed my mouth to hers and gave her a gentle embrace. Her lips were slightly dry from the night before but she still tasted delicious. When I pulled away, I looked at her face.

She had a dreamy look in her eyes, like she was light-headed and confused. "You're a really good kisser..."

I grinned. "No. I think you make me that way."

"I really don't think so. Because every other guy I've kissed slobbered like a dog."

I laughed. "That's gross."

"You're telling me..." She snuggled closer to me, her hand moving across my stomach. "I don't want to go to class."

"Neither do I." My hand trailed through her hair and to her neck.

"Let's just stay here—forever."

"You won't get much of an argument from me. But knowing you, you'll get hungry at some point."

Right at that moment, her stomach growled. "Ugh. You know me so well."

"I do." I pressed my lips to her forehead, loving the touch.

She sighed then sat up. "I guess I should get ready then. Why does the weekend have to go by so fast?"

"I wish I knew."

She leaned over and gave me another quick kiss on the lips.

I melted, like always.

"I'll see you at school." She crawled off me then stood up.

I grabbed her arm then yanked her back to me. "One more."

"Cayson, no. You know what will happen."

I gave her a mischievous grin. "I don't care." I pulled her to the bed then moved on top of her.

"I haven't even brushed my teeth."

"Don't care about that either." I pressed my lips to hers then felt her legs wrap around my waist.

Skye turned into mush below me. Her lips sought mine, the passion deep within.

I was going to be late to my first class.

Oh well. I couldn't care less.

***

Slade spotted me down the hallway. He shielded his eyes with his hand, like he was trying to spot something across a desert. "No…it couldn't be."

I rolled my eyes, knowing what was coming.

"Could that be Cayson…my old best friend that I haven't seen in three weeks?"

I closed the gap between us. "You know I've been busy."

He narrowed his eyes while he stared at my face. "What the hell is this?" He slapped his hand against the side of my face. "Are you a lumberjack?"

"I haven't had time to shave."

"You can't be having sex every second of the day. You got to shower sometime."

I felt the hair on my face then lowered my hand. "It's not that. I've just forgotten about a lot of things since we got together."

"I hope a condom isn't one of them."

I never talked about my personal life, and now it was even weirder because Skye was the woman I was dating.

"Because Uncle Sean would kill you if you knocked up his daughter. I mean, like actually kill you." His eyes widened then he acted like he pointed a pistol at his head then pulled the trigger. "Boom."

"Thanks for the demonstration," I said sarcastically.

"I always wondered if theatre was my calling." He gave me the same cocky smirk he constantly wore.

"Skye and I aren't having sex, not that it's any of your business, so we have nothing to worry about."

Slade's jaw almost hit the floor. "Then what the hell have you been doing? Painting each other's nails?"

"We've been spending time together…talking."

He gripped his skull. "You've been talking since we were two. What more could you possibly have to say?"

"I don't know…it's different now that we're together."

"Seriously, you guys are the lamest couple I've ever heard of."

"I'm not in a hurry. I've got the rest of my life to make love to her."

"Make love?" His face contorted like he might vomit. "What are you? A girl?"

"Well, I'm not fucking her."

"You should be," he snapped. "Have you at least fooled around?"

"I'm not having this conversation with you." I turned on my heel and walked down the hall.

"Come on, spill it." Slade walked beside me. "I'm your best friend."

"Skye is different. I don't want you gossiping about her to other people."

He sighed and rolled his eyes at the same time. "You know I would never do that, man."

"You've done it with every other girl I've told you about."

"Because they were fuck buddies. I know Skye is different. Shit, everyone knows she's different."

"And she's your cousin...why would you want to know anyway?"

"Not in detail," he hissed. "Just in general. Come on, I tell you everything."

I sighed, knowing I was going to regret this. "We haven't done anything."

Slade froze on the spot. "I...I hope I didn't hear you right."

"We've kissed—a lot. But we—"

"Please tell me this is a damn joke."

"We're taking it slow."

"Like the 1800s?" he snapped. "Why don't you sit for an oil painting too?"

"I just don't want to mess it up. She's not just some other girl."

"I get that. But she's not your friend anymore. She's your girlfriend. By definition, you should be tit-fucking her."

I glared at him. "Could you be more PG?"

"No. Sorry, man. Grow a pair."

I should have expected this from him.

"All kidding aside, did Skye say she wanted to take it slow?"

"No…"

"Then I'm confused. She probably is too."

"I don't see what the big deal is." I shook my head.

"Because you've been in love with her for five years and now she's finally yours…I just assumed you'd want to fuck her."

I gave him a threatening look.

"I mean, make love. Whatever."

"I think about it…among other things. But I'm not in a hurry."

"Clearly…" He started walking down the hallway again. "Want to play ball tonight?"

"Skye is coming over."

"Aren't you sick of her by now….and all the *talking*?"

I smirked. "I love talking to her."

"You've been blowing me off for three weeks, man. I gave you a grace period because I thought you were getting laid, but that extension is over."

I had been neglecting Slade lately. Now I felt like a horrible friend. "Tomorrow night."

"No. Tonight. I'll be at your place at seven."

"Slade—"

He walked away before I could get another word in.

I sighed then walked to class, knowing I needed to concentrate.

Chapter Two

Skye

I wore leggings and a loose sweater. Gold earrings my mom gave me hung from my lobes. Light make up gave my face some color. The winter chill made my cheeks paler than the snow on the ground. When I deemed myself to look as nice as possible, I drove to Cayson's house.

Being with him was indescribable. He was a boyfriend that was also a best friend. I could tell him anything and I knew exactly what to say to make him laugh. He stared at me with affection in his eyes, making me feel beautiful without the use of words. It was more than I could ever have hoped for.

But I was scared.

What if it didn't work out? What if we walked our separate ways? What would that do to our friendship? I feared getting in too deep. Because in a short amount of time, he became air and water to me. I couldn't imagine my life without him. It was an existence I feared.

I came to his door and knocked.

He opened it in a flash, like he'd been waiting for my arrival. His eyes were bright with emotion. They were blue and icy, reminding me of a winter storm by the sea. His broad shoulders could carry the weight of the world, and his chest was strong enough to lift a mountain.

My eyes moved to his chin, seeing the lack of stubble. "You shaved."

His arm hooked around my waist and pulled me inside. "Do you like it?"

"I think you look handsome either way."

He rubbed the fresh skin then smirked. "Slade called me a lumberjack today."

"Oooh...I'd like to watch you chop down a tree shirtless any day."

He smirked then cornered me into the door, pressing my body flat against it. Then his face moved close to mine. His eyes suddenly turned dark, serious. I recognized the look because he'd given it to me countless times. "You look beautiful."

"Thank you."

His hand moved up my neck and into my hair. He fisted it before pressing his lips to mine, giving me a hot and aggressive embrace.

I melted at his touch. I couldn't get over how well he kissed. He knew exactly how to brush his lips against me. His tongue danced with mine, always lighting me on fire just enough before he pulled away. Every kiss was purposeful and precise. Sometimes he would pull away altogether, his lips moving past mine in a devilish tease. Then he kissed me, knocking the wind out of me.

His hands moved to my hips under my shirt. That was where he always touched me, never going higher or lower. I knew Cayson respected me and didn't want to rush a physical relationship, but I couldn't deny how anxious I was. If he was already an amazing kisser, what else was he amazing at?

He finally broke the kiss then rubbed his nose against mine. "I could do that all night. But I suspect you're hungry and thirsty."

"For you."

His eyes softened then his hand trailed to my neck. "I can't believe you're mine."

"I can't either…"

"I've waited so long for you…but you were worth all the heartache."

I hated thinking about the way I hurt Cayson all these years. My ignorance and naivety was ludicrous. Everyone told me how he felt but I never listened. It was hard to understand. "I'll make it up to you."

"Please do." He gave me another kiss before he stepped away. "I made chicken and rice pilaf."

"That sounds good."

"The chicken just needs a few more minutes. Can I get you something to drink?"

"I'm okay."

He grabbed my hand then led me into his living room. He had a small apartment with a single bedroom. But it was enough space for one person and a friend. He sat on the couch then pulled me into his lap. We faced one another and he leaned his head back, just staring at me.

Cayson usually touched me at all times. His embraces were innocent, massaging the back of my neck or my legs. But desire burned in his eyes. And I could feel his arousal against my hips, legs, and ass whenever we cuddled. From what I felt, it was impressive.

"Skye?" He pulled down one side of my loose sweater, exposing my shoulder. Then he leaned in and gave me a slow and torturous kiss. He knew how to ignite me without trying.

How was I oblivious to him for so long? Cayson was hot—like really hot. "Cayson?" I bit my lip while I felt his warm mouth against my shoulder.

He pulled away then sat up, his face just below mine. "I see you every day, but when we're apart, I still miss you." He kissed the freckle in the corner of my mouth, making me yearn for him more than I already did. "I miss you like crazy."

"I miss you too..." I felt my nipples harden and the area between my legs burn. I wanted more than just the heated kisses we shared. His perfection and mind-blowing touch, even in the most innocent places, were driving me wild, making me want him more than I already did. Passion and heat burned between us, but neither one of us had acted on it—yet. I knew Cayson was waiting until I was ready. And I already knew he was wondering when that would be. "You must be wondering why we haven't done anything more than kiss..."

He leaned back and stared into my eyes. "I can't deny how much I want you. You're the sexiest woman I've ever seen. Every curve of your body excites me in a way I can't explain. I want you more than any other woman I've had in my life. But, Skye, I'm not in a hurry. And I'm not going anywhere." His hands gripped my waist, his fingers spanning my back. "I'm a very patient man, and I will wait as long as you want me to. There's no pressure. So please don't worry about it."

"That's the thing…I don't want to wait."

Fire leapt to life in his eyes. It cracked and sizzled, turning into slow burning embers. His hands dug into my skin slightly.

"But…I'm scared."

The desire evaporated. "Scared of what, baby?"

I didn't know how to verbalize it, at least in a way that wouldn't offend him. But he must be thinking the same thing…or at least thought it at one point. "There's no turning back if things don't work out or something bad happens in our relationship. Our friendship will be ruined—forever."

He processed my words for a second, his eyes conveying his thoughts. "I never want to be just your friend again, Skye. And I don't plan on it."

"I don't either," I said immediately. I cupped his face, looking into his eyes. "You mean the world to me, Cayson. And you've made me happier than I've ever been. This is where I belong."

"Then there's nothing to be scared of."

"But…what if something happens?"

He grabbed my wrists then brought them together in his hands. "Don't think like that, Skye."

"But what if it does? What will happen to us? I just feel better talking about it…just in case."

He sighed then kissed one of my wrists gently. "No matter what we promise, no matter what we say, it won't change what's already come to pass. We'll never be what we used to be—even if we broke up now."

"But down the road..."

He looked me in the eye. "No matter what happens between us, I'll never stop loving you and I'll never stop caring. If you were another girl, it would be different. But you're special to me. You've always been special. And I never want to lose you from my life. Even if you cheated on me and broke my heart, I still wouldn't turn my back on you. I wouldn't leave the group and I wouldn't avoid you. I'll always be around—forever."

"Me too..."

He kissed the other wrist. "Most ex's can't be friends. But we're different, Skye. We are far more mature than anyone else our age. And I know our love is strong. Nothing will keep us apart."

I nodded.

"Do you feel better now?"

"Yeah...we're family. And we'll always be."

"Exactly." He leaned back and rested his hands on my thighs, rubbing me gently. He stared at my face, never looking away.

I leaned forward, my head pressed to his. Then I closed my eyes, enjoying the silence. Cayson moved his hands to my waist, gripping me. I leaned down and found his lips, feeling their softness.

His hands tightened around me slightly, conveying the pleasure my mouth was giving him. They moved up my sweater, feeling my bare skin.

My hair fell around his face, blocking him in. I deepened our kiss, feeling his lips with my small mouth. His tongue found mine, dancing slowly. He breathed hard into my mouth, showing his excitement.

Finally giving into what I wanted, I broke our kiss then grabbed the end of my sweater. Slowly, I pulled it off then dropped it on the couch. I wore my black lacy bra. It pushed my breasts together and made them look bigger than they already were. Cayson stared at them for a moment with desire burning in his eyes. Then he looked back at me, his lips desperate for my touch. He pulled me toward him, kissing me again.

I felt his chest beneath his shirt. Every groove and line was hard. He worked out and was in great shape, but I didn't realize just how strong he was. How was I immune to him for so long? Now I couldn't stop picturing him shirtless. I couldn't stop imagining how he would feel inside me. My lips were constantly desperate for his. I needed him—all the time.

I lifted his shirt then yanked it off. I tossed it aside then stared down at his body. His chest was wide and strong. His stomach was lined with hard abs. He was thick like a slab of wood and strong like a concrete wall. My hands moved down, feeling every inch of his perfection. "Damn, you're so hot," I blurted.

Cayson stared into my eyes while I touched him. It didn't seem like he heard me. His hands fingered the waistline of my leggings but he didn't pull them down. Then he gripped me and pulled me closer, his lips finding mine. He sat up, holding me close to him.

My chest pressed against his. Our stomachs almost touched. I moved my arms around his neck, my mouth devouring his like I couldn't get enough. Cayson moved his hands up my back, feeling the small muscles underneath. He moved past my bra clasp to my shoulders. Then he came down again and back to my waist.

I knew he didn't want to push me. He wanted me to make it clear what I wanted. I doubted he was always this sensitive when he was fooling around, but since our relationship was different, he was cautious. While I continued to kiss him, I reached behind me and unclasped the strap. My bra was immediately loose on me and it started to fall.

I broke our kiss and stared at him, wanting to see his reaction to me.

Cayson felt a strap in his hand but he didn't pull it down. His breathing was hard and he didn't stare at my chest. His eyes were glued to mine, like he was afraid to look. I grabbed the hand that held the strap then pulled it down. His breath hitched. The rest of the bra came with it.

I hated my chest. Guys constantly stared at it instead of my face. It was hard to tell if a guy was really into me because of my personality or just my appearance. It seemed like they were immediately smitten with my rack. But with Cayson, it was different. I already knew he loved me for me, that my chest had nothing to do with it. And I wanted him to enjoy my body.

Cayson still wouldn't look. His eyes were locked to mine.

I grabbed his large hands then placed them over my breasts, making him squeeze them. He swallowed the lump in his throat then moaned quietly. "Touch me."

That seemed to unwind him. His hands moved back to my waist and he pulled me closer to him, his mouth closing around a nipple. He kissed it then sucked it hard, taking it into his mouth.

Seeing the passionate way he took me only made me more aroused. I loved feeling him suck my skin, tasting me. He kissed my entire chest, exploring each breast while he dug his fingers into my skin, trembling slightly.

My head rolled back and I closed my eyes while I enjoyed how good it felt. It never felt this way before, this amazing. With every other guy, I felt used and tarnished. Cayson made me feel loved and sexy at the same time.

"God, you're beautiful." He licked the valley between my breasts. His mouth moved all the way to my throat, tasting me. He stopped when he reached my chin, placing a gentle kiss there.

My hands moved to the button of his jeans and undid them. Then I tried to yank them down.

Cayson hooked one arm around my waist then stood up, still kissing my neck. He pulled his jeans down with one hand then kicked them off, not breaking his focus on me. Then he sat back down, in his briefs.

His hands moved to the top of my leggings then he yanked them down. He got them over my ass before he rolled me to the couch then pulled them the rest of the way off. I wore a matching black thong. I wasn't sure what would happen tonight, but I wanted to be prepared.

Cayson stared at me for a moment, taking me in. His eyes lingered on my legs before he grabbed them and adjusted me on the couch. Then he pulled one over his shoulder and kissed the inner thigh.

My body had never been worshipped like this. My hands fisted his hair, feeling the soft strands.

His mouth moved to the opposite thigh, kissing it in the same way.

My head rolled back, loving the way he was making me feel. He was already an amazing lover.

Then he moved up my stomach, kissing the skin around my bellybutton. He kissed the area of my ribs then moved back down to my hips. He pulled down my thong slightly and he kissed the now exposed area, lighting me on fire.

"Cayson…"

He immediately moved up my body and crushed his lips against mine, like he needed the embrace in order to survive.

My hands glided down his strong back, feeling every muscle. When I reached his briefs, I gripped the brim then slowly pulled them down, exposing him. I didn't look because our lips were engaged but I felt every inch of him as he was revealed. His length lay against my stomach, and I didn't need to look at it to know how large it was. He definitely put Zack to shame. I pulled the fabric down to his knees and he kicked them off the rest of the way.

When he was naked, he ended our embrace and stared at me, waiting for me to look.

I gripped his biceps and glanced down. Instinctively, I licked my lips, liking what I saw.

Cayson moaned while he watched me, the excitement in his eyes.

I wrapped my hand around his shaft and rubbed him gently, massaging the tip with my thumb.

He breathed hard while he felt me. Then he grabbed my thong and slid it off. When it was gone, he stared at me for a moment before his eyes moved to mine again.

I didn't kiss him. Instead, I felt his naked body against mine. We'd been friends my entire life and I never thought of him this way before. But now we're together. And it felt right. It made me wonder why we hadn't done this a long time ago. "You're beautiful."

"Not as beautiful as you," he whispered. He hooked his arm around my waist then pulled me to him as he stood up. My legs instinctively wrapped around his waist, and he carried me into his bedroom.

He carefully laid me on his bed, my head hitting his pillow. Then he pressed his head to mine. "I want to taste you."

I knew what he meant. "I do too."

He kissed my chest and stomach as he moved down. When he reached the area between my legs, he gently kissed me.

And I went wild.

He rubbed his tongue against my clitoris, making a circular motion. Then he slipped his tongue inside me, applying the right amount of pleasure in all the right places.

I writhed on the bed, gripping his hair with one hand and the sheets with the other. "Cayson…"

His thumb moved to my clitoris, applying the same circular motion.

My head was spinning. My heart was racing. I couldn't control my breathing. He was making me feel so good, better than I've ever felt. His mouth was warm and inviting, sending me to a climax so strong I almost didn't recognize it. "Oh my god…"

Cayson continued to please me, making it last as long as possible.

When the sensation passed, I was out of breath. My hand moved through my hair, unsure what else to do. I was disoriented, caught off guard by how good it felt.

Cayson moved back up my body slowly, my moisture still on his lips.

"Why the hell did we wait so long?" I blurted.

He smirked slightly. "You tell me."

"God, you're good at that. You're fucking hot."

His cheeks blushed slightly. "I'm glad you think so."

"Like, really hot. Wow."

He kissed my chest, probably trying to hide his face. "I'm glad I can please you. I've never gotten so much pleasure out of it."

"Until now." I pushed him to his back then climbed on top of him.

His head hit the pillow and he looked up at me with desire in his eyes.

I moved down his body until I met his cock. It was thick and long, and it twitched when I came near. I grabbed his shaft then put his tip in my mouth, moaning as I did it. I hated giving head. It was the worst. But with Cayson, I enjoyed it, despite his large size.

Cayson breathed hard while he lay back on the pillow. His hands moved to my hair, pulling it from my face. Then he gripped it with one hand, fisting it.

I took him deep in my throat, as far as I could go.

"Skye..."

I moved up and down, doing my best to give him the most amazing blowjob of his life. He certainly gave me the best head I'd ever received.

His other hand rested on the back of my neck, guiding me slightly when he got really into it. "Fuck, that feels good."

I sucked his tip then ran my tongue across it before I took him deep again.

He breathed hard, his chest rising and falling. "Skye...I'm going to come." He cupped my neck, getting ready.

I didn't pull him out. I kept going, wanting to taste him.

He continued to breathe hard. "If you don't want me to come in your mouth, pull me out."

I deep-throated him again.

He took a few more breaths before he suddenly tensed. A deep moan from the back of his throat escaped his lips. He gripped my neck, holding on. "Mmm..." He filled me, releasing into me.

I swallowed it as it came, noting how much it was. When I was certain he was finished, I licked his tip then pulled him out.

He was still catching his breath, winded.

I crawled up his chest then leaned over him.

"You're really good at that..."

"Only because I enjoyed it."

He cupped my face and kissed me gently. The kiss lasted for several seconds, the connection passing between us. Then he pulled away, affection in his eyes. "You blew my mind."

"I think I blew your load."

He chuckled then smirked at me. "That too, definitely."

I lay next to him, getting comfortable on his bed.

Cayson pulled the sheets over him then snuggled close to me. His hand moved through my hair while he stared at me, his eyes boring into mine. "I've never seen or shared anything so beautiful in my life."

My heart convulsed at his words. I never expected Cayson to be such a gentle lover. Nor did I expect him to be so romantic and tender. He was thoughtful, passionate, and sexy. "Nor have I."

He continued to move his hand through my hair, his eyes never leaving my face. He stared at me like I was a work of art, a piece on the wall of a great museum. I realized then that I recognized that look. He'd given it to me hundreds of times. I just didn't recognize it before. "I can't believe I didn't notice..."

"I wasn't very discreet about it."

"And everyone told me...but I thought they were just joking."

"No, definitely not." His hand moved to my shoulder, touching the skin lightly. "But it's okay. It took us awhile to get here, but it happened. And that's all that matters."

"Yeah..." I grabbed his hand then brushed a kiss across his knuckles.

His eyes softened when he looked at me.

"Is that why you never wanted to talk about your personal life?" I whispered.

"Yeah."

"I feel so stupid now."

"Don't," he said gently.

"Is that why you hated Zack?"

He chuckled slightly. "No. That guy was a dick. I hated him regardless. But more so because you noticed him and not me."

"I wasn't thinking clearly…" Zack would always be one of my biggest regrets.

"It's in the past. Let it go."

My hand moved to his chest, feeling the mound of muscle underneath. "Can I ask you something?"

"Skye, you can ask me anything. You know that."

"It's about your personal life."

"You can ask about that too."

"How many girls have you been with?" I was just curious. Since he never talked about his rendezvous, I really had no idea.

He thought for a moment. "I'm not sure. More than fifteen but less than twenty."

That was more than I expected. "Were they ever serious?"

"No. A lot of them were similar arrangements to the one I had with Jasmine."

"Oh." I didn't like thinking about her. I got jealous all over again. "On the plane, you told me you were in love with a girl. Who was it?"

He smirked. "Seriously? You haven't figured that out yet?"

"I just wanted to make sure…"

"I guess you *are* stupid," he said with a laugh.

I hit his arm gently. "Hey. Don't be mean."

He pulled me closer and kissed my forehead. "You're the only one, Skye. It's always been you."

My heart melted at his words. I felt special, cherished. Cayson was the perfect guy and he only wanted me. "I can't believe I was immune to your charms for so long. Now, I can't stop thinking about kissing you when I'm in class. At night, I think about you in ways I never did before."

"I like what I'm hearing."

I smiled. "I just can't believe it took me so long to open my eyes."

"Tell me more about these fantasies." His hand moved to my waist.

"I just…think about us."

"Doing what?" He rubbed his nose against mine.

"Making love."

"I've been thinking about it for five years. And I'm looking forward to the real thing."

"I am too…"

He kissed my forehead again.

"When did these feelings start?"

He shrugged. "A long time ago. I can't recall the exact moment. It wasn't something you did or said. It just happened. I started to notice the sound of your laugh, the way your hair shined in the sun. I hung on to every word you said. I didn't think about other girls, only you.

And it hit me one day; I was in love with you. And the fact those feelings never went away only solidified that."

"Well, I'm glad you're mine now, Cayson. I never want to be without you." I clutched him tightly.

"Neither do I, baby." Emotion filled his voice as he said it. His hand moved through my hair again, being gentle like always.

I rested my head on his chest and listened to the beating of his heart. It was slow and steady. His chest rose and fell with every breath of his lungs. It felt like the rising tide on the shore. I listened to him breathe, treasuring the quiet companionship. Feeling his body wrapped around mine in his sheets felt right, felt perfect. It was what I'd been missing my whole life. He was the guy for me, the one I had all along. I just never noticed.

The front door opened and closed. "It's time to play ball. Cay, get your ass out here!" It was Slade.

Cayson sighed. "Damn."

"What's Slade doing here?"

"He said I've been ditching him for weeks. He wants to hang out. I told him you were coming over tonight but he obviously doesn't care."

"How did he get in?"

"I have no idea." He pulled the blanket off then pulled on his sweatpants. "I'll be right back." He walked out and shut the door, leaving it cracked.

I heard their conversation.

"Can you stop barging into my apartment?" Cayson demanded.

"Could you stop being a dick and actually hang out with your best bro?"

"I said tomorrow."

"I want to play today." Slade bounced a basketball on the hardwood floor.

"Thanks for getting my floor dirty," Cayson said sarcastically.

"If we were at the courts, it wouldn't matter."

"How did you get in anyway?"

"Through the front door, idiot." Slade bounced the ball again. "I'm starting to think Uncle Sean paid your way into this school too."

"But it was locked."

"It's called a lighter."

"What?" Cayson asked. "How did you get in with a lighter?"

"I'll show you."

"I don't want you to show me," Cayson said immediately. "I just want to know how you broke into my apartment."

I left the bed and pulled on one of Cayson's shirts.

"I'm not breaking in. Do you see me stealing anything?" Slade asked.

"That's looting," Cayson corrected. "What you are doing now is breaking in."

"Potato-potato."

"Slade, I think it's time for you to leave."

"What are you guys doing in the bedroom anyway?" Slade dropped the ball then moved to the kitchen. "What smells good?" He opened the oven door. "Ooh…chicken."

I opened the door then stepped out. "Cayson, go play ball with him."

"Listen to your woman." Slade came to the living room then spotted me only wearing Cayson's shirt. Then he glanced at Cayson's naked chest. A wide smirk spread on his face. "About time you guys started to get it on. Shit, I thought you were waiting until marriage for a second. I was about to call a psychiatrist."

Cayson didn't bother commenting to that. "Baby, it's okay. I made plans with you first."

"No, you should spend time with Slade. I've been hoarding you."

"Damn right you have," Slade said.

"Can I have a private conversation with my girlfriend?" Cayson asked, giving him a glare.

"I don't know," Slade said. "Can you have a girlfriend and keep your best friend at the same time?"

"Conrad, Theo, and Roland haven't complained once," Cayson argued.

"Because they're rubbing their dicks together. They're fine," Slade said.

Cayson rolled his eyes.

"Babe, just go," I said. "I'll see you later."

Cayson's eyes lost their light. It was obvious he didn't want our time together to end. "Okay."

"Thank god," Slade said. "Let's go. Then we're hitting the bar after that. I need a wingman to pick up chicks with."

"Having a girlfriend means I can't pick up girls anymore," Cayson reminded him.

"But you can help me. You know, distract the fat ugly ones so I can go for their cute friends," Slade said.

"That doesn't sound fun at all," Cayson said.

"Then dump Skye," Slade said.

I laughed then looked at Cayson. "Just go and have a good time."

Cayson sighed then joined me in the bedroom. "I'll be out in a second, Slade."

"'Ight. Hurry up," Slade said. "No quickie before we go."

Cayson shut the door and sighed. "I'm sorry."

"Don't be sorry. I've been neglecting Trinity and Silke too. We've both been bad friends."

"Yeah..."

I changed back into my clothes then fixed my hair.

Cayson put on his gym shorts and a t-shirt. Even in that, he still looked hot. "What?" He caught my look.

"You're just...really hot."

He smirked. "I'm always uncomfortable when girls say that, but I really like hearing it from you."

"I'll say it more often then." I grabbed my purse then walked out.

Cayson grabbed his wallet and keys. "Alright, Slade. I'm coming. But don't light your way into my apartment again."

"Don't be pussy-whipped and it won't be a problem." Slade dribbled the ball as we walked out.

Cayson walked with me to my car. Slade was beside him, spinning the ball on one finger.

"I'll see you tomorrow." Cayson cupped my face and kissed me.

"Okay. Have fun."

"Thanks." He kissed me again before he stepped back and watched me get into my car. Then, like a perfect gentleman, he watched me drive away.

As soon as I got back to my apartment, the longing hit me. I missed him like crazy, needing him desperately. I thought about when my mom talked to my dad on the phone when she visited. She would always say she missed him even though she saw him just a few hours earlier.

Now I knew exactly how that felt.

Chapter Three

Slade

The house was crowded with people. One side of the wall was stuffed with kegs, and every one held red Solo cups while they mingled. A haze of smoke filled the air. The scent of cigarettes and marijuana came into my nose.

I took a deep breath. "Man, I love that smell."

Cayson cocked an eyebrow. "Of pollution and body odor?"

"It's the smell of a party."

He shook his head and sighed.

I practically had to drag Cayson here. "Loosen up, man."

"I just feel weird coming since I'm not single."

"Please don't tell me you're going to be one of those guys that stops living his life because he has a girlfriend." I gave him a firm look.

"No. But I don't want to pick up girls with you either."

"Just calm down. Skye trusts you. And she knows you're whipped hard. She hasn't got anything to worry about."

Cayson sipped his cup then looked bored.

I rubbed my hands together. "Now…who should I ruin tonight?"

"Why do you have to *ruin* anyone?" Cayson asked.

"It's not fun otherwise." I eyed the girls in the room, noting their curves in their sweaters and jeans. "There's a lot of talent here tonight."

Cayson glanced at his watch. "The sooner you get laid, the sooner I get to leave."

"You're no fun anymore."

"I was never any fun before."

"True."

"Where are the other guys?" Cayson asked.

"I don't know. They said they were coming." I glanced at my phone to see if I missed any messages.

A loud commotion happened in the center of the room. Girls were pulling down their pants and having a thong contest. They were shaking their asses, making their bright underwear turn heads.

Cayson turned away, more interested in a picture on the wall.

"Now this is my kind of party."

"Why don't you try to meet a nice girl? I'm telling you, the sex is so much better if you're with the same partner."

"How would you know?" I snapped. "You aren't even having sex with your girlfriend."

He didn't bother to respond.

"Besides, we both know I'm not the girlfriend type."

"I think you could be if you wanted to—for the right person."

"Nope." I crossed my arms over my chest and tried to pick someone to take back to my place. I narrowed my eyes on a cute brunette. "She's cute."

"Yeah…" Cayson didn't seem impressed.

"But her thighs are too big." I scanned the crowd again.

Cayson laughed. "You're such a jackass."

"You act like you didn't know that already." I continued to look, my eyes searching for the perfect girl to hit my sheets.

"Cayson!" A geeky guy with glasses came over. "Isn't this party awesome?"

He had 'loser' written all over him. "First-timer?" I teased.

The guy didn't catch on. "Did you finish that lab report?"

"No." Cayson sighed. "I'll probably do it Sunday night…or Monday morning, actually."

"I never considered you to be the procrastinator type."

"He's pussy-whipped now," I explained.

Cayson rolled his eyes. "I have a girlfriend so I've been distracted…"

"Oh." The guy nodded. "Cool. I got a lot of girls hanging around but I can't make up my mind."

I tried not to laugh. "I'm going to go for the kill." I patted Cayson on the shoulder then walked away.

Cayson continued to talk to his geek twin.

When I came closer to the other brunette I was looking at, I realized she wasn't as pretty as I thought. Distance and darkness had that effect. I continued to move through the crowd, looking for something worth my time. The house was packed and it was difficult to scan my options. Then I spotted a blonde on the other side of the room. She had long thin legs that stretched for days. Brown heeled boots were on her feet and skin-tight black jeans clung to her form. Her ass was toned and prominent. Her waist was petite, and her hour-glass figure was noticeable. I couldn't see her face, just her back. But I liked what I saw. Her long blonde hair trailed down her back in slight curls. "Bingo."

"Just drop it in. It will dissolve in seconds." The guy standing nearby held the red cup out.

He dropped the pill inside and stared at it. "Alright. You're good."

The hair stood up on the back of my neck. I knew what they were doing. And I didn't like it one bit. If you had to use date rape drugs to get laid, you were lower than dirt.

"I'm going for it." The guy with the cup walked across the room. And he headed right to the girl I had my eye on. He reached her and engaged her in conversation. When she turned slightly, my heart fell.

The beautiful girl I targeted was someone I knew. *Trinity.*

Her deep green sweater clung to her curves tightly, showing off her flat stomach and boobalicious chest. For a moment, I felt awkward. She was annoying as hell yet I was stalking her like prey.

Then she took the cup from his hand, accepting his offer.

Fuck. No.

Anger exploded inside me like a lit stick of dynamite. I was livid, seeing red. My hands were shaking, and I couldn't see straight. My head was about to ignite because I couldn't hold the blood rage.

I marched through the crowd, time suddenly slowing down. Every one moved like a snail. The music stopped. Trinity slowly brought the cup to her lips, about to take a drink. That sped me forward.

I slapped the cup to the ground, watching it spray across the girls' boots and jeans.

"Slade, what the hell?" Trinity snapped.

My fury was focused on the piece of shit. Without thinking or speaking, I slammed my fist against his jaw so hard he flew to the ground. "Fucking asshole."

The entire crowd backed up, knowing a serious fight just broke out.

"Slade?" Trinity's eyes widened. "What the hell are you doing?"

I grabbed her arm and pulled her behind me. "Stay out of the way. Now."

The guy rubbed his jaw then came back to his feet. He squared his shoulders and stared me down. Then he rushed me. Using my Krav Maga training, I spun him around then threw him to the ground. He groaned when his bare back hit the tile.

"Slade, behind you!" Trinity's voice came to me.

I figured his boys would come to his aid. I turned around then grabbed the first one by the neck. I choked him hard then threw him on top of his buddy. A third guy came after me and I took care of him too. Taking on three guys at once was no problem for me. I kicked their ass, making everyone in the vicinity gasp and step back.

"Slade, knock it off." Cayson grabbed my arm. "You're going to kill them."

I jerked away. "You think I care?"

Roland came out of the crowd. "Knock it off. Seriously. You made your point."

"What the hell did they do?" Conrad asked.

The guys were lying on the ground, gripping their bloody noses and choking.

I spit on them. "If anyone else thinks about using roofies around me, they'll meet the same fate as these guys."

The crowd was deadly silent, hanging onto my words.

I turned around and grabbed Trinity by the arm. "Come on. Let's go."

"But—"

"Don't argue with me," I snapped. I dragged her out, parting through the crowd and pushing people aside. When we were outside, our feet crunched against the hard snow. Trinity was struggling to keep up. She was wobbling on her heels, clearly drunk off her ass.

"What the hell is going on, Slade?" She tried to turn me around but only managed to fall over.

She was going to break her ankle at this rate. I pulled her back into my arms. "What the hell is going on?" I yelled in her face. "You were about to take a date rape drug. The only thing I should be hearing from you is your gratitude."

"How do you know?" Her words were slurred.

"I saw them. Now what the fuck is wrong with you? You don't take an open drink from a random dude! How many times have I told you that?"

"I…he was nice."

"You just put out for any guy?"

"You're one to talk," she snapped.

"I'm a dude. I don't need to worry about being raped. It's not the same thing at all, Trin."

She pushed me away. "Just leave me alone."

"To do what?"

She tried to walk back to the house but she was struggling through the snow.

I grabbed her arm and pulled her in the opposite direction. "We're heading home."

She twisted her arm away. "You don't care about me anyway. What does it matter to you?"

"I don't care?" I asked incredulously. "I just beat the shit out of three guys for trying to fuck with you."

"Whatever."

"No. Not whatever. Now come on."

"Just leave me alone, Slade." Her voice was becoming quiet. "You hate me."

"I don't hate you!" I picked her up and pulled her to my chest. "Now stop talking. You're fucking annoying."

"See?"

"See what? Like you aren't a brat to me every other second."

She tried to squirm out of my grasp. "I'm just going to drive."

"You're drunk, Trinity."

"Fine. Then you drive."

"Didn't bring my car." I carried her across the snow toward my apartment. My place was much closer than hers, at least by a mile.

"I can walk!"

"No, you can't. And you can't take off your shoes." She was light in my arms. Weighing a little more than a hundred pounds, she was like an easy day at the gym.

She finally shut up and rested her head against my chest. Her hand grabbed my shoulder then loosened.

Silence finally fell. My feet crunched against the snow while I walked. Small flakes fell from the dark sky, landing on my nose. My phone kept vibrating in my pocket, telling me everyone was calling me to ask what the hell happened. I ignored it and kept walking, hoping Trinity would fall asleep so I wouldn't have to hear her bitching about how I beat up that 'nice' guy.

I finally ascended the stairs to my apartment then got the door open.

She stirred when she realized where we were. "I thought you were going to take me home?" Her voice was hoarse.

"I'm not walking a mile in the snow. You'll have to stay here." I put her down on the ground, but she wobbled. "God, you look like Bambi."

"You look like a douchebag."

"Good one," I said sarcastically.

I moved into the hallway then grabbed an extra blanket. My apartment was packed with shit. My guitar leaned against the TV in the corner and my *Playboys* sat on the coffee table.

Trinity walked to the kitchen table and cringed. "Why do you have a hundred condoms sitting there?"

"That's a stupid question," I snapped.

"But a hundred?" she asked incredulously. "*A hundred*? That's ludicrous."

"Stop talking. You're more annoying when you're drunk."

"You're a bigger dick when you're drunk."

"I'm sober. So, I'm just a dick in general." I tossed the blanket and pillow on the couch. "Now shut up and go to bed."

She stared at the couch. "I'm not sleeping there."

"Then have fun sleeping on the floor."

"No." She stumbled as she headed to my room.

"I don't think so..." I chased after her.

She lay on the bed and tried to kick off her shoes.

"I'm not sleeping on the damn couch," I said with a growl.

"Neither am I. The cushions are going to make me break out."

"You think my bed is any cleaner?" I snapped.

"I'm sure even a disgusting pig like you washes his sheets."

"You'd be surprised."

She finally got one shoe off then tried to catch her breath.

"God, you're pathetic. Why do you always need to get so drunk that you don't know your nose from your ass?"

"I could ask you the same thing."

"No, you couldn't. Now go to the couch. I'm sleeping in my bed."

"Take me home or I'm sleeping here." She got her other boot off then lay back on the bed.

I growled. "I take it back. I do hate you."

"The feeling is mutual, asshole."

"Yeah, I'm such an asshole," I said sarcastically. "I saved your ass from getting raped."

She lay on the pillow and said nothing.

"Whatever." I pulled my shirt off then kicked off my shoes.

She glanced at me, seeing the tattoos along my ribs. Then she looked away.

I pulled my jeans down and stood in my boxers.

"Um...do you mind?"

"Don't act like you don't like it." I pulled the covers back and got between the sheets.

"Why are you always so cocky?"

"Because I have a lot to be cocky about."

"Anyone can get a tattoo. That doesn't make you a bigger man."

God, she was annoying. "How about we play a game?"

"A game?"

"Yeah. Who can shut up and stay that way the longest."

She sighed then pulled her shirt off. Then she took off her pants.

I didn't look at her once.

She got under the covers and stayed on her side of the bed.

My phone rang again. It vibrated on the floor where it sat in the pocket of my jeans. I groaned then fished it out before I answered it. "What?"

"Dude, what the hell happened?" Conrad snapped. "Where's my sister? Is she okay?"

"I thought you hated her?"

"I do. Now is she okay?"

"She's fine. She's staying with me tonight. We're both too drunk to drive."

He breathed a sigh into the phone. "Did those guys really try to…do what you said?"

"Yeah." It pissed me off just thinking about it.

"I'm glad you were there."

"Yeah…I just wish I had killed them."

"I'm going to have a big talk with my sister when I see her next."

"I don't think you need to. I'll give her a good speech when she wakes up tomorrow."

"Don't mention this to my dad, okay?"

"You think I'm crazy?" I asked.

"I'm glad we're on the same page."

"Yeah…"

"Well, I'll talk to you later."

"Yeah." I hung up and tossed the phone on the nightstand. I ran my fingers through my hair then closed my eyes, trying to find sleep. But it was a struggle. My heart wouldn't stop racing. I kept thinking about what would have happened to Trinity if I weren't there. It was something that made my stomach clench in pain. It was a fate I couldn't even stand to consider. She drove me crazy, made me want to slap her, but I couldn't deny what she meant to me. She was my family, someone I'd known my whole life. I would die if that happened to her, to any of the girls in my inner circle. I knew I was a jackass that treated people like shit, but there were a few people I really cared about—even if I never showed it.

***

When I woke up the next morning, the sun was beating on my face. I forgot to close my curtains the night before. I took a deep breath before my eyes fluttered open. What I saw caused me to do a double take.

Trinity was cuddled into my side, her arm around my torso. Her face was rested in my neck, her warm breath falling on me. My arm was around her waist and I could feel the dip in her back.

What the fuck?

I immediately moved away, trying to untangle our bodies. I didn't do that cuddling shit.

She stirred when she felt me move. "God, my head..."

I opened my nightstand, riffled through all my handcuffs, bondage, and condoms until I found the bottle of aspirin. "Here." I tossed it at her.

She fumbled with the cap until she got it off. "How do you expect me to swallow this?"

"With your throat," I snapped.

"I need water."

"God, you're high maintenance." I got out of bed then retrieved a glass of water. I practically threw it at her.

She swallowed the pill then rubbed her head. She was only wearing a pink bra. Her breasts were pushed together, and her skin was pale, like winter morning. Her lips were red from her make up from the night before. Her eyeliner and eye shadow were smeared.

"You should wash your face. You look like shit."

She grabbed the pillow then slammed it hard into my face. "Go to hell, Slade."

"I will—one day." I walked into the bathroom then took a whiz.

She came in behind me and turned on the sink.

My back was to her but I was mid-stream. "Um…do you mind?" I snapped.

She ignored me and washed her face.

I growled then finished.

She wiped her face with toilet paper and dried her skin. Then she tossed it in the garbage, where she saw a pile of used condoms. "You're so disgusting."

"I'm disgusting?" I barked. "At least guys don't come inside me. Now that shit is gross." I walked out and headed into the hallway.

"Aren't you going to wash your hands?"

"Not when your fat ass is in the way."

She grabbed the towel then chucked it at me.

"This is me caring." I walked into my room then changed.

She followed me a moment later, wearing just her bra and matching thong.

As much as I knew I shouldn't look, I did anyway. I'd seen her in a swimsuit so I knew what her body looked like but I still took a peek. Her stomach was flat and her navel was pierced. Her breasts curved out, being perfectly proportioned to her size. Her legs were long and thin, and her ass was toned and lifted. I knew she hardly ate and worked out like crazy. It showed.

She pulled her clothes on and got dressed, not looking at me. "What time is it?"

"Noon."

She adjusted her top then fixed her hair. "Are you going to take me home?"

"Yeah, sure."

She walked to the front door and waited for me.

I grabbed my keys and we walked out together. We got into my truck then headed toward her house. She rested her face against the window, her eyes closed.

I turned on the radio.

"Turn that off," she snapped. "I have a headache."

"It's my car. I can do what I want."

She hit the button and turned it off. "You can not listen to music for a few minutes."

I didn't want to argue with her so I let it go.

When we arrived at her house, she jumped out then slammed the door. She didn't say bye or even look at me.

I don't think so.

I killed the engine to my truck then went after her. "Why are you being a bitch right now?"

"A bitch?" She got her keys in the door. "I didn't do anything."

"Are you at least going to thank me?" I snapped. "I saved your ass."

"You don't need me to stroke your ego. It's already big enough as it is." She got the door opened and stepped inside.

I chased after her. "This is serious, Trinity. You shouldn't go to parties alone and get that drunk. And don't take drinks from strangers. Ever."

She crossed her arms over her chest and said nothing.

Was I missing something? "Why isn't this a big deal to you? Do you understand you could have been raped? By multiple guys? They would have taken you—"

"Stop." She held up her hand. And finally, the emotion was in her eyes. "I get it. I learned my lesson. I'm sorry."

At least she admitted it. "Don't say you're sorry. Be smart and take care of yourself. What if I weren't there, Trinity?"

"I get it, okay? Stop repeating yourself."

"I just want to make sure you understand how serious this is."

"I do. Now go." She turned away, hiding her face.

I sighed, not knowing what to do. I knew she was upset but I wasn't sure what to do to fix it. I wasn't good with the whole emotional thing. I didn't know how to comfort someone, especially a girl.

She sniffed then breathed hard.

I knew she was crying.

Ugh, this was awkward.

I sighed then came close to her. I put my hands on her shoulders and rubbed her gently.

"Thank you, Slade. I do appreciate it."

My hands stilled. "You're welcome, Trin."

She turned back around, the tears gone. "You can go now."

Something was keeping me there. "I need to know you'll be smarter about this. No more taking drinks from random guys, okay? If something happened to you…I couldn't bear it."

Her eyes softened. "I will. I promise."

That was what I needed to hear. "Okay."

Tension stretched between us.

"Well, I'll see you around…" I turned and walked away.

"Okay."

I walked out the front door then closed it behind me, not looking at her again.

Chapter Four

Trinity

I knew I made a stupid decision. And it frightened me that the consequences of that stupidity could have been dire. What was wrong with me? What if Slade hadn't been there? It freaked me out so much that I forced myself not to think about it.

When I went to the library on Monday, Skye was there.

"Hey." She studied me for a moment with concern in her eyes.

Being in a tight group meant everyone knew everything the moment it happened. "I'm okay," I said proactively.

"I'm glad Slade taught those guys a lesson." She highlighted a few sentences in her textbook.

"That Krav Maga should be illegal," I said.

"Good thing he knew it." She adjusted her glasses over the bridge of her nose.

I sat there, not in the mood to read or do anything.

"Do you want to talk about it?"

"Not really." I looked out the window, trying to think of other things.

"Maybe you and Slade will get along better now…"

I tried not to laugh. "I doubt it." I didn't want to talk about Slade or that horrible night anymore. "How's it going with Cayson? I haven't seen you to ask."

She couldn't hide the smile on her face. "Wonderful."

"He's the whole package?" I gave her a playful grin.

"Ooooh yeah."

I chuckled. "Lucky you. Have you been humping like rabbits?"

"No…we haven't done it yet."

"What? Why?"

She shrugged. "Just taking it slow. But we fooled around the other night. That was fun. Mucho fun."

I laughed. "I bet it was. Cayson is a good-looking guy."

"I'm not sure why I was immune to him for so long."

"Because you're stupid," I blurted.

"Apparently."

"This is when I get to say, told you so. Every time I said Cayson was in love with you, you never believed me."

"I know…I'm not sure why I was in denial."

"Like I said, you're stupid."

She glared at me through her spectacles.

"I'm just saying…"

Cayson entered the library then spotted us at our table.

"Your boyfriend is coming."

Skye immediately pulled her glasses off like she was embarrassed.

"He's seen you wear them before," I said.

"But now he's my boyfriend."

"I really don't think he cares."

"Hey." Cayson only had eyes for her. He leaned down and kissed her. "I missed you."

"I missed you too." She couldn't wipe away the grin on her face.

He put his backpack down and sat beside her. "Why aren't you wearing your glasses?"

I grinned. "Because she's embarrassed."

Skye gave me that look that clearly said, "Shut your mouth."

"Embarrassed of what?" he asked. He leaned toward her. "I think you look cute when you wear them."

"You don't think I look like a nerd?" she asked hesitantly.

"Well, since I'm a nerd, I find that attractive." He grabbed the glasses then slipped them over her nose. "That's better." He kissed her forehead before he pulled away.

"You guys are ridiculously cute," I said.

"I know," Skye said with a sigh.

Cayson rested his hand on her thigh while he opened his textbook. "Anything new?"

"No," I said immediately.

Cayson looked at me with concern in his eyes. But he didn't say anything. He probably picked up on the tension.

Slade stepped into the library with an energy drink in his hand. He found our table and made his way over. For some reason, when I saw him, my heart rate increased slightly. He wore a gray t-shirt and dark jeans. The colors of his sleeves brought out his blue eyes. He walked past the table with an air of indifference. Then he slid into the seat beside me, downing his energy drink.

I eyed it. "Those are so bad for you."

"Taking drinks from random guys is bad for you," he snapped.

I would never live that down. "I'm just trying to help you."

"Thanks, Mom."

Seriously, I wanted to slap him sometimes.

"She's right," Cayson said. "The epinephrine in that can really mess up your heart, especially over a long period of time."

"Well, I choose to live my life how I want. Did you know stress can really mess up your heart?" Slade countered.

Cayson shrugged. "I tried."

"You want to head to the bar to watch the game tonight?" Slade asked. "The Steelers are playing."

"Um…" He eyed Skye.

Slade rolled his eyes. "You're so lame, man."

"I'm not asking her for permission," Cayson said immediately. "I just had plans with Skye tonight."

"Change them. She can come too." Slade finished his drink then crushed the can with his hand. "Invite everyone. I don't care."

Cayson looked at Skye. "What do you think?"

"Yeah, let's watch the game," Skye said. "I want fries and hot wings anyway."

Cayson gave her a fond look. "I should have known food would be the deciding factor."

Skye shrugged. "I like food."

"You coming?" Slade asked. He looked at his can when he said it.

Who was he talking to? "Sorry, are you talking to me?"

"Who else would I be asking?" he snapped.

"Well, look at me when you talk to me."

He rolled his eyes. "Okay, Princess."

"Do you even want me to go?"

"Would I have asked you if I didn't?" He finally looked at me.

Cayson sighed. "Peace—just for a few minutes."

"Please," Skye said.

Slade rolled his eyes then crushed the can into a thin strip with his bare hands. "I'll see you guys there at six." He stood up and left his trash on the table.

"I hope you don't expect us to throw that away," I noted.

He growled then grabbed the can. On his way out, he tossed it in the recycling bin.

"You guys are so weird…" Skye stared at me as she said it. "He beats up three guys to protect you but then you argue like hyenas fighting over a dead carcass."

"He and I will never get along." I leaned back in my chair, trying to forget about how pissed off Slade made me.

"Yeah…we're figuring that out." Cayson smirked.

***

As soon as I got home, there was a knock on the door.

I put down my bag then looked through the peephole. My brother was standing on my doorstep. I sighed then opened it, knowing I'd have to get this over with sooner or later.

He walked inside then looked at me. His eyes were dark and focused, like he was furious or on the verge of tears.

I decided to speak first. "Look, I know what you're going to say and I don't want to deal with this right now. I made a mistake and I learned my lesson. I'll be smarter from now on. Get off my ass." I turned around then opened the refrigerator, looking for a bottle of Evian.

Conrad stayed behind me and said nothing.

I grabbed the bottle then took a drink. I set it on the counter and waited for him to scream at me and call me a stupid whore.

Conrad stepped closer to me. He wore a gray hoodie and his hair was slightly messy. He had dark hair like my father. We hardly looked anything alike. Only our eyes seemed to be similar. "I'm not here to yell at you."

That was a first.

"I just wanted to see if you were okay." He rested his hand on the counter next to me and put the other in his pocket.

"Nothing happened, Conrad. I'm fine."

"But…I'm sure you were shaken up about it."

"Not really. I was drunk so everything was numb. And Slade dragged me out before I could really think about anything."

He sighed. "I'm so glad he was there."

"I'm not sure how he knew what was going on. But he did."

He stared at me, concern in his eyes. "Are you sure you're okay?"

"I'm fine. Really."

"Please be more careful. Most of the time I can't stand you and I think you're annoying as hell...but...I do love you."

Warmth flooded my heart. "I love you too."

He coughed into his hand then shifted his weight. "Should we hug or something?"

"I guess we could."

He closed the gap between us and hugged me quickly. Then he pulled away.

"You aren't going to mention anything to Dad, right?"

"No. You never tattle on me and I'll never tattle on you."

"Thanks. I'm not worried about how he would treat me. Honestly, I'm terrified of how he would react to those three guys."

"I know, right?" He chuckled slightly. He put both hands in his pockets. "Are you watching the game tonight?"

"Yeah, I'll be there."

"Cool." He ran his fingers through his hair. "I know you and Slade argue a lot...but maybe you should try to be nice to him since he...you know...obviously cares about you."

"He's the one that's an asshole every second of the day. It's hard to be nice to him."

"It's just some friendly advice." He walked out and shut the door behind him.

I didn't need any advice when it came to Slade. He was the definition of an asshole. And just because he saved me didn't mean I'd let him treat me like dirt. No way.

***

We got a booth in the corner and faced the large screen TV.

"Come on!" Conrad shouted. "Score, goddamn it!"

"Go...go...go!" Roland thumped his hand against the wood of the table.

Slade leaned forward on his elbows. "I'm about to be a thousand bucks richer."

The player made it to the end zone.

"Yeah, baby!" Slade clapped his hands. "Alright."

"Who did you bet a thousand bucks with?" I asked.

"Online sport betting," he answered.

"Isn't that illegal?" I asked.

"Anything worth doing is illegal." He spoke without looking at me then drank his beer. His arm was covered in various tattoos. A black squid moved up his forearm and a grizzly bear was on his bicep. His body was a canvas of random images. But he used color in every single one. Instead of traditional black ink, he was covered in bright hues, like red, green, blue, and orange.

"Does your dad know?" I asked.

"Duh. He bets too." He finished his second beer but didn't seem affected by it.

Cayson had his arm around Skye while his free hand held his beer.

Roland watched them. "This is so strange..."

"What?" Conrad asked.

"Seeing them together," Roland said. "I thought it would never happen, and now that it finally has, it's hard to understand."

"Get used to it." Skye leaned in and kissed Cayson on the cheek.

Cayson smirked then gave her a fond look.

Roland cringed. "Just keep it PG, alright?"

"You talked about fucking that married woman countless times," Skye countered.

"Totally different." Roland drank his beer then wiped his lips.

"No, it isn't," Skye snapped.

"You're my sister," Roland said. "It is different."

"Sexist pig," she mumbled.

"Annoying brat," Roland mumbled back.

Slade stared at the screen like it was the most fascinating thing in the world. "If they win with a score of 28 to 22, I win ten grand."

"Shut up," Conrad said. "How?"

"The odds are slim but it could happen," Slade said. "I did a lot of research."

"Imagine how well you would do in school if you used all the time you spent on gambling, doodling, and playing your guitar toward your classes," Cayson said.

Slade didn't seem to care. "Nah."

I sipped my wine but couldn't drink most of it. I was sick of alcohol from the previous weekend. My body needed a break.

"Do you want some more hot wings or fries?" Cayson asked Skye.

She shrugged. "I guess some fries wouldn't hurt."

"We just ate," Roland snapped. "How can you possibly be hungry?"

"Because I am," Skye argued.

Roland rolled his eyes. "I hope you like fat girls, Cayson. Because Skye is going to be huge."

"I like it when a girl knows how to eat." Cayson leaned toward her. "I'll be right back. Keep my seat warm."

"Or I could just sit in your lap," she whispered.

"Don't make me gag," Roland said.

Cayson left and headed to the bar.

I sighed in sadness. I couldn't deny how envious I was. I wished I had a great guy that loved me the way Cayson loved her. All I had were a string of guys that meant nothing. And I meant even less to them. Good guys were hard to find, nearly impossible. I'd given up at this point.

Cayson retrieved the basket of fries and placed them in front of Skye. "Eat up."

"Thank you." She gave him a bright smile before she started to munch.

I glanced at Slade. His eyes were glued to the screen. "Fucking refs. It seems like none of them are even qualified."

"Maybe they paid their way through school," Cayson said.

"They have referee school?" Slade asked with a raised eyebrow.

"Yeah, it's in Australia." Cayson drank his beer and avoided Slade's look.

I didn't know anything about football but I knew that was totally off.

"Australia?" Slade asked. "But they don't even have football over there."

Roland tried not to laugh.

Conrad was struggling too.

Cayson shrugged. "They want the refs to have absolutely no distractions during their training."

Slade's eyes narrowed. "But how would they practice if there're no football games?"

"They have all virtual testing," Roland said.

Slade stared at them suspiciously. "Wait a second…"

Cayson smirked.

"You're fucking with me, aren't you?" Slade asked.

Roland laughed. "I can't believe you bought that."

"Idiot," I murmured.

"You're one to talk," he snapped.

I sipped my wine and ignored his look.

"I'll get you back, Cayson," Slade threatened.

"Oooh…I'm so scared." Cayson laughed.

"You should be." Slade returned his eyes to the TV.

We watched the rest of the game then squared the tab. Cayson and Skye immediately paired off then headed home together. Roland and Conrad were inseparable so they drove together. I was the only one who drove on my own.

"See you later." Slade headed down the sidewalk, his hands in his pockets.

"Did you walk?" I asked.

"Yes, genius."

"You want a ride?" I asked. "It's cold."

"And sit with you in a car? I'm good." He kept walking.

I knew he was a dick but I was getting sick of his attitude. "Do you ever get tired of being a jackass?"

He didn't turn around. "No."

***

I got a text message from my father a few days later.

Breakfast on Sunday? He usually came down every other week. It was a routine we established a long time ago. It was unspoken but always acknowledged.

Sure.

I'll pick you up at 9.

Okay.

My father never brought my mom. It was always something only he and I did. I loved my mom but we weren't nearly as close as my father and I. I still remember going to work with him when I was younger. He'd let me play with my toys in his office, and he even took me to meetings with him. When he finished his workday, we would go by McDonald's and never tell my mom. He and I were always rule breakers.

On Sunday morning, he knocked on my door.

I wore my black leggings with boots and a thick sweater. A gold bracelet hung on my wrist and my hair was pulled over one shoulder. When I opened the door, I saw him wearing his usual attire. He wore dark jeans and a t-shirt. A dark blue blazer covered him, keeping him warm. My dad was at least a foot taller than me, if not more.

"Hey, Trin."

"Hey, Dad."

He stepped across the threshold and gave me a warm hug. He held me for a long moment before he pulled away. "Hungry?"

"Do you know me at all?"

He smirked then walked out. "Then let's get our grub on."

I walked out then locked the door behind me.

"The usual?" he asked.

"Yes, please."

He walked to his Porsche then opened the passenger door, letting me get inside. Then he walked around the car and got into the driver's seat. My dad was the only guy I knew who treated me like a lady. Every other guy couldn't care less about chivalry. My brother wasn't even nice to me.

My dad pulled onto the road and headed to the diner we always went to. It was a tradition that we never broke. When we arrived, he opened the door for me and even pulled out my chair.

"How's school?" He sat with his back perfectly straight then looked at the menu.

"Good. Nothing too interesting." I looked at the menu even though I already knew what I would order. It was the same thing I always got. "How's work?"

"Good. Nothing too interesting." He smirked while he read through the menu. "Are you getting the strawberry waffle with bacon and eggs?"

"When do I ever order anything else?" I said with a smile.

"Well, you always look at your menu so I know you consider it." He put the menu down. "New York steak and eggs for me."

"A very hearty meal."

He nodded. "I'm a big guy."

My dad wasn't fat. He was thick with muscle and strength. His eyes were blue, but most of the time they looked gray. He had an intimidating look about him. He looked like his brother but he had his own distinct features. I knew my father boxed for exercise and trained in martial arts. He was an intense person sometimes. "How's Mom?"

"Good. She's doing Cross Fit now."

"That doesn't surprise me. She's always been super fit."

"She's a fit chick. A hot one." A grin was on his face.

My mom was still pretty, even after all these years. "She could outrun you."

"Now let's not get carried away…"

The waitress approached our table. "I already know what you want, Trinity." She smiled then turned to my dad. "What can I get you, sir?"

"Mike," he answered. "Steak and eggs. Medium well, please."

"You got it." She took the menus.

"And some coffee, please," I blurted.

"Make that two," my dad added.

"Of course." She walked away.

My dad stared at my neck. "That's a nice scarf."

I felt the purple fabric. "Thanks. I got it on sale."

"It's a good color on you. Brings out your eyes."

"Thanks, Dad."

"Anything new?" he asked. He leaned back in his chair then rested his hands in his lap.

I thought about the party I went to last weekend and what almost happened. No, I couldn't bring that up. What could I talk about? "Cayson and Skye are cute together."

He nodded. "Your uncle Sean is very happy about that. I am too."

"Yeah...I can't believe it took them so long to figure out their feelings."

He shrugged. "Sean took longer."

"So I've heard from Skye." I crossed my arms over my chest and leaned back.

"Your brother behaving himself?"

"As far as I know. But if he wasn't, he wouldn't mention it to me."

"Like you would tell me anyway." He had a playful look in his eyes.

I shrugged. "I've never been a tattle-tell."

"Good. Those are annoying."

I chuckled. "Yeah, they are."

"Juggling any guys?" he asked.

My dad always asked this question in a calm way, almost like he didn't care. But I knew how protective he was of me. The last time I had a boyfriend, he insisted on meeting him and his entire family. It was an ordeal... "No."

He nodded. "Seeing just a single guy?"

"No guys at all," I answered. I hadn't dated in a while. I was getting tired of it. Most guys were jerks, boring, and horrible kissers. I wanted a guy to sweep me off my feet but I was quickly realizing that would never happen. I shouldn't bother waiting.

"Any reason why?" he asked.

"No...I just haven't met anyone who's worth my time."

"Good. I'm glad you're picky. You deserve nothing but the best, honey."

I smiled slightly then dropped it.

"You have the rest of your life anyway. And I don't want to have a heart attack anytime soon."

"Then you probably shouldn't order a steak," I noted.

He smirked. "I'm a man. I order what I want."

"You sound like a caveman," I said with a laugh.

"Me like meat," he said in a deep voice.

I laughed again.

"So, how are your classes?"

"You already asked me that."

"And you didn't give me a sufficient answer." He stared me down, suddenly becoming serious.

I shrugged. "Classes are alright."

"Conrad made it sound like you don't like school much."

"He did?" *When did he say that?*

He nodded. "He said you were more interested in fashion." He stared at me like he was waiting for a response. When I didn't say anything, he kept going. "Trinity, is that true?"

"Well, I do like fashion..."

"More than business?" he asked.

I guess I should just be honest. I could tell my dad almost anything. Sometimes I feared I would disappoint him for not wanting the company, something he spent his life doing. "I guess I'm not that into it…"

He nodded slowly. "Do you have any desire to take over the company with Skye?"

Not really. What should I say?

My dad leaned over the table. "Honey, you can tell me anything."

I looked down. "I guess I don't want to disappoint you."

"You could never disappoint me." Thick emotion was in his eyes. "Honey, I want you to be happy. Don't do something you don't want to do. Talk to me."

"I guess…no, I don't really want to do that. I think it's amazing that you and Uncle Sean have done such a great job growing the company into the empire it has become but…my heart isn't into it."

He stared at me for a long time, taking in my words. "Okay."

Okay? That's it? "What?"

"Trin, it's your life. I want you to do what makes you happy. If you don't want the company, you don't have to take it."

"But I know how important it is to you…"

He shrugged. "What does it matter? You need to live your life for yourself, not other people. No matter what you do or how aware you are of other people's feelings, you aren't going to make everyone happy. So don't bother. My dad started that company out of his garage when he was eighteen. When I graduated college, he wanted Sean and I to take over. But neither one of us wanted it. I did my own thing for years. I didn't come to it until I was ready and knew I really wanted it. Sean did the same. Do what you want, Trin. You have my support no matter what."

My dad made it so easy. "Thanks…"

"But you should really think about it before you make any hasty decisions. That's all I ask."

"You're right."

"So…what would you like to do?"

I never entertained the idea before. "Well, I like fashion."

"You could do modeling. Are you interested in that?"

I rolled my eyes. Of course my dad thought I was model material. He was blinded by his love. "Maybe design. I really like putting outfits together."

He nodded. "I know a lot of people in the city. I can set you up with something or even a designer. Or we could launch your own clothing line. Whatever you want, Trin."

Sometimes I forgot all the power my father had. "Thanks. I'll think about it."

"Okay."

The waitress returned with the food. "Plates are hot. Be careful." She set everything down then walked away.

I picked up my fork and started to eat. "What do you and Mom do now that Conrad and I are out of the house? Are you guys bored?"

He laughed. "Bored? Definitely not. It's nice having time to ourselves again. And the peace and quiet…" He shook his head. "There's nothing like it."

"We weren't that loud," I argued.

"Maybe not in high school but you certainly were growing up."

"You said I was a cute baby."

"Oh, you were. You were adorable, still are. But that doesn't mean you weren't a pain in the ass."

I glared at my dad and kept eating. "Conrad was the terror, not me."

He laughed. "You have some odd perceptions of yourself. You guys both drove your mother and I up the walls. You both had your golden moments, but also times of pure terror."

"How sweet," I said sarcastically.

He smirked. "Your mother and I miss you guys—sometimes."

"I miss being home sometimes," I said with a sigh, feeling the emotion come out.

He caught the look. "Is everything okay, Trin?"

"Yeah…I guess I miss living in a fairy tale."

He studied me for a moment. "I don't understand your meaning."

I took a deep breath. "I just expected being an adult would be awesome. It would be all fun and games. All I would do is enjoy my freedom. Life would be good, it would be great. But…"

"But what?" he pressed.

"I guess it's a lot harder than I thought."

His eyes softened when he looked at me. They turned blue for a moment, showing his vulnerability.

"I feel like I don't know where I belong. I keep making mistakes. I just want to fast-forward to the next stage. I want to find the perfect guy and marry him. I want to be married with kids. I just want to find the place where I belong…" I realized this conversation became too serious. "I'm sorry. I'm just rambling."

He processed my words for a long time. "When I first became an adult, I struggled. I was a much different man before your mother came into my life. I was a jerk, frankly. I wanted to be a bachelor all my life. All I cared about was racing fast cars and picking up different girls every night. I went through the motions, just having fun. But in reality, I was sad. When your uncle Sean got married, I realized how empty and meaningless my life was. All I did was waste time and break hearts. I had nothing to show for it. The depression hit me hard. I was a single guy, alone and broken. But then your mother came into my life, bringing the light with her."

His words echoed in my mind long after he said them.

"My point is, even though I went through a hard time, I wouldn't change it for anything. Because when you do finally find where you belong and the person you belong with, you realize you wouldn't have appreciated it so much unless you struggled to begin with." He rested his hand on mine. "You will find the place where you belong and the guy you belong with. But never speed up time. Because we really don't have long on this earth. Appreciate what you have. Because before you know it, it's gone."

My father pulled his hand away then sipped his coffee. Silence stretched between us. My dad and I always had serious conversations, but we never went as deep as this. He was a friend as well as a parent. It felt good to get that off my chest. Because, like always, he made me feel better.

Chapter Five

Cayson

I sat down at our usual table in the library but Skye wasn't there. It was only Trinity and Slade.

"All I'm saying is, you're stupid and annoying." Slade ate his burrito while he spoke, forgetting his manners. "So just shut the hell up."

"You aren't supposed to eat in the library," she hissed.

"And you aren't supposed to talk," he snapped. "Do the world a favor and become mute."

"Ugh." Trinity looked like she might slam her textbook into his head.

I eyed them both. "Best friends, I see…"

"I wouldn't be her friend if you paid me," Slade said, still eating his burrito.

"I'm so close to smashing my book into your skull," she threatened.

"You would never hit your target." He crammed the rest of the burrito, nearly half of it, into his wide open mouth. He could barely close his lips around it.

"Gross…just take a bite and chew," Trinity said. "Why do you have to shove it down your throat like a seagull?"

"At least I eat. You're a twig."

"At least I'm not disgusting."

I couldn't stand this much longer. "Kids, knock it off. Or time-out for both of you."

Slade rolled his eyes. "I'm about to wipe a booger on her."

"Gross…" She crossed her arms over her chest and sighed.

"Have you seen Skye?" I asked. "She's usually here about now."

"No. I haven't seen her all day," Trinity said.

She usually came to the library for her two-hour break. I couldn't recall a time when she skipped it. "That's odd."

"Just text her and ask where she is, genius." Slade balled up his foil then threw it right at Trinity's face.

"Jackass." She swatted it away and it fell on the floor.

I typed the message. *Babe, I'm in the library. Where are you?*

"Excuse me." The librarian stood at our table, looking pissed. Her glasses made her eyes look three times as big. She looked like a bug under a magnifying glass.

Trinity stiffened.

"No food in the library." She was staring at Trinity, annoyance and disapproval heavy in her eyes. "You know the school rules. Now pick up that trash and throw it away."

Trinity turned to Slade, glaring at him.

Slade covered his mouth and tried not to laugh.

"I'm waiting..." The librarian crossed her arms over her chest. "You think just because you're a rich kid that you don't have to follow the rules?"

The librarian was being awfully harsh but none of us told her off.

Trinity sighed then picked up the foil from the ground. Then she threw it away.

"Now was that so hard?" The librarian gave her one final glare before she walked off.

Trinity turned her rage to Slade. "You dick!"

Slade laughed hard, hitting his hand against the table. "Oh man, that was hilarious."

"It was not," Trinity hissed.

"Dude, that book nerd hates you." Slade couldn't stop laughing. "That was priceless."

"Go to hell, Slade." She grabbed her bag and marched off.

Slade kept laughing even after she was gone. "She had it coming."

I didn't comment on it. I never understood their odd relationship. Slade treated her like dirt but he was willing to stick out his neck to protect her. He tried to act like a macho and careless guy on the outside, but he had a heart of gold underneath. That was the reason why he was my best friend. There was a lot of good to him—he just never showed it.

I turned my attention back to my phone. Skye never texted me back.

"Dude, leave her alone," Slade said. "Don't be one of those obsessive and stalker type boyfriends."

"I'm not," I said immediately. "It's just out of the ordinary for her. And the fact she isn't messaging me back is worrying me."

"Chill, man. Girls hate clingy guys."

"I'm not clingy," I said firmly. "I'm just concerned."

"She's probably taking a dump," Slade reasoned. "No reason to get upset."

I ignored his comment and called her. It rang several times then went to voicemail. What was she doing? Did she go home? If she did, why? And why wasn't she texting me back? "I'm going to look for her."

"Overreacting…" He shook his head slightly.

"When you fall in love with someone, you'll overreact too."

"Fall in love?" He leaned his head back and laughed. "Stop with the jokes. My stomach hurts."

I left the library to search for her. I walked past the classes she already had and hoped to find her there. She was nowhere to be found. I headed to her apartment but she wasn't there either. I was starting to get uneasy. The situation wasn't adding up. Where was she?

***

I headed through the school grounds toward the main building. I still couldn't find Skye so I was backtracking. The fact no one knew where she was and she wasn't answering her phone was making me panic. I wasn't sure if I should call the police or her dad. I tried to stay calm and remain logical. There was obviously an explanation for her disappearance.

When I reached the path, I heard voices.

"No, you aren't running away from me. I want to talk about this!" a man yelled, sounding threatening.

"Leave me alone!" It was the voice of a woman. And I recognized it immediately.

I turned the corner and saw Zack gripping Skye by the elbow. He was holding her phone in the opposite hand, keeping it out of her reach.

"Give it back to me," she hissed. She tried to knee him in the groin but he moved out of the way.

I suspected Zack would make a reappearance at some point, but not like this. Seeing him grip her arm sent me to the brink. If it were any girl, I'd be pissed. But since it was Skye, I was livid.

"No," he snapped. "How do you think I felt when I was stuck in the hospital for two weeks?"

"I didn't put you there!" She hit him in the stomach and tried to grab the phone.

He pushed her back. "Don't act innocent. I know it was your dad. You—"

I grabbed him by the neck and viciously slammed him into the concrete.

Skye stepped back then looked at me, relief written all over her face.

Without thinking, I raised my foot over his face and stomped down, making his nose crack and blood spew out.

"Fuck!" He clutched his face and rolled over.

"You think that hurt?" I savagely kicked him in the side, right where his ribs were. "Since you miss the hospital so much, I'll put you back there." I kicked him again. "Fucking dick."

He curled into a ball and moaned, trying to protect himself.

"Let's get this straight. Come near Skye again and I'll make it a million times more painful." I stomped on his hand, snapping two fingers.

"Fuck!"

"Cayson, that's enough." Skye's words washed over me.

Only her voice could hold me back. Like a scabbard, she could sheath my anger like no one else. The blood lust was suddenly gone. I turned away from Zack and looked at her. "Are you okay?"

"I'm fine." She walked around Zack then yanked her phone out of his grasp. "I'll be needing that." No sympathy was on her face. She came back around, joining me.

I was so relieved she wasn't hurt. I immediately pulled her into me and formed a steel cage around her with my arms. "You're safe now. Don't be scared."

"I wasn't scared. He was just being a dick."

"Well, I won't let him be one anymore." My hand moved through her hair, treasuring her.

She rested her face against my chest then sighed.

Zack climbed to his feet slowly then wiped the blood from his nose. One hand was pulled to his chest and his fingers were bent in an odd way.

I stared him down, not feeling any remorse. "She's mine now. And I won't hesitate to kill you if you give me a reason to."

He gave me a final glare before walking away.

Skye sighed then pulled away. "Please don't mention this to my father."

I would do whatever she asked. "Okay."

She looked at her phone and saw all the messages and missed calls. "I'm sorry, Cayson. You must have been worried."

"Don't apologize," I said immediately. "I'm just sorry he had you cornered like that."

"It's okay. I'm not scared of him."

That didn't mean I wasn't. I'd have to keep a better eye on her. "Is there anything I can do?"

"No. I just want to go home and eat something."

"Okay." I pulled her close to me and kissed her forehead.

"Thanks for getting rid of him. I was so relieved when I saw you."

"I'll always take care of you." I never meant anything more in my life.

She grabbed her bag off the ground and shouldered it. "Let's go."

***

Two empty pizza boxes were left on the coffee table. Skye could down a whole one by herself. Her brother teased her for it, but I thought it was hot. She had curves in all the right places, and she wouldn't have them unless she ate like a normal person.

"Poker?" she asked as she pulled out a deck of cards. A mischievous grin was on her face.

It was past nine. Since it was a Friday night, I didn't care about the time. I'd probably stay with her all weekend, and before I knew it, it would be Monday again. Time flew by with her. I never had enough of her. "Sure. But I'm not playing for money."

"Because you know I'll win."

I smirked. "No. Because I'm a gentleman."

"I don't want a gentleman. I want you."

When she said things like that, my heart fluttered. It was hard to understand that she wanted me the way I wanted her. So many years had gone by when she didn't notice me. Now everything was different. "Well, that's what you're going to get."

She pouted her lips. "You don't have to be perfect all the time, Cayson. I wouldn't mind a darker side to you."

My eyes narrowed when I looked at her.

She pulled out the cards and started to shuffle them. "Can I ask you something personal?"

"Like I said, you can ask me anything."

"Were you like this with your other girls?"

"Like what?"

"Sweet, considerate, compassionate...stuff like that."

When I remembered my time with Jasmine, I knew the answer. "No. I was a dick most of the time."

"I can't picture it..." She shuffled the cards again and started to deal.

"I'm only sweet to you, Skye. Honestly, I'm not that great of a guy. I have a lot of regrets."

"Like what?" She placed the deck on the table and looked at me.

This was a new realm for her and I. "Jasmine is one of them."

She stared at me, waiting for me to go on.

"I told her we were just..." It was hard to find an appropriate description. I watched my language around Skye, being a gentleman. "Someone to pass the time with. Our relationship was only physical but she always wanted something more. I told her I couldn't give it to her. But then she told me she loved me…and that I was the one to her."

Emotion flashed in her eyes but she said nothing.

"I wish I'd never gotten involved with her. I know firsthand what it's like to love someone you can't have. I never wanted that to happen to her…but it did."

She stared at the cards in front of us, considering my words. "It's hard not to fall in love with you, Cayson. I'm not surprised. I'm sure it happens more often than you think."

Did that mean she was in love with me? I knew she loved me but…was it the same? "Do you have any regrets?"

She smirked. "I think it's pretty obvious what my biggest regret is."

Zack. She didn't need to say it. "Any others?"

She pulled her hair over one shoulder, revealing her slender neck. It caught my eye immediately. "You."

"Me?" *What did she mean?*

"I wish I had realized how I felt before…all the time we wasted."

"We have the rest of our lives, Skye. Don't beat yourself up over it."

She gave me a slight smile before she dropped it. "There are a few things here and there but nothing major. I never really had a serious boyfriend when I was younger because my dad would have shot them."

I chuckled. "Yeah…I could see that happening."

She rolled her eyes. "I'm glad you aren't scared of my dad."

"Who said I wasn't?" I teased.

"He loves you."

"Yeah. But that could change if I crossed a line."

She stared at me across the table. "But you never would."

Snow was falling lightly outside. The windowpanes were starting to frost. She and I were alone in winter bliss. I treasured the silence, feeling like we were secluded from the world. She was mine—and mine alone. "I'm glad you realize that."

"I trust you more than anyone, Cayson. There's no room for doubt."

"I'm glad you feel that way." Because I worked hard for that trust. I stared at the skin of her neck, wanting to press my lips against it. Her flesh would feel warm against my mouth. But there would be time for that later.

She grabbed her deck and looked at the cards. "How about we make it interesting?"

"What are you thinking?" I picked up my cards and looked through them. Uncle Mike taught me how to play and I was pretty good at it, definitely better than Skye. But I always let her win.

"Strip poker?" She gave me a seductive grin.

That caught my attention. I wanted to see Skye naked all the time—ever since I hit puberty. "I'm game if you are."

"I am too. But I'm going to be fully clothed while you're naked."

Not this time. "We'll see."

We started the round. I had a good hand and all I needed was to trade a single card. Skye thought she had a clever poker face, and maybe she fooled everyone else, but she couldn't fool me. I'd studied her face for too many years, saw it in every dream, to not understand all of its secrets. She gave a quick smile, a fake one, and then traded a card.

She was bluffing.

"You ready?" she asked.

"Yeah."

"Are you sure you don't want to fold?"

"No." I kept a stoic face, hiding everything.

"Alright...what item of clothing is this for?"

I immediately wanted to blurt "shirt" but I didn't want Skye to know that, like every other guy, I was obsessed with her chest. "Shoes."

"Okay...your feet are about to get cold." She put down her cards. She had two pairs.

I smirked then put mine down. I had a full house.

She narrowed her eyes. "Lucky hand."

"Yeah." She was going down. "Now take off those boots."

She yanked them off then tossed them aside.

"Those socks will be next."

"Don't get cocky," she warned.

Too late.

We played another round. Skye pulled her typical tricks on me but I didn't let them slide. My hand beat hers—easily.

"Now take those socks off." I stared at her, waiting for her to comply.

She sighed then pulled them off.

I smirked. *I was loving this.*

"Your luck has run out." She dealt the cards again and we picked up our piles. I had a bad hand but I knew how to play it cool. I only traded one card instead of all five.

Skye watched me, studying my face. Then she looked back at her hand.

"For the pants?" I asked.

She seemed unsure. Then she put her cards down. "I fold."

I smirked. "Someone is dropping the ball."

"Shut up. It was just a bad hand."

"Someone's touchy…"

She kicked me playfully under the table then dealt the new hand. Now she was watching me closely, trying to gauge my features like she never had. She studied her cards for a long time before she swapped them. I did the same.

"Ladies first," I said.

She gave me a cocky smirk before she put them down. "Flush. I want to see some drawers."

I put my cards down. "Royal flush."

Her smile dropped.

"I want to see some knickers."

She growled then rolled her eyes.

"Come on." I snapped my fingers. "We don't have all day."

"Why are you winning all of a sudden?"

I shrugged. "Stop talking and start undressing."

She stood up then unbuttoned her jeans.

My eyes were focused on her hands, watching everything she did. I tried to seem indifferent but I couldn't. My cock grew in anticipation. Then she lowered her jeans and kicked them away. She wore a purple thong that barely covered anything. My cock twitched in my pants. Then she sat down and was hidden from view.

Now I was even more motivated to win the next hand.

Skye dealt the cards. "I'm winning this round."

So she thinks…

We put down our cards. Skye's face fell when she saw mine. "You have two aces and two kings?"

"Yep." She only had pairs of twos and fours. "Now the top."

She growled at me then yanked it off. Her bra pushed her breasts together and made her cleavage more prominent. Her pale skin was perfect and unblemished. She was a vision, she was a muse. Nothing had ever turned me on as much as she did. My cock twitched again. And again.

Now I just had to get that bra off.

"Are you cheating?" she demanded.

"How would I cheat?" I looked at my cards and tried not to gawk at her.

"Well, you always lose. All of a sudden, you're the best poker player I've ever seen."

"I guess I'm extremely motivated." I arranged my cards then swapped them.

She eyed me suspiciously before she continued with the game.

To no one's surprise, I won the next round. I held out my hand. "I'll take those."

"You want my panties?" she asked incredulously.

"I won them."

She stood up then pulled them off.

I blatantly stared at her, unable to control myself. Her legs were toned and smooth, and my eyes went to the nub between her legs. I wanted to taste her again, to feel her dig her fingers into my hair because I made her feel so good.

She sat down again, hiding her waist from my sight. "I'll offer you another deal."

I smirked. "You can't stand losing."

"It's not that."

"Whatever you say…"

"It's not."

"Sure." I nodded my head slowly.

"You want to listen to my offer or not?"

"I'm all ears."

"Winner takes all. If I win, you have to do something…sexual to me. If I win…then I do something sexual to you. The victor gets to choose."

It sounded like I won in either case. "Sounds good. I guess I should start brainstorming now."

"I wouldn't waste your time." She shuffled the cards then passed them out.

I glanced at mine and realized I had a good hand. I wouldn't even need to try. Skye stared at her cards for a long time, biting her nails. That was a dead giveaway that she was stressed. I pretended not to notice and swapped my cards. I had two pairs. Not amazing, but I had a feeling it would beat hers. "Ready?" I asked.

"Yeah..." She placed her cards on the table. She had a pair of aces.

I smirked then put mine down.

She sighed when she looked at it.

I held out my hand. "Now the bra..."

She unclasped it in the back then let it fall. The second I saw her nipples, I was practically on the edge of my seat. She pulled it off then threw it at me. "There. Congratulations."

I grabbed the panties off the table and stuffed them into my pocket. I held her bra in the other hand. Completely clothed, I stared at her chest, liking what I saw. I was excited for what was next.

She stood up, showing me a full view. "I'll be in the bedroom." She walked away, her ass shaking.

I adjusted myself in my jeans then followed her. My heart was beating fast and I felt hot all over. The last thing I felt like doing was being a gentleman. Skye drove me wild and I wanted to be inside her.

I walked in and saw her sitting on the bed.

"What do you want to do?" she asked.

"Anything?" I asked.

"Yep." She crossed her legs and stared me down.

I came closer to her, wanting to crush my mouth against hers.

She held me back. "Nope. You have to choose one thing. If it's kissing, that's all you get."

"You have a strict set of rules."

"Yep."

"Have you played this before?" I asked suspiciously.

"Nope. Just you. Now what do you want to do, Cayson?"

We already did other things so I was eager to try something new. But I felt like a jerk for even thinking about saying it. Skye was already sensitive about it and I didn't want to irritate her. But I couldn't deny what I wanted.

"Cayson, spit it out."

I guided her on her back. "I want to kiss you."

She tried not to laugh. "Be real, Cayson. That can't be what's on your mind."

"I love kissing you."

"Come on. What do you really want?"

I said nothing, just staring at her.

"Why won't you tell me?"

"I don't want to make you uncomfortable."

"I wouldn't have made this bet if I were uncomfortable."

I glanced at her chest and looked away.

She caught the look. "You want to tit-fuck me."

Was I that obvious? I didn't respond. She didn't ask me a question so I wasn't obligated to say anything.

"Why are you ashamed to admit that?" She smirked while she ran her fingers through my hair.

"Skye, I know you hate it when men are obsessed with your chest. I don't want to remind you of them."

She cupped my face and kissed me. "You're so sweet, Cayson."

My lips burned the moment I touched hers.

"But that doesn't apply to you."

"It doesn't?"

"No. You're different. I want you to enjoy my body."

"You hated it when Zack did it."

"But I didn't love him," she blurted. "I love you."

My heart fluttered at her words. "I love hearing you say that."

"Well, you better get used to it." She kissed me again, slipping her tongue inside.

I melted at her touch, feeling vindicated for my perverse thoughts. She grabbed my arm then turned me on my back, making me hit the sheets. Then she moved off me, standing at the foot of the bed.

I'd tit-fucked a few girls but I never was excited for it before. Skye was my ultimate fantasy, the woman I used to jerk off to when I was growing up. But my desire never died out.

She unbuttoned my jeans then yanked them off, pulling my briefs with them. She left my socks on and didn't think twice about them before she pulled off my shirt. "I want to see all of you." She kissed my chest then moved down toward my waist. My cock was twitching, yearning for her. When she reached me, she took me into her mouth, shoving me far into the back of her throat.

"Fuck..." Now that she said she was okay with my lustful obsession with her, I was more open about it. I was strongly sexually attracted to her and I wasn't afraid to hide it.

Once I was wet, she kneeled at the bed, her chest level with my waist. Then she wrapped her tits around my cock and pushed them together.

Oh my fucking god.

Then she moved up and down.

I raised myself on my elbows and watched her slide up and down my shaft. I couldn't tell what felt better. Her tits sliding past my cock or watching her do it. She gave me a dark look while she did it, driving me wild. I already wanted to explode. Unable to control myself, I grabbed her tits on either side and smashed them together, thrusting my hips up and down. "Shit, that feels good."

She bounced up and down my dick, keeping her breasts together.

I was about to crumble. She was the most beautiful woman in the world and we were playing out my dirtiest fantasy. I squeezed her tits as I came, moaning as I did it. I squirted on her chest and the area below her chin. I rested my head against the mattress while I recovered from the pleasurable sensation in my groin.

Skye wiped off then climbed up my chest until her face was close to mine. "Did you like that?"

"That's the dumbest question I've ever heard."

She smirked then kissed the hair on my chin. "I'm glad you liked it."

"Shit, I loved it."

"Did Cayson Thompson just curse?" she teased.

I chuckled then rolled her onto her back. Then I showered her breasts with kisses. "I love your rack, Skye. I think it's sexy as hell and I'm not going to hide it anymore. If that makes me a pervert, so be it. I love you for a lot more, but I won't deny how these things get me going."

She ran her fingers through my hair, amusement in her eyes. "That doesn't bother me in the least. You're the only man I've ever wanted to look at them in that way."

"Well, mission accomplished." I gave her a gentle kiss before I slid down her stomach. "Now, how about your turn?"

She fisted my hair. "I thought you'd never ask."

***

"Did you see that play?" Slade put his feet on his coffee table and kept his eyes on the TV. We were watching the game at his place but I wasn't sure why. There were usually women hanging around, used condoms in places where they shouldn't be, and it was usually a mess.

"How do you fumble the ball when you're the quarterback?" I asked.

Slade rolled his eyes. "You would think the pros would have their shit together by now."

I adjusted myself in my seat but felt a lump. Unable to get comfortable, I pulled aside the cushion and looked behind it. A pink bra was lodged inside. "Gross." I pulled it out and tossed it on the floor.

Slade didn't blink an eye over it. "Oh yeah. I remember that one girl was wondering what happened to it."

"Why don't we just watch the game at my place?" Who knows what else was hidden in the crevasses of his couch.

"Because my place is better."

I eyed his closed bedroom door. "There better not be a girl in there." I couldn't count the number of times that happened. They stepped out, totally naked, and didn't even care if I saw.

"No. Calm down."

I settled back into my seat.

"What happened with Skye the other day?" He rested his beer on his thigh.

"Oh…" I hated thinking about it. "Zack cornered her and was giving her a hard time."

Anger moved into his eyes. "Kick his ass?"

"And his ribs…and his face. I got it covered."

"Fucker." Slade clenched his jaw and shook his head. "She's okay, right?"

"She's fine. She didn't seem upset about it—just annoyed."

"What did you guys do this weekend?"

"We stayed at her place and hung out."

"Hung out?" he asked.

"Played poker."

"Are you guys twelve?"

"When you're in a relationship, you do more than have sex all the time."

He shook his head. "That's why I'm going to be a terminal bachelor. So, how's her rack?"

I cocked an eyebrow. "She's your cousin…"

"I'm not asking for a description," he snapped. "Are they as good as everyone makes them out to be?"

"Definitely." I got red in the face from thinking about our last rendezvous.

He grinned then nudged me in the side. "You dog."

I wasn't going to deny it.

"What did you guys do now?"

I didn't see the harm in telling him. "I tit-fucked her."

He raised his hand to give me a high-five. "Man, those are the best. They come in a close second to blow jobs."

"For me, it comes in first."

"Skye gives horrible head?"

"No," I said immediately. "I just…really liked it."

"I tit-fucked this one girl who insisted on it even though she was flat." He shook his ahead. "It was awkward and didn't feel good. So I just fucked her ass instead."

"TMI, Slade."

"What?" He shrugged. "I'm an open guy."

"I've noticed."

"You've done anal, right?"

"Not with Skye."

"I'm sure that will be fun." He wiggled his eyebrows.

Slade was all about getting to home base. He lacked the understanding that running around the bases was the best part. Cultivating a relationship and adoring your partner made it a million times better. I hadn't had sex with Skye yet, but everything we'd done up to that point was way better than anything I ever did with someone else. "Slade, when is this going to end?"

"At seven. The Simpsons come on after that."

"No, I meant your lifestyle. This can't be as satisfying as you claim."

"But it is." He stared at the game while he said it, half listening to me.

For as long as I'd known Slade, he never had a girlfriend. He didn't even have a junior high love. Ever since he hit puberty, all he cared about was getting girls in the sack. "It's going to get old after awhile."

"Maybe when I'm forty. Then I'll reconsider some stuff. Until then, I'm very happy with my life."

"Don't you want someone that you like to be around for longer than five minutes?"

"Five minutes?" He raised an eyebrow. "Sorry, man. If you only last five minutes, I feel bad for Skye."

I gave him a hard look. "Slade, I'm being serious."

He sighed then put down his beer. "Look, it's cool that you've finally found the one girl you can settle down with. But aren't you forgetting all the years before this? How many girls did you sleep with that meant nothing to you? How many one night stands did you have?"

"Not nearly as many as you. And I was depressed the entire time."

"You enjoyed it and you know you did."

"At the time, yes. But I was definitely lonely."

"This is how it is." He talked with his hands, which he usually did when he was being serious. "You're the type of guy who's going to be rich and successful. And not just any rich, but respectable rich. You're going to be loved by your community. Everyone already adores you as it is. You'll have a wife with a house and a picket fence. You'll pop out three kids and save money for their tuitions. That's you, Cayson. Not me. I can't see any of that happening for me."

"And what do you see, Slade?"

He thought for a moment. "Living out of a bag. Inking in different parts of the world. Playing in a band for a few tours. Getting so drunk in a country I don't recognize that I can't even tell where I am. Picking up girls in various places. Just living my life."

"What about when you turn thirty? Then forty? What will you have then?"

"Why would anything change?"

"Not a lot of chicks dig old guys."

"That's not old. And I'm good-looking. You should see my dad at the shop. The girls still throw themselves at him. I'm surprised he doesn't cheat on my mom. She's so annoying that I wouldn't blame him." He laughed then drank his beer.

"I know you don't mean that."

He didn't comment.

"You're one of the greatest guys I know and I just want…the best for you." Awkwardness filled the room. I stared at the TV, feeling the tension. I wasn't an emotional guy and neither was Slade. All we did was joke around and never took anything seriously.

Slade was quiet. The silence stretched for so long that I didn't think he would say anything at all. "I know, man. I want the same for you too."

"Just think about what I said, alright?"

He shrugged. "I might."

We returned our attention back to the TV. The game continued on until it ended at seven. A rerun of the Simpsons came on.

"I love this show," Slade said.

"Me too." I put my empty beer bottle on the coffee table. "I guess I'll see you later."

"'Ight. Tell Skye I said hi."

I stared at him.

"Like you aren't going over there," he teased.

I didn't see the point in denying it. "It was nice coming over here without a naked chick walking around."

"That's a sentence no man should ever say."

I chuckled. "And make sure you throw that bra away."

"I'll probably rub one out on it."

I cringed. "TMI, Slade."

The door to his bedroom suddenly opened. A blonde with a sheet wrapped around her body came out with her eyes squinted. "Where am I?"

I glared at Slade. "I thought you said there wasn't a girl in there?"

He grinned. "Wait for it..."

Then another blonde appeared. "Please tell me you have aspirin and a beer."

Slade stood up then squeezed my shoulder. "I said there wasn't a girl in there—not *girls*."

Chapter Six

Skye

Trinity sat across from me in the library.

"How's your dad?" I asked.

"Good. Pretty much the same."

"Did you go to the same diner?"

"Always," Trinity said with a smile. "I told him I want to do fashion instead."

My heart stopped. "Seriously?"

She nodded.

"What did he say?"

"He supports it. He says I should do whatever I want to do. He gave grandpa the bird when he became an adult and I should do the same."

"That's really cool. So what now?"

She shrugged. "He said he wants me to think about it first. I mean, I'm almost done with college. It would be a waste to just drop out now."

"Did he say that?"

"No, but I know he's thinking it. He offered to get me in contact with designers in the city. And he even offered to fund my own clothing line."

"Uncle Mike is a good guy," I said. "I knew he would be supportive."

"He said the doors are always open if I want to change my mind. I guess it's not a big deal."

I smiled then patted her on the hand. "I'm excited for you. I know how much you want this."

"Thanks...I feel better about it now that I got it off my chest."

"Did you...get anything else off your chest?" I asked hesitantly.

"No," she said immediately. "I would never tell him that."

"A wise decision," I said with a laugh.

She closed her textbook and rested her chin on her hand. "How's it going with Cayson?"

I felt my cheeks lift with a smile. "Absolutely amazing and fantastic."

She smirked. "I can tell. How's he in bed?"

"I don't know yet."

She rolled her eyes. "Fuck his brains out already."

"I know. I want to."

"Then do it."

"I just don't want to rush anything. And he's good at everything else so I'm okay."

"How's he look down below?" she asked with a mischievous grin.

"Trinity!" I swatted her hand.

"What? It was just a question."

My cheeks blushed.

"He's big, huh?"

I covered my face because I was beet red.

"Bigger than Zack?"

"Much, much bigger."

"Oooh...lucky you."

I tried not to giggle. "He's definitely a lot to take in..."

"Did you gag when you went down on him?"

"I'm only answering your questions because you're my best friend."

"You think I'd ask you this if I weren't your best friend?"

She had a good point. "No. But I don't put the whole thing in there."

She rubbed her chin. "Maybe I should have gone for Cayson first..."

"Hey, he's mine."

She laughed. "Whoa...I'll back off."

"You better."

"But I can tell you won't be able to handle him at your back entrance."

I scanned the tables around us, making sure no one heard. "Shh!"

"I'm just saying...if you've never done it before, trying it out with a huge dick isn't the best idea."

"Okay...enough of this conversation."

"I haven't had sex in forever... I miss it."

That surprised me. "Trinity, you're gorgeous. Just go pick up some guy."

She shrugged. "I haven't really found anyone worth my time."

"Maybe you haven't looked hard enough."

"I've been to all the parties. Believe me, I've seen everyone," she said.

"Maybe you're looking in the wrong place," I said. "A party isn't the best location. Maybe you should try an online dating site."

"Is that a joke?" she snapped. "I'm not doing that. Only weird serial killers do that."

"It was just a suggestion." I backed off.

"Why can't Cayson have a brother?" she demanded.

"How about Theo? He's cute."

She shook her head. "No chemistry."

"Well, you have a lot of chemistry with Slade. Every time you're around him it's like the bomb dropping on Hiroshima."

"Don't even get me started with him. He makes my head want to explode."

"I think that's a universal feeling," I said with a laugh.

Cayson and Slade entered the library and headed for our table.

"Ugh. Just looking at him makes me want to hit him in the face." Trinity rolled her eyes.

"I hope you're talking about Slade."

"Obviously, I'm not talking about your boyfriend and his huge dick."

My eyes widened. "Shh!"

The guys reached our table just as I finished hushing her.

"Hey, baby." Cayson leaned down and kissed me.

"Hey." My spine shivered as soon as I inhaled his scent. His powerful arms made me feel safe, and I couldn't stop picturing him naked. It was such a beautiful image.

He sat beside me then kept his arm over the back of my chair. "Hey, Trin."

"Hey, Cayson." She batted her eyelashes at him then waved.

I kicked her under the table.

She giggled then looked away.

Slade sat next to her. "Let me clear the air right now." He pulled out a sandwich from his bag. "This is my lunch. And I'm going to eat it—right here and right now. I suggest you keep your trap closed if you don't want to pick up my trash."

Trinity took a deep breath, controlling her anger, and then said nothing.

"Good, she finally gets it." Slade bit into his sandwich.

I needed to change the subject. "How was the game last night?"

"Good," Cayson said. "Slade won five hundred bucks."

"Online sport betting. It's pretty awesome." Slade kept eating.

"Do you gamble too?" I asked him.

Cayson shook his head. "Not my thing. Besides, I got to take out my girlfriend."

"You know we can trade off paying."

He laughed. "That's a good one, baby." He rubbed the back of my neck while he continued to laugh.

Trinity shrugged, not bothering to say anything.

Slade finished his sandwich then crumpled his trash into a ball. "Zack hasn't been bothering you, right?"

Of course Cayson told him. "No. If he does, I'll handle him."

"No." Cayson's voice was cold. "I'll take care of it."

I didn't want to challenge him in front of our friends so I said nothing.

"I hear through the grapevine that your tits are great for fucking," Slade blurted.

Cayson flinched beside me, clearly not expecting him to say that.

I guess I wasn't surprised Cayson told Slade what happened. They were best friends. I told Trinity everything.

"Personally, I like big tits but they got to be proportional." He rolled the ball of trash between his hands on the desk.

Cayson cleared his throat. "Thanks for that info." The irritation was clear in his voice.

"No problem." Slade obviously hadn't caught on to the tension.

Cayson turned toward me like he might say something but then he changed his mind.

Trinity caught the interaction. "Skye just told me Cayson's dick is huge so now you're even."

Slade's eyes widened. "Um…gross."

I glared at her viciously. "You're the worst secret-keeper ever."

"Hey, I just saved you guys from your first fight," Trinity said. "You're welcome."

Cayson smirked at me. "You like my package?"

I hoped my face wasn't red. "Why wouldn't I?"

He chuckled then kissed my cheek. "And yes, I do like your rack—a lot."

"How romantic," Slade said sarcastically.

"I'll be right back." Trinity stood up and walked to the rear of the library in my line of sight.

Slade stared straight ahead, still playing with his foil. Crumbs from his sandwich scattered across the table. Pieces of lettuce and tomato were sprinkled everywhere.

Cayson leaned in and pressed a gentle kiss to my neck. "I love kissing you there." His lips were near my ear, his voice coming out as a whisper.

"I like it too."

"I'll do it a lot more—tonight."

That reminded me of something. "My parents are coming to town tonight and want to have dinner. I'm sorry. I totally forgot to tell you."

"As in, I'm included?" he asked.

"Yeah."

Slade smirked. "Oh no. Cayson is officially meeting the parents."

"I already know them, idiot," Cayson said.

"As her friend—not her boyfriend." Slade winked. "Good luck with that."

I rolled my eyes. "My parents already love you, Cayson. They just want to spend some time with us."

"I would love to go," he said. "A little further notice would have been appreciated…but of course I'll be there."

"We can fool around later."

"Yippie."

"And you can tit-fuck me since you like it so much." I gave him a seductive grin.

His eyes darkened in desire.

"Gross…I can hear you," Slade snapped.

"Then don't listen," Cayson said.

"It's kinda hard when I'm a foot away from you," Slade said sarcastically.

Trinity came back to the table but she wasn't alone.

"No eating in the library!" The librarian shrieked then pointed at the mess Slade made. He was caught red-handed, the trash balled up in his hands.

"Oh shit," he whispered.

"You're going to clean this up right now and you're going to serve one hour of clean up as punishment." She put her hands on her hips and glared at him.

"Can you even do that?" Slade snapped. "This isn't kindergarten."

"You bet your ass I can," she hissed. "Do you want me to call the dean and double check?"

I tried not to laugh. This was hilarious.

"Do it," Slade said. "Like I care."

"Then I'll call your mother."

That changed Slade's attitude immediately. Aunt Janice wasn't someone that just let things slide. She was strict and controlling, definitely the alpha of the house. She even kept her husband in check. "Fine. I'll do it."

"I'll see you when the library closes." She stormed off, her anger obvious in the movement of her limbs.

Slade gave Trinity the most hateful stare I've ever seen. "You fucking—"

"Payback's a bitch, huh?" She put her bag over her shoulder and strutted off, her nose held high.

Cayson and I tried not to laugh. Hearing them constantly bicker and argue was annoying, but moments like these reminded me why I put up with it.

***

Cayson arrived at my door wearing a suit.

I stared at his broad shoulders and long legs. His blue eyes stood out against the dark colors, and his chin was cleanly shaved. "Wow…you look yummy."

He smirked. "I was going to say the same thing about you." He stepped inside then moved his hands around my waist, gripping me. He kissed me long and hard. His hands moved downward to my ass. Then he squeezed it. Cayson had been a lot more forward in our relationship since I made it clear it was okay. Now he was aggressive and forward, just the way I liked. "I like this dress."

I wore a champagne pink dress that was tight on my body. This color looked good on my fair skin so I tried to wear it whenever I got a chance. A gold bracelet was around my wrist and it matched my earrings.

Cayson took a long look at me. "You look so lovely." His hand tucked a loose strand behind my ear.

My face flushed. "Thanks."

He moved closer then placed a gentle kiss on my neck, making me hot. "I could eat you," he whispered.

"Please do."

When he pulled away, his eyes were dark. "I'd love to. But it'll have to wait, unfortunately. I couldn't look your father in the eye if I saw him right after…doing that."

I smirked. "That would be awkward, wouldn't it?"

"Slightly." He reached into his pocket and pulled out a thong. "I forgot to return these the other day."

I snatched them away then tossed them in my room. "You're such a pervert."

"What? I like your underwear."

"Exactly something a pervert would say."

He shrugged. "I guess I am—at least for you."

"As long as it's only for me, I'm okay with that."

"Definitely only for you." He came to me again then pulled me against his chest. He looked down at me, his eyes lingering on my lips. "Every day feels like a dream. I just can't believe when I look at you, you're looking back at me. I can't believe this is real, that these lips are only mine to enjoy." His thumb moved across my lower lip, making my breath hitch.

Cayson was sexy without even trying. "You're confused. I'm the lucky one out of the two of us. Every girl knows it. And I'll never forget it."

His eyes twinkled in amusement. "You couldn't be more wrong, Skye. But there aren't enough hours in the day to argue with you." He leaned in and kissed me, his lips conveying everything his voice didn't. He gripped my lower back, crinkling my dress, and deepened the kiss. I wanted to drag him into my bedroom so the kiss would escalate but I knew that wasn't the best idea.

A knock sounded on the door.

Cayson pulled away, reluctantly.

"That would be my parents."

He stepped away and put his hands in his pockets.

"You don't have to not touch me just because they're around."

He sighed. "This is going to take me a while to get used to. Your father will watch me like a hawk, with the eyes in the back of his head and the cameras he has everywhere."

"That's so creepy it's not even funny." I walked to the door and opened it.

My mom was wearing a dark blue dress with matching heels. Her wedding ring sparkled in the light, and her bracelet did the same. "Hey, honey. You look beautiful."

"Thanks, Mom. You do too." I hugged her tightly. Even when I was happy, she somehow made me happier.

My dad stepped inside, wearing a black suit just like all his others. Each one was created by the top designers in the world and not a single wrinkle existed in the fabric. A Rolex shined from his wrist, and his wedding band was still in place, the one he never removed. "Hey, pumpkin." He pulled me in for a long embrace. "You look lovely—as always."

"Thanks, Dad. You look stiff—as always."

He laughed then pulled away. He studied my face for a moment. "It's nice to see you smile."

"I always smile."

"But not quite like this." He gave me a knowing look then walked to Cayson.

"Hello, sir. How are you?" Cayson stuck out his hand to shake my father's.

My dad smirked. "Just because you're dating my daughter doesn't mean you have to behave differently around me. Loosen up." He patted his shoulder then pulled him in for a hug. "You're a son to me, Cayson."

"Thanks, Uncle Sean." He patted his back then stepped away.

"Cayson." My mom opened her arms and hugged him. "You're more handsome every time I see you."

"Thank you, Aunt Scarlet."

"You look so much like your father." She pulled away and stared at his face. "It's remarkable."

"I'm not sure if that's an insult," he said with a laugh.

"It is," my dad said.

My mom glared at my dad then turned back to Cayson. "It's a very, very big compliment."

My dad gave her a hard look. "Don't forget the man you married…"

"The most handsome man in the world. Yes, dear. I know." She came to his side and hooked her arm through his. "Like you would let me forget."

"I remind you every night." He gave her a dark look.

"Okay…let's go before I throw up." I headed for the door.

Cayson opened it for me then walked out behind me.

"They're gross, huh?" I whispered.

He shrugged. "I think it's cute."

"Of course you would. You're brown-nosing."

"Am not," he argued. He put his arm around my waist and walked with me to the car.

My mom's car was in the driveway. Cayson opened the backseat for me to get inside then he sat beside me. My parents joined us.

"How about French?" my father asked from the front seat.

"Sounds good to me," Cayson said.

"I eat anything," I said.

"I know that too well," my dad said. "And my wife will eat anything, even if it's been expired for a few days."

My mom shrugged. "I don't like to waste food."

"Menton's?" my dad asked. It was a restaurant we went to a few times in Boston.

"Let's do it," I said.

He put the address in the GPS then eyed my mom's safety belt, making sure it was on. Then he looked in the rearview mirror. "Everyone buckled in?"

"Yes," I said. "But we aren't five."

"Sometimes you act like it so I have to double check," my dad said.

Cayson chuckled.

"Don't laugh at him," I whispered. "You'll just egg him on."

"He's going to tease you either way." He rested his hand on my thigh then looked out the window.

My dad drove to the restaurant, holding my mom's hand the entire time. They were so affectionate that I didn't even notice it anymore. If my dad needed both hands for the wheel, my mom rested her hand on his thigh.

When we arrived at the restaurant, the valet took the car then we walked inside.

"Reservation?" the host asked.

"No," my dad said. "But I have a party of four—for Preston."

The guy studied my dad's face and seemed to recognize him and his name. "Right this way, sir."

Cayson leaned toward my ear. "See that—power."

"No. The guy just knows my dad is loaded," I whispered.

"Same thing." He kept his hand around my waist as we walked to the table. Like always, Cayson pulled out the chair for me and let me sit down first. My dad did the same for my mother. I noticed my dad glanced at Cayson, watching him. But he didn't say anything.

My dad grabbed the wine list. "How about a bottle for the table?"

"Sure." My mom sat with perfect posture and looked like a queen.

"What are you in the mood for, baby?" my father asked.

"Anything. You have better taste than I do," she said.

"That's debatable…" He scanned the list then put it down. "Chardonnay it is." His hand moved to her thigh.

Cayson rested his ankle on his knee and placed his hand on my thigh, acting normal.

My father turned his look on Cayson. "How's school?"

"The same," he responded. "But I'm just eager to be done at this point."

"You're almost there," my mom said. "Don't get senioritis."

"I'll try," Cayson said with a laugh. "I have a few interviews coming up for medical school. I'm a little nervous."

"Congratulations," my father said with a nod. "I'm sure you'll do well."

He had interviews? He didn't mention that to me. I decided to bring it up later.

Humble as always, Cayson didn't say anything else.

My dad noticed his arms. "Your arms look like trees. Are you hitting the gym as often as you're studying?" Amusement was in his voice.

"It's the one thing Slade and I can do together that doesn't get us in trouble," he said with a smirk.

My mom laughed. "Slade is something else, but he has so much life in him—just like his father."

"I like Slade too," my dad said.

"You mean you love him," my mom pressed.

"Obviously, baby." He rolled his eyes. "I'm just glad Roland isn't so extreme."

"Why didn't you invite Roland?" I asked.

"Of course we did," my mom said immediately. "He said he had to study."

"And he didn't want to," my dad started to use air quotes, "attend our lame tea party double date."

I smirked. "That sounds like Roland."

"Has he been staying out of trouble?" my father asked.

"Even if he wasn't, I wouldn't tell you," I said.

My dad nodded. "Sounds about right."

The waitress came over and took our order. My dad ordered for both himself and my mom.

"What are you getting, baby?" Cayson asked.

"The French brie," I said.

"Okay." He took our menus and put them to the side. Then he ordered for both of us.

This was the first time I ever went out with my parents and my boyfriend at the same time. And it was really nice. My dad was calm and normal. He wasn't watching Cayson's every move. It was clear he loved Cayson, and not just because he had to. He genuinely loved him—especially for me. My mom felt the same way. It was something I never expected to happen.

"So, is my daughter driving you crazy yet?" my dad asked Cayson.

"No, surprisingly," Cayson answered.

I hit his arm playfully. "I would never drive you crazy."

"You drive my wallet crazy with how much you eat," Cayson said.

I rolled my eyes. "I don't eat that much."

Cayson chuckled. "Sure, baby."

My mom smiled while she watched us together. "How did this happen? How did you two get together?"

Cayson and I looked at each other, unsure who should tell the story.

Cayson took the lead. "Well…I've had a thing for Skye for a very long time."

"You fooled us," my mom said.

"Good," Cayson said with a laugh. "That's what I was going for. Anyway, I kept hoping something would happen between us, but it was pretty clear Skye didn't feel the same way about me. So I moved on…"

Then I took over. "When I saw him with Jasmine at Thanksgiving it just hit me. I missed him and I couldn't stop thinking about him. Everyone kept telling me he was in love with me but I never listened…I should have. And, well, you guys influenced it too. I want what you guys have, and…Cayson is my best friend."

My dad nodded his head in approval. "I'm glad it didn't take you ten years like it did with your mother and I."

"Me too," I said with a smile.

Cayson gave me a playful look then rubbed his nose against mine.

The waiter returned with the dishes and wine. We immediately dug in. I was starving so I practically inhaled my food.

Cayson smirked while he watched me.

"What?" I said.

He used his napkin to wipe my chin. "I always know when you're really hungry because you get food all over your face."

"Whoops." I shrugged and kept eating.

Cayson ate with perfect manners and acted like himself. "How's work, Uncle Sean?"

"A big snooze fest," my dad said. "Nothing worth mentioning."

"I'm so excited to work there…" I said sarcastically.

My dad sipped his wine then smirked. "Well, I've been working there for twenty years. It gets old after a while. Plus, it keeps me away from your mother."

"Don't you get tired of her anyway?" I asked.

"Do you get tired of Cayson?" my dad countered.

No…definitely not.

My dad drank his wine again. "Your mom comes to work with me sometimes but I never get anything done that way…"

"TMI, Dad." I cut into my food and kept eating.

"Your father tends to share too much sometimes." My mom gave my dad a flirtatious smile.

"When you have a hot wife, it's hard to resist her," my dad said, wiping his lip with a napkin.

Cayson looked at me. "I hope you don't distract me at work or I might kill someone."

Did he mean if we were married? "Just make sure I'm fed and that won't be a problem."

My mom looked at me. "How's Trinity?"

"She's good," I said. "She wants to go into fashion."

"That's what your uncle Mike was telling us." She sipped her wine.

"I'm happy for her," my dad said. "Life is too short to live someone else's dream."

"Did you work for the company right after college?" I asked.

"No. I worked for a stockbroker for a few years then I worked for a recycling company. Then I took over the company with Uncle Mike."

"Did Uncle Mike do anything else first?" Cayson asked.

"He worked on Wall Street," my dad answered.

My mom rolled her eyes. "The Preston boys are very accomplished."

"So are the Siscos," my dad countered, mentioning my mother's maiden name, the one Uncle Ryan shared.

"Is Slade still intent on being a tattoo artist?" my mom asked.

Cayson nodded his head immediately. "I don't think he'll ever change his mind. He's not very interested in school."

My mom shrugged. "I told my brother to let his son make his own decisions but he didn't take my advice."

"He just wants to make sure Slade keeps his options open," my dad said. "You can't blame him for that."

"Of course not," my mom said. "How's Clementine?" she asked Cayson.

"Good. We don't talk much during the school year, but I think she's good," Cayson said. "She's still a violinist with the New York Symphony as far as I know."

"She's very talented," my dad said. "Every time I tried to get Roland to learn to play the violin, he kept trying to play it like a guitar." He rolled his eyes.

I laughed, recalling the memory.

"Maybe our son is destined to be a rock star," my mom said.

"He would give his grandmother a heart attack," my dad said.

"But Grandpa would be on the tour bus," Cayson said.

I laughed, thinking about Grandpa as a roadie. "I can see it."

"So can I," my mom said with a laugh.

I wiped my plate clean then pushed it away. "I'm stuffed."

"It's a miracle," Cayson teased.

I hit his arm again. "Don't make fun of me."

"Baby, I'll always make fun of you. Sorry." He winked at me.

"Good," my dad said. "I want her to have a man who treats her like a princess but keeps her down to earth at the same time."

"Then I'm your man," Cayson said.

"I can tell," my dad said.

The waiter came over with the tab.

Cayson immediately grabbed it then slipped his credit card inside. "Dinner is on me."

"I don't think so, Cay." My dad snatched it away then switched their cards.

My mom rolled her eyes. "Here we go..."

"Then at least let me pay for Skye's dinner as well as mine," Cayson said.

"No." My dad handed the waiter the tab. "We're done with this."

"Of course, sir." The waiter walked away.

Cayson sighed in defeat.

"I'm sure feeding my daughter is already enough of a financial burden," my dad said with a smile.

"Why is everyone picking on me tonight?" I asked.

"You're an easy target," Cayson said. He turned back to my dad. "Well, thank you for dinner, Uncle Sean."

"You're very welcome, Cayson," my dad said gracefully.

The waiter returned with the receipt then we headed back to my apartment. The drive home was spent in silence. Since I was full and warm, I was sleepy. I leaned my head on Cayson's shoulder while he held my hand. Whenever I opened my eyes, I caught my dad glancing at us in the rearview mirror.

When we arrived at my apartment, my parents got out and hugged me.

"Until next time," my mom said. She never said goodbye. She always made her departure as easy as possible. I've always clung to her since I could remember and it was hard to let her go.

"Okay, Mom. I love you."

"I love you too, honey." She kissed my forehead before she pulled away.

My father hugged me hard. "I hate saying goodbye."

"I do too."

"I love you so much, pumpkin. I miss you every day."

"I miss you too."

He continued to hug me. "I could stand here all night..." He finally dropped his embrace. "Call me if you need anything."

"I know, Dad."

He hugged Cayson before he headed back to the car.

Cayson put his arm around my waist, and together, we watched my parents drive away.

When their taillights were gone, I felt sadness in my chest. "Do you feel sad when you say goodbye to your parents?"

He kissed my forehead. "I do."

"Good...it's not just me."

"Of course not."

"Cayson, can I ask you for a favor?"

"Anything, baby."

"When we settle down...can we live in Connecticut?"

He dropped his arm and looked at me with emotion in his eyes. He said nothing for a long time, just staring at me. His blue eyes faded to gray slightly, and the depth of his eyes seemed to travel indefinitely. He cupped my face then brushed his thumb over my cheek. "Of course."

Chapter Seven

Slade

If I didn't refuse to hit girls, I'd slap the shit out of Trinity.

I spent an hour cleaning the library with the librarian watching me. There was dust everywhere and I had to empty the garbage cans. It wasn't flattering work and I clenched my jaw the entire time. I couldn't believe Trinity threw me under the bus like that. She got me good.

Cayson texted me as soon as I stepped out of the building. *Roland is having everyone over for poker.*

I could use some relaxation. When?

In an hour.

K. I'll be there.

I went home and showered, getting the grime and garbage off my hands, before I changed and walked to Roland's apartment a few blocks over. Normally, I would have driven since it was freezing cold but I planned on drinking. Driving wasn't a good idea.

I walked inside without knocking and placed the six-pack on the counter. "Blue Moon—the good stuff."

"Good." Roland grabbed it and shoved the beers into the refrigerator.

A circular poker table was set in the center of the room along with chips and cards. I grabbed a beer then sat down.

Conrad sat across from me. "How's the janitor life?" He had a smirk on his lips.

"Fuck you," I snapped.

"Did you have to clean the toilets too?" Roland sat down then shuffled the cards.

"I'm about to shove this bottle up your ass." I pointed my beer at him.

Roland laughed. "I wish I could have gotten a picture of that."

I sighed then sipped my beer, wishing no one knew about my afternoon cleaning the library.

"Slade in all his glory…" Conrad chuckled. "I'm sure the girls would have loved that."

"I can still land more pussy than you," I snapped. "Whether I'm cleaning the library or not."

"Whatever, man," Conrad said. "My sister got you good."

"Brat," I mumbled.

The door opened and Skye and Cayson walked inside, holding hands.

"I thought this was a guy's night?" I demanded.

Roland shrugged. "Skye is pretty good at poker."

"Not as good as Cayson." Skye gave Cayson a flirtatious look.

Roland ignored her words. "Anyway…it's more money in the pot."

I decided not to argue. Skye was already there.

Cayson sat beside me with Skye on his other side. He grabbed her a beer and a plate of pretzels, waiting on her hand and foot.

I rolled my eyes but didn't comment. "Let's get this game started."

The door opened again and my sister walked inside. "Hey, janitor."

You've got to be kidding me...

She held out a broom. "I got this for you. I figured you'd appreciate it."

Everyone laughed.

"I'm about to shove it through your gut," I threatened.

She laughed then leaned the broom against the wall. "My brother is the messiest guy I know. Who knew he would be a professional cleaner."

"Look, I just tidied up the library for like an hour," I said. "Let's move on."

"Slade can dish it out but he can't take it." Roland laughed then sipped his beer.

"Just shut up, alright?" I peeled the paper off my bottle because I didn't know what else to do.

"Mom and Dad will be so proud," Silke said.

"That I killed you?" I snapped.

She messed up my hair with her hand then sat on the couch. "Whatever, Brother."

I flattened my hair then leaned back in my chair. "If we're done with that, let's—"

Trinity walked through the door. "I brought Heineken."

Son of a bitch.

She put the six-pack down then gave me a smirk. "I was wondering why it smelled like garbage in here. Just got off work?"

Everyone laughed.

I glared at her, wanting to pull out that pretty blonde hair.

Cayson seemed to know I reached my limit. "Okay, guys. He's had enough. Just drop it."

Trinity sat across from me, a gloating smile on her face.

I gave her another threatening glare before I dropped it.

"Let's get this game started." Roland passed out the cards. After everyone scanned their hands, they tossed their chips in. I did the same.

Trinity kept watching me, a victorious look on her face.

She was going down.

We put all our cards down, and Conrad was the winner of the hand.

"Looks like I'm going to run you guys dry tonight." Conrad pulled the pile toward him.

"It's just the first round, man." Roland dealt the cards again.

Trinity finished her first beer and moved onto her second one like she was drinking water.

"Did you not learn anything?" I snapped.

She understood my meaning. She lifted up her bottle. "Sealed bottle. And I don't think anyone here has any interest in raping me."

Roland shook his head immediately. "Definitely not."

I downed my beer then grabbed a second one.

"Slade is just insecure that I can best him in every way possible," Trinity said. "If it's not in intelligence, it's in drinking."

I tightened my grip on my bottle. "No one can match me." I chugged the bottle in seconds then left the empty glass on the table.

She did the same. "That was easy."

"At least they'll be easy to beat in the game," Roland said.

We played a few more rounds. Cayson won a few times then I took the pot. Trinity surprised everyone with a full house and we all took a huge hit. I kept drinking and she kept up with me.

She poured herself a seven and seven. Then she downed it without blinking an eye.

"Beer then liquor, never been sicker. Liquor then beer, have no fear." I stared her down, putting her on the spot.

She poured another. "If you can't handle it, that's fine. I know you probably have to work tomorrow scrubbing some toilets."

God, she was a bitch. I made myself a brandy. "Go to hell, Trinity."

We finished the poker game then settled down on the couch to watch TV. Roland and Conrad were still drinking beer. Skye hadn't had another since her first one, and Cayson stopped after his second beer. Trinity and I, however, were fighting to the death.

She had another seven and seven. Her eyes were heavy and she seemed a little tired. Her words were slurred, but she seemed fine in every other way. I was already drunk and wasn't hiding it very well. I tried to play it cool but it was becoming more difficult.

Conrad snatched a glass out of Trinity's hand. "I'm cutting you off."

"I'm cutting *you* off." She tried to hit his arm and missed. Instead she hit Skye's thigh.

"Yeah…she's drunk." Conrad returned the empty glass to the kitchen.

"You've had enough, Slade." Cayson took my glass away.

"Come on," I snapped. "Don't be a girl."

"Too bad." Cayson took the liquor away.

I lay back on the couch then turned to Roland. "You have a weird ass name."

He was buzzed too. "What kind of name is Slade? It's like blade but not really…"

"But Roland sounds…stupid."

"You're stupid."

"And don't get me started on Conrad," I said. "He sounds like a park ranger."

"What kind of name is Skye?" Roland said. "It makes my parents sound like hippies."

"Because they are," I said.

Silke sat on the other couch and quickly fell asleep. She couldn't hold her liquor like the rest of us.

"Cayson, let's go home and have sex," Skye blurted.

Cayson did a double take.

"Gross!" Roland said. He covered his eyes. "I don't want to listen to that."

Conrad moved his hands to his ears. "There you go."

Cayson's face flushed red. "All it takes is three beers and a whiskey, huh?"

"Come on," Skye said. "Why haven't we done it yet? Your dick is huge!"

Cayson's face was beet red.

"Just go do it," Trinity said with slurred words. "Ride him like there's no tomorrow."

"You're right, Trin," Skye said while laughing. "You're right about everything."

"I know." Trinity gave a victorious smile. Her cheeks were reddening from the alcohol.

Cayson was thoroughly embarrassed. "Baby, it's time for us to go home."

"What? It's just getting fun." Skye pouted.

"Come on." He pulled her up and hooked one arm around her waist. "Say goodnight."

"Nighty-night." She waved then laughed.

Once they were gone, Conrad put his feet on the couch. "Dude, these couches are so comfy."

"I know," Roland said. "And they are perfect for fucking."

"Eww." Conrad cringed then rolled onto the hardwood floor. Then he laughed. "Shit, the ground is hard."

Silke started to snore.

"You guys are lame." Trinity flipped her hair then stood up. "I'm heading home."

"You aren't driving," Conrad blurted. He tried to get up but he fell again.

"I walked, idiot." She marched to the door.

My mind was becoming hazy. I had a strong urge to sleep but I didn't want to sleep there, on the couches Roland did god knows what on. "I'm out of here too."

"Good," Conrad said. "Walk with my sister."

"I don't give a shit about your sister." I walked out and slammed the door a lot harder than I meant to.

I tightened my jacket around me then headed down the stairs. It was cold and icy outside. Piles of snow were on the ground everywhere. I loved the winter even though I preferred the summer. Girls wore short dresses with flowers in their hair. It was easy to tell who had rocking bodies and who didn't. And girls were always a little heavier during the holidays.

When I turned the corner, I saw Trinity picking up her phone from the ground. "Damn it." She wiped it off on her coat.

I laughed, watching her wipe the snow from her screen.

She looked up when she heard my voice. "Following me?"

"Why would I follow you? I'd prefer to run from you."

She checked her phone and the screen lit up. "Phew, it's not broken."

"Phew, I don't care." I walked down the path through the trees.

Trinity came up behind me and caught up to me.

"Why are you walking with me?" I snapped.

"I live this way, jackass."

I shook my head and kept my hands in my pockets. "Of all the people in the world, I can stand you the least. I can't believe you threw me under the bus like that!"

"You did it to me first! The librarian thought it was me and you never told her otherwise. Coward." She gave me a look of disgust.

"But I didn't tattle on you like a four-year-old."

"You act like a four-year-old."

"You look like a four-year-old."

She hit my arm. "So, you like to fuck four-year-olds?"

"Excuse me?" I hissed. I stopped in my tracks.

"Don't act like you don't stare at me. I've caught you so many times."

"Because you were parading around my room in a bra and thong. If you were a fat ugly cow, I still would have looked."

"Whatever." She crossed her arms over her chest and kept walking. "You have the hots for me and I know it."

I laughed because it was so absurd. "You sure think highly of yourself, don't you?"

"I know you do."

"Fuck no. I hate you. I absolutely despise you."

"Then why did you save me?" she demanded. "You could have looked the other way, picked up some girl, and went on with your life. If you despise me so much, are so indifferent toward me, you wouldn't have done a damn thing."

God, I wanted to slap her. "I would have done it for any girl. Men who take advantage of women like that should be killed."

She kept walking, keeping her jacket close around her. "All you ever do is treat me like shit. I'm sick of it.

And when I stand up for myself, you throw a hissy fit like a damn girl."

"I don't treat you like shit," I argued. "I treat everyone exactly the same way. I'm not sure why you think you're special. Because, Princess, you aren't."

"Shut up, Slade."

We reached my apartment building. "Thank god."

"You aren't going to walk me home? Or invite me inside?"

"Why the hell would I do that? You walked all this way. You can make it the rest of the way." I moved to the side of the building and headed to the staircase.

She came up behind me and pushed me. "What is your problem? You act like you care about me one second then you're a dick a second later."

I stumbled forward then caught myself by my hands. The road was freezing cold. I got back to my feet and wiped my palms on my jeans. "Don't push me!"

She used all her strength and pushed me again. "It wouldn't kill you to just try and be nice to me. I'm never going to go away. We can be frenemies for the rest of time, or you can actually try to be my friend."

I stumbled back, disoriented from the alcohol and the cold. I stopped myself from falling but I couldn't stop my rage. Unable to control myself, I shoved her into the wall, making her back collide with the wood. "Push me again and I'll break your neck." I gripped her wrists then pinned them against the wall. "Got it?"

She breathed hard, staring into my face. The snow was falling lightly around us. I didn't know what time it was, but judging by the temperature and lack of people,

I would guess it was past midnight. She stared into my eyes, her chest rising and falling with every full breath she took. Her blonde hair framed her face, and the dark green eye shadow around her eyes made them look big and beautiful. Black eyeliner marked the edges, making them pop. Her lips were ruby red despite the cold. Her pale skin was a reflection of the winter bite. It was fair and light, reminding me of a snowflake.

I didn't know what the hell was going on. The alcohol made me confused and bipolar. One moment, I wanted to rip her throat out, and the next, I wanted to feel her warm breath in my mouth. She stared at me then looked at my lips, thinking the same thing.

At exactly the same moment, she crushed her mouth against mine while I ravaged hers.

My mouth aggressively took hers. I caressed her, tasting her. Her lips reciprocated, brushing past mine before her tongue slipped into my mouth, lightly touching mine. I crushed my body against hers, feeling her chest push against me.

Her hands moved into my hair, messing up the strands. Then she moved under my shirt and felt the muscles of my back. Her hands were cold but it felt good. Her nails lightly dragged across my skin, applying just the right pressure.

I ripped open her coat then shoved my hands under her shirt, groping her breasts over her bra. She moaned into my mouth while she felt me take her, squeezing her.

Her hand snaked into my pants and grabbed my cock. She stroked it like she'd done it a thousand times.

Her touched relayed her experience. She was making me pant, making me hot.

I moved to her jeans then unbuttoned them, still kissing her. Our tongues danced together, making me forget about the cold. I breathed hard, my cock throbbing every few seconds.

When her jeans were loose, I yanked them down and helped her kick them off. She was probably freezing but it didn't seem like she cared. She undid my fly then pulled my jeans down with my boxers, revealing my cock.

My lips moved to her neck and I sucked the skin while my hand moved beneath her underwear. I found her clit immediately and rubbed it. Then I slipped two fingers inside, feeling how wet she was.

She licked her hand then rubbed me hard, doing it exactly as I did it when I beat off. She was a pro and it was making me hornier than I already was.

I didn't want to wait any longer. I wanted to be inside her and forget the foreplay. My hand gripped her thong and pulled it off. I tossed it aside, leaving it in the snow. Then I grabbed her ass and lifted her, pinning her against the wall. Her legs automatically wrapped around my waist.

Neither one of us cared that someone could walk by at any second. My jeans were low, showing my ass, and her legs were spread to me. Like a magnet, my cock found her entrance and felt the moisture pool between her legs.

"Fuck. Do you have a condom?" I blurted.

"No. I'm on the pill." She wrapped her arms around my neck and kissed me again, her mouth touching me the way I liked.

That was all I needed to hear. I gripped her ass and tilted her hips slightly. Then I slid inside with little resistance. "Holy fucking shit." She felt so damn good. I'd never fucked a girl without a rubber and now I knew what I was missing.

She moaned then gripped me, trying to hold on.

After I took a moment to recover, I thrust my hips and moved inside her. There was no way to describe how good it felt. It was heaven, pure heaven. She was so wet and smooth. Her tightness was perfect for my big dick. I could do this all night.

"Slade...yeah." She used her arms to move up and down slightly, rocking with me.

I started to move faster, wanting as much of her as I could get.

"Fuck me." Her head rolled back while she enjoyed what I was doing to her. "Fuck me, Slade..."

I went as fast as I could, loving the feel of her skin against my shaft. My tip pierced her over and over, throbbing from how good it felt. I was breathing hard and moaning, wanting to go even faster.

Minutes passed and we clung to each other while we moved together. Trinity made noises in my ear, exciting me more. She pressed her lips to my ear and kept whispering dirty things, making me crumble. I fucked her hard and good, and I knew when I hit her in the right spot. She practically screamed when I made her come.

"God...yes."

Even though it was freezing out, I started to sweat. I'd never worked this hard during sex. I was giving her everything I had, loving the way her bare pussy felt against my dick.

When I felt the warmth pool in my stomach, stretching to every nerve in my body, I knew the orgasm was coming. Like a ball of raging fire, it burned every single part of me. It hadn't even hit me yet and it was the best sensation I ever felt. I was spiraling, plummeting hard. Then it hit me.

"Fuck yeah." I held her against the wall while I tensed up and released. I never came inside a girl before and it felt a million times better than anything else. I filled her, squirting hard. I kept my body against hers, clinging to her warmth.

When I was finished, I stayed that way, suddenly feeling exhausted. She breathed hard underneath me, trying to catch her breath. The world started to spin, and the cold suddenly hit me.

Still holding her, I grabbed her clothes off the ground and carried her to my apartment. I was still inside her. She lay her head over my shoulder and wrapped her arms around my neck.

When we entered my bedroom, I tossed her on my bed then lay beside her. It only took a few seconds for me to pass out. I didn't know if Trinity was asleep but I was too drunk and tired to care.

Chapter Eight

Trinity

A massive migraine was thudding behind my eyes. It slammed into the front of my skull, putting me in a horrible mood before I even started my day. Last night was a blur. I remembered drinking—a lot. Everyone was there. And Slade…he…

Oh shit.

It all came flooding back to me. We fought like we were across a battlefield, and then suddenly, we were going at it against the wall of his apartment. I remembered the cold air moving into my lungs, burning me, with every desperate breath I took. I remembered the concrete wall against my back. I remembered our kiss, our tongues dancing. And I remember him inside me.

Holy fucking shit. I slept with Slade.

My eyes flashed open and I stared at a ceiling I didn't recognize. Where was I? I looked at the nightstand and spotted two pills and a glass of water. Was that for me? Then I realized I was in Slade's bed. It must have been where we passed out. I turned to my other side, expecting to see him passed out next to me.

He wasn't there.

I sat up and felt my tangled hair move around my shoulders. I still wore my jacket and shirt, but I didn't wear any bottoms. My jeans and underwear were on the floor, forgotten. Slade's side of the bed was wrinkled like he slept there the night before. But he wasn't around now.

"Slade?"

No response.

I moved to the end of the bed and felt my head pound harder. I was disoriented for a moment. I breathed through the nausea then focused my thoughts. My hand immediately grabbed the pills and shoved them into my mouth. I downed them with the glass of water.

Oh god, this was bad.

I took a few moments before I rose to my feet. My head hurt again but I pushed forward and got dressed. My phone was still in my coat pocket and so were my keys.

"Slade?"

He still didn't respond.

I walked through the house and didn't spot him anywhere. The TV was off and there weren't any dirty dishes. It was pretty clear he already took off. Did he take off because of me? Wanting to head home and get into the shower, I left his apartment.

***

I still couldn't believe what happened. Slade had been my enemy for as long as I could remember. We fought and bickered like two people who despised each other. I hated him and he hated me.

So what the hell happened?

I knew alcohol lowered inhibitions but I had to stoop pretty low to sleep with Slade, the biggest manwhore I'd ever met. My fingers moved through my hair anxiously as I processed what happened. I couldn't believe we fucked outside in the cold like that, like animals.

Even though it was Sunday, I didn't go to Skye's. She was having people over for the football game but I wasn't going to set foot in that place. What if Slade was there? God, that would be so awkward. What would I say? What would he say?

My phone lit up with a message.

Please don't be Slade. Please don't be Slade.

It wasn't. It was Skye. *Are you coming over or what?*

I couldn't ask if Slade was there. *I'm going to stay in today.*

Are you okay?

Why was she asking? *Yeah, totally. Why wouldn't I be? I'm awesome. I'm fantastic.* Okay…that was a little over the top…

I just wanted to make sure everything was okay. Slade didn't come over today so I thought something was up.

Nope. I'm peachy.

Have you talked to Slade?

Why would I have talked to Slade? I haven't seen him. No. Geez, I sounded defensive.

Well, if you see him, tell him Cayson wants to talk to him.

Since I won't be seeing him, don't depend on me.

Are you okay, Trin?

I'm peachy. I needed to stop using that word.

Skye stopped texting me so I assumed I was in the clear. I tossed my phone aside then lay in bed, wondering why I was so damn stupid and made such idiotic decisions.

***

I avoided Slade all week. Anywhere I thought he might turn up, I skipped. I didn't go to the library during my break for classes, and I steered clear of everyone in the gang. Seeing him would be the most awkward thing in the world. I wondered if he told Cayson what happened? It was my biggest fear. Nothing happened in the group that everyone didn't know about. But if he did tell Cayson, he would have told Skye…who would have confronted me. Since she hadn't, I assumed Slade kept the truth to himself.

Thank god.

The week went smooth. I didn't see him anywhere. Maybe we could just keep avoiding each other and pretend it never happened. But, of course, Skye knew something was up.

Trinity, where have you been?

God, was she a detective? *I've just been busy. Did you and Cayson do the deed yet?* I didn't really care at the moment but I tried to sound normal.

Doing what?

Homework. I knew that was a bad response the moment I sent it.

You never do homework.

Ugh. *I'm sick.*

Which is it? You're busy or you're sick?

I dug myself into a hole. I stopped texting her altogether. That was probably the best idea.

A few days later, I was walking across campus through the trees when I spotted Slade just a few feet away. His hands were in his pockets and he stared at the ground. His black blazer kept his body warm from the cold.

Oh shit. I needed to hightail it out of there.

Right at that moment, he looked up. His eyes met mine and panic moved into them. Suddenly, he turned around on his heel then walked away. I did the same, trying to pretend that didn't just happen.

The next week went better than the last. Slade and I did a better job of avoiding each other. But everyone else in the group had caught on.

Did something happen with you and Slade? Skye texted me.

Fuck. Fuck. Fuck. *No.*

Then why has no one seen either of you?

At least Slade kept our secret. I'd take it to the grave. But I needed to spit out an excuse. *We got into a fight.*

What's new? That doesn't explain why you guys are avoiding us as well as each other.

I'll see you soon, alright? You got Cayson to entertain you.

I don't care about that. I just want to make sure you're okay.

Having a best friend sucked sometimes. *I'm fine. Don't worry about me. I'll talk to you later.*

I'm always here, Trin. Don't forget that.

Like you would ever let me.

***

By the end of the second week, I knew this couldn't go on any longer. By avoiding each other, we were avoiding all the people we cared about. I wasn't looking forward to the conversation, but we needed to have it. I decided to be the bigger man.

I don't want to talk about this any more than you do but we need to.

Slade didn't respond for hours. *There's nothing to say.*

Can we just talk? We can't avoid each other forever.

Another hour passed before he responded. *Fine. Where do you want to meet?*

I don't care. I'm home right now.

I'll be there in an hour.

I spent the next hour dreading his arrival. I was nervous to see him and I wasn't sure why. Flashbacks of our night came to me as time passed, becoming more vivid with every passing minute. Our tongues moved together like we were desperate and our bodies were starving for one another. Even though it was outside in the middle of winter with my back against the wall, I had to admit the sex was pretty good...damn good. But that was beside the point. It was with Slade.

And that was a big no-no.

Slade arrived at my door an hour later.

I answered it, trying to remain calm.

His hands were in his pockets and he wouldn't make eye contact with me. He stared across the lawn then at my doorbell, finding it more interesting than my face.

"Come in." I left the door open and headed to the living room.

He followed me then sat on the opposite couch, as far away from me as possible.

"You think I'm going to rape you or something?"

He finally looked at me, annoyance etched onto his face. "Let's just get this over with."

"Did you tell anybody?"

"Fuck no. You think I'm crazy?" He looked at me with wide eyes. "If your dad found out, he would kill me. And I don't mean figuratively. Literally. He would stab me in the gut and watch me bleed to death."

My dad had this reputation as an overprotective father but he really wasn't that bad. It could be worse. "He wouldn't do that."

"Either way, I don't want him to find out." He ran his fingers through his hair in frustration. "Did you tell anybody?"

"No."

He breathed a sigh of relief. "Not even Skye?"

"No."

"Good. She's got a big mouth."

I crossed my legs and tried to think of something else to say. "Are we going to be weird around each other forever?"

He was quiet for a long time. "I hope not."

"Then why have you been avoiding me?"

"I figured you were in love with me and wanted a relationship or some shit like that."

I cringed. "No. I despise you as much as I did before."

He leaned his head back on the couch. "Thank god. I despise you too."

"So we really shouldn't have trouble returning to normal, right?"

"I guess not." He looked at me, a thoughtful expression on his face. "As long as we don't tell anybody."

"Believe me, I don't want anyone to know." I shook my head. "I'd never live that down."

"Like you're much better," he snapped.

"I am, actually. You're a manwhore."

"Like you aren't. Believe me, I can tell you've been around."

"What's that supposed to mean?" I demanded.

He said nothing.

"You think I'm good in bed?" I cornered him into a wall.

He still kept his mouth shut.

"You don't need to confirm it. I already know I am."

"Well, now you know I'm good too."

I refused to feed his ego so I didn't compliment him. "So, we're friends, right?"

"Yeah. Let's just never speak of it again."

"That sounds great."

"Alright." He stood up. "Um…I guess I'll see you around."

"Yeah." I walked him to the door.

"Bye." He walked out without looking back.

I shut the door, trying to forget him the second he was gone.

Chapter Nine

Cayson

Slade had been weird for weeks. He was unusually quiet around me, not making jokes like he normally did. His eyes showed a depth they never had before. It seemed like he was lost in thought most of the time, even in the middle of a conversation.

"Skye asked me if we could live in Connecticut when we settle down. You think that means when we get married? That's what she was implying?"

Slade sipped his beer and stared at the table. A whole minute went by without a response. He didn't even blink.

"Slade?"

"Hmm?" He came back around. "What?"

"Dude...what's up with you?"

"Nothing. I was just thinking....about a paper that's due."

"You never think about schoolwork—ever."

"What was the question again?" He tried to change the subject.

"Skye asked me if we could live in Connecticut when we 'settle' down. What do you think that means?"

He kept his hand on his beer. "She's probably referring to marriage. What else would she mean?"

That's what I was hoping for. When she said those words, my heart grew wings and took flight. It was something I constantly thought about, coming home from work and seeing her every day. I wanted her to be the mother of my kids, the woman I made love to every night. It was my dream since I could remember. The fact it was a real possibility made my hands shake. "That's what I was hoping for."

"Why are you surprised?" He stared at the TV, a bored look on his face.

I shrugged. "She dated Zack for a long time but never considered marriage. And we haven't been together very long and she's already talking about it."

"It's pretty obvious how much she loves you, man. And I don't see why she would date you unless she thought it would go somewhere. Why ruin a friendship for nothing?"

"Yeah..."

"Just be happy. Don't overthink it."

"You're right." Wait a second...Slade was never right. Where were all the jokes? All the comments? "We still haven't had sex." He should take the bait.

He stared at the foam in his cup. "It'll happen when it happens."

What the hell was wrong with him? "Okay, you're really freaking me out."

"What?" He looked offended.

"What's up with you? You're all quiet and serious and stuff."

He shrugged. "I'm just tired."

I wasn't buying it. "What happened with you and Trinity?"

"She's hideous," he blurted. "I would never sleep with her."

Okay... "I didn't say you would."

"We just had a fight and we're cool now. What's the big deal?" He drank his beer and spilled a little on his shirt.

"Well, what did you fight about?"

"The usual stuff..."

"But you've never avoided each other before." What was he hiding?

"She was just being annoying and I didn't want to talk to her anymore. End of story. Shit, get off my back. Are you a detective or something? Calm the hell down. Who cares if she and I weren't talking for a while? Why don't you..." He rambled on for a full minute about me getting off his case.

I wasn't buying his bullshit. I knew something more happened but he obviously wasn't going to spill. I decided to drop it. "Got it. I'm sorry."

"You should be sorry, dick face."

"Damn, you're defensive today...."

"I just don't appreciate being called a liar!"

I raised my hands. "I never called you a liar."

"Yeah, you did. Now stop asking me about her. I told you she was ugly."

"What does her appearance matter?"

"Just...this conversation is over." He downed half of his beer then wiped his lips. His eyes were glued to the TV, pretending I wasn't there.

Geez, he was being weird.

Roland and Conrad slid into the booth, their beers in hand.

"Have you seen Trinity?" Conrad asked. He looked at me when he said it.

"Why would I know where she is?" Slade blurted. "I don't fucking know. I don't even like her. She's disgusting." He was breathing hard, practically having a panic attack.

Roland raised an eyebrow. "You okay, man?"

"I'm groovy," Slade said without looking at him.

Conrad raised an eyebrow and looked at me. He gave me a look that clearly said, "What's his deal?"

I shrugged in response.

Slade ordered another beer and downed it like water. He was clearly on edge.

Skye stepped into the bar, looking like a vision. She wore black pants that were skin-tight and a maroon sweater that went well with her skin tone. A pink scarf was around her neck and a gold bracelet was on her wrist. She looked beautiful, like always. I hardly noticed Trinity behind her. She was just a blur to me.

I got out of the booth, eager to reach Skye.

Skye gave me a breathtaking smile when she came near. Her eyes lit up like Christmas morning, and they sparkled with their own inner light. I've never seen her give this look to anyone before—just me. "Hey." She moved into my chest and hooked her arms around my waist. "I saw a really good-looking guy when I walked in, but then I realized it was you."

"I'm glad I'm the only one who catches your eye." My hand automatically moved to her neck, the place I loved to touch her most. I placed a gentle kiss on the corner of her mouth, treasuring the moment as it happened.

A quiet moan escaped her lips while I touched her. Her small hand clenched my side, holding on during the embrace. When I pulled away, she gave me a look full of love. "I love kissing you."

"I love kissing you." I gave her another kiss.

"If you don't mind moving your fat asses, we're trying to watch the game," Roland barked.

I sighed then broke the kiss. "Can I get you something to drink?"

"Can I just sip some of yours? I'm not really craving anything."

"Whatever you want, baby." I guided her to the booth and sat next to her. Trinity sat on the end, directly across from Slade.

We all watched their interaction, wondering what they would do or say. They ignored each other, like always.

"Did you have a lame time with Mom and Dad last weekend?" Roland asked.

"No, it was fun," Skye said. "You should have come."

"Ha. Yeah right." He rested his elbows on the table and watched TV.

"Mom and Dad said they wished you were there," Skye said.

"Of course," he said. "I could only imagine how boring you and Cayson were."

"Could you not be a dick for like a second?" Skye demanded.

"Nope." He drank his beer then turned his attention on Trinity and Slade. "So what happened between you guys?"

Both of them flinched.

"We just got into a fight," Slade barked.

"Why is everyone so interested in us?" Trinity stammered.

Roland raised his hands. "Sorry, I was just curious…"

"Well, don't be." Slade watched the TV again.

I finished my beer. "You sure you don't want anything?" I asked Skye.

"No, thank you."

I left the booth and headed to the bar. The bartender was busy taking drink orders so I patiently waited for him to notice me. If I were a girl who looked like Skye, I wouldn't have to wait for anything.

"Cayson?"

I recognized that voice. I turned to see the blonde hair I fisted more times than I could recall. She smelled the same way, like vanilla. Her hair was silky like I remembered. It framed her face. It was a little shorter than the last time I saw her. She must have gotten a haircut. "Hey, Jasmine." I knew I would run into her eventually.

She wore a smile but it was clearly forced. "How's it going?"

"Good. You?"

"Good." Sadness was in her eyes.

The last words she said to me on the night we broke up came back to me. She said she loved me the way I loved Skye. And I felt like a damn asshole. It was clear she still felt that way.

"I know this is awkward…but I figured it would be better just to say hi rather than pretend I didn't see you."

"I'm glad you said hi. It's nice to see you."

She nodded, loosening up a bit. "How's school?"

"Lame, like always."

She chuckled. "I can imagine. And Skye…?"

I felt the guilt in my stomach.

"She was going to come up eventually, right?"

"Yeah. She and I are great. I'm very happy." I didn't want to downplay my feelings for Skye. The last thing I wanted to do was give Jasmine the impression she had a chance with me.

She nodded slowly. "Good. I'm glad to hear it."

No, she wasn't. "Are you seeing anyone?"

"I date here and there…I'm actually on a date now." She didn't seem too thrilled about it.

"Is he weird?"

She shrugged. "He's just clingy and brags a lot. I like a guy who's humble." She gave me an affectionate look.

"You'll find the right guy. Just keep looking." There was hope. I didn't want her to lose it.

"Yeah…hopefully." She tucked a strand of hair behind her ear, something she used to do when she was nervous. "You look good."

I felt awkward. What should I say in response? "Thanks…"

"You're still working out all the time?"

"Every day with Slade."

She nodded. "It shows."

I couldn't compliment her appearance. It would feel like I was cheating on Skye in a complicated way. "Well…it was nice seeing you."

"Yeah…" She played with her hair again.

An arm moved around my waist and rose hips came into my nose. Skye moved into my side, hugging me like a teddy bear. "Where's that beer?" she asked with a playful look. She pressed her breasts into my side and practically smothered me.

Jasmine looked at the ground, clearly uncomfortable.

"Uh…I'm getting it now." This was weird. "I'll be back in a second."

"I'll wait." Skye didn't move.

Jasmine didn't look at us. "I'll see you around…" She drifted away and returned to her table.

When she was gone, I gave Skye an incredulous look. "What was that?"

"What do you mean?" She raised an eyebrow.

"You didn't have to scare her off like that." It was already difficult for me to get mad at her as a friend, but it was even harder since she was my girlfriend. But I couldn't deny how upset it made me.

"I didn't scare her off," she said, offended. "You're my boyfriend and I can touch you whenever I want."

I turned to her, trying to keep my voice down. "Don't bullshit with me, Skye. I know exactly what you were doing."

She flinched when I cursed. She was used to me treating her like a princess.

"You already won, Skye. You don't need to rub your victory in her face. Honestly, I never thought you'd be one of those girls."

"I wasn't rubbing anything in her face," she argued.

"Seriously, just stop. She already knows I love you. You don't need to come over here and claim me. You either trust me or you don't."

"I never said I—"

I walked off, not letting her finish her sentence. I stormed out of the bar then headed home. Anger consumed me, making my hands shake. I couldn't believe I turned my back on Skye like that. But just because I loved her didn't mean I'd let her get away with whatever she wanted.

Not gonna happen.

***

A few hours later, there was a knock on my door. It was almost midnight and only one person would come over at this hour. Skye and I usually slept over at each other's houses. I was so used to it by now that I knew I wouldn't be able to sleep without her.

I looked through the peephole and saw her standing on the other side. She was bundled up in a jacket and scarf. Her arms were crossed over her chest.

I sighed then opened the door, keeping an indifferent façade. I stood in the doorway so she couldn't walk in. I kept my silence, waiting for her to speak first.

She stared at me for a while, the fear in her eyes. "Can I come in?"

"No. I may be in love with you but I'm not going to let you walk all over me. Say what you came to say and leave."

Skye flinched at my aggression. "I just wanted to say I'm sorry..."

I waited for her to elaborate.

"I…I shouldn't have acted like that. You're right."

"Then why did you?"

She kept her arms across her chest. "I guess I just love you so much."

"That's not an excuse," I said darkly.

"I was jealous," she blurted. "I admit it. Seeing her talk to you with that look on her face hurt my stomach. You're mine and I…just wanted to make sure she knew that."

"Skye, she knows. I made it pretty clear when I dumped her for you."

She pressed her lips tightly together.

"I've known you my entire life, Skye, and you've never pulled this number before. You've always been trusting and calm. You've never gloated to other people and you've certainly never intentionally tried to hurt another person. And that's why I fell in love with you. I don't want that to change."

"I know…I was being a bitch."

I didn't deny it. "And it hurts me that you don't trust me."

"It's not that," she said immediately. "It was all jealousy—on my part."

I studied her face under the light from my porch. Her hair was over one shoulder and her lips were ruby red.

"It's not going to happen again, right?"

She shook her head. "No."

"Good. That's what I wanted to hear."

She stared at me, the longing in her eyes. "Do you still want me to go?"

I grabbed her arm and pulled her inside. “No. I want you to make it up to me.”

Her eyes lit up. “I can do that.”

Chapter Ten

Skye

I messed things up with Cayson and I knew it. When I saw Jasmine talking to him, I don't know what came over me. And everyone at the table wasn't helping.

"Oooh…she's after your man." Slade watched them by the bar.

"She wants him to stick it to her good," Roland said. "Break up sex, you know."

"Shut up," I said.

"And she's down for anal," Conrad said. "So you have a lot to compete with."

The idea of Cayson having sex with her, any kind of sex, made me sick. "Knock it off."

"Someone's getting jealous." Roland nudged me in the side.

"If my boyfriend's ex was all over him, I'd strut over there and make it clear she'd have to go through me first," Trinity said.

"But you don't have a boyfriend," Slade noted. "You aren't sleeping with anyone…"

She gave him an irritated look.

"If you don't claim him, she's going to snatch him up," Conrad said. "And I wouldn't blame Cayson for having his cake and eating it too. You being the cake and Jasmine being the too."

They were getting under my skin even though I tried to act like they didn't. It was pretty clear Jasmine was in love with him. It was obvious every time she looked at him. I gave into the jealousy and made a stupid decision.

And now I felt guilty about it.

I knew Cayson wouldn't leave me over something like that, but I didn't like upsetting him. Our relationship was perfect. He was perfect. I didn't want to ruin it over something stupid. Honestly, I've never been jealous before. Cayson was the only one who instilled that emotion in me. I guess it's because I was head-over-heels in love with him and I've felt that way for years—even if I didn't realize it at the time.

Whatever the reason, it wasn't right. Jasmine was a very nice girl and what I did was very uncool. I admit it, and I didn't feel good about it. Luckily, Cayson let it go the moment I apologized. I learned my lesson.

Trinity sat across from me in the library and placed her magazines on the table. "I just got *Vogue* in the mail yesterday."

"Anything cute?" I asked.

"A lot of cute things." She pulled out a sketchpad and handed it to me. "I was inspired by a gown I found in this magazine. But I think mine is better."

I examined the picture, immediately impressed. "Trinity…this is really good."

"Really? You aren't just saying that?"

"No…" I was being genuine. "Do you have any others?"

She laughed. "I have hundreds. They are at home in my office."

"You should show your dad. He would open up your clothing line in a heartbeat."

She sighed. "I think I'm going to finish my bachelor's first."

"Really?"

She nodded. "I'm almost done and my dad already paid a lot of money…I may as well finish."

I agreed. "I'll support whatever you decide, Trin."

"Thanks." She gave me a smile. "So…you and Cayson okay?"

I rolled my eyes. "Yeah. I was just being childish."

"Are you still fighting?"

"No. He forgave me the moment I apologized."

"That's a relief. Knowing Cayson, he couldn't stay mad at you for long."

"I don't know…he was pretty mad."

"It all worked out, right?"

I nodded. "It did."

"And I'm sure Jasmine will keep her paws off him."

The idea of Jasmine touching him still got my heart racing. "Yeah…"

Trinity returned her attention to her magazine and flipped through the pages.

I opened my textbooks and began to study.

An hour of silence passed until I heard the chair move beside me. I turned, hoping to see Cayson. It wasn't him.

Zack was staring me down. His face was back to normal and no bruises lingered behind. Judging by the anger in his eyes, he wasn't here to discuss ponies and rainbows. "So, you and lover boy, huh? I shouldn't be surprised."

"Zack, go away."

He grabbed my wrist. "No. I'm going to talk and you're going to listen."

Trinity glared at him. "Let go or I'll break your dick."

He ignored her, still staring at me. "So, first your dad beats the shit out of me, then I find out you're fucking the guy you spent all your time with when we were together. I'm not happy, Skye. You claim I played you but it's the other way around."

"I said let her go," Trinity threatened.

I wasn't scared of Zack and I refused to act like it. "I suggest you let go of me. Otherwise, you're going to get your ass kicked by two girls."

He dropped his hand but didn't move away. "You owe me."

What? "Owe you what?"

"An apology. You totally played me."

I rolled my eyes. "You're so pathetic."

"Apologize to me or I'll make your boyfriend pay for it." His eyes held his mirth.

"Did you just threaten Cayson?" Now I was pissed. Zack could do and say whatever he wanted to me and it didn't make me blink twice. But threatening someone I cared about was another story.

Trinity left her chair and came around the table, coming behind him. Then she grabbed him by the hair and yanked him to the ground.

"Fucking bitch," Zack mumbled.

We were the only ones in the corner so no one noticed the disturbance. The Harvard library was enormous. We were practically alone.

Trinity kicked him hard in the balls. "You think that makes me a bitch? I'm not even done." She kicked him again.

He curled in a ball and moaned.

"Nobody threatens Cayson and gets away with it." She kicked him again but Zack caught her leg. Then he pulled her foot out from under her, making her fall down.

"Shut the hell up." Zack moved on top of her and held her down. "As I was saying..."

I stood up and kicked him hard in the arm.

He pressed his lips together and took the hit. "If you don't want me to hurt your friend, I suggest you knock it off."

"You're psycho. I can't believe I ever dated you," I said.

"Maybe I wasn't so bad in bed, after all."

Trinity tried to wiggle free. "Get off of me, jackass!"

The sound of approaching feet caught my attention. And Zack's. I turned and grabbed my ethics textbook, preparing to slam it on Zack's head.

"What the fuck?" It was Slade. He took one look at Zack on top of Trinity and snapped. "Fucking piece of shit!" He rushed Zack then yanked him off, thrusting his head into the carpet while he did it. "You want to die? Because it seems like it." Slade punched him hard in the jaw then rushed to Trinity. "Trin, are you okay?" He pulled her up so she was sitting. He kept his arm around her then grabbed her chin, examining her face.

"I'm fine," she said immediately. "He didn't hurt me."

Relief filled his eyes.

"But you better bust out that Krav Maga and kick his ass."

"You got it." He stood, but Zack was gone. We were both concerned for Trinity and forgot him for a moment. Slade searched the aisles then came back when he couldn't find him. "I'll see him again. And when I do, he'll have no teeth." He came back to Trinity and helped her stand up. Then he looked at me. "Skye, are you okay?"

"I'm fine," I answered.

Slade pulled out a chair for Trinity and helped her sit down. "What the hell happened?"

"Zack wanted to talk but Trinity tried to kick his ass instead," I explained.

"I kicked him in the balls a few times. I would have done more damage if it wasn't so cramped," Trinity said.

Slade rested his hand on her back and rubbed her gently. "You sure you're alright?" Concern was in his eyes.

"He didn't do anything except pin me down," she said.

I'd never seen Slade be so affectionate with Trinity—or any girl.

He breathed a sigh of relief. "I'm glad you girls are alright."

"We aren't scared of him," Trinity said. "He's a fucking pussy."

"Yeah," I agreed.

Slade gave me a firm look. "I think it's time to tell your dad, Skye."

"No." That wasn't an option.

"He's obviously not going to leave you alone," Slade pressed.

"I got myself into this mess and I'll get myself out," I said. "Zack isn't dangerous. He's annoying but not dangerous."

Slade wasn't so sure. "What does he want?"

"He keeps saying my dad put him in the hospital, which he didn't."

Emotion moved into Slade's eyes but he didn't react in any other way.

"And he thinks I had a thing with Cayson while we were together. He wants an apology."

"Weirdo," Slade said.

"He is," Trinity said. "I can't believe you were fucking him."

"Don't remind me," I said miserably.

"Cayson isn't going to be pleased when he finds out." Slade shook his head.

"I know…" I didn't want to tell him.

"He'll be hovering around you every second of the day," Slade said.

That didn't sound so bad.

Slade continued to rub Trinity's shoulder. "Can I get you something to eat?"

"We aren't supposed to eat in the library. Remember?" she teased.

He smirked. "How could I forget?"

What was going on? "I thought you hated each other?"

Slade dropped his hand immediately. "We do. I just wanted to make sure she was okay…not that I care or anything."

They were the weirdest people I knew…

***

Cayson came over that night with a vase of flowers. Green stems left the glass and erupted into beautiful red roses. There were a dozen and they smelled wonderful.

I studied them for a moment before I grabbed them. "They are beautiful."

His eyes shined in adoration. He stepped inside then placed a gentle kiss on my lips. "I know your favorite flower is the lily, but I also know that's your dad's territory."

I smirked. "It is a tradition."

"Roses are more romantic anyway."

"They are." I filled the vase with water then set it on the table. "But you shouldn't be getting me anything. I should be the one kissing your ass."

He grinned. "It's water under the bridge, Skye. Just forget about it."

"You let me off the hook so easily."

"Well…you gave me an incredible apology." He came close to me and hooked his arms around my waist. His nose rubbed against mine gently.

I felt redness move into my cheeks. "I guess I know what to do in the future."

He chuckled. "It looks like you do."

I rested my face against his chest, feeling it rise and fall. His scent came into my nose and I felt relaxed, comfortable. The cotton of his t-shirt felt good against my cheek.

"How was your day?" he whispered.

I immediately thought about Zack. I really didn't want to get into it until after dinner. "Fine. How about yours?"

"Pretty lame. But, then again, my life is always lame when you aren't around." His hand moved up my back and rested between my shoulder blades.

"Mine too." I felt warmth move through my body.

He pressed his forehead against mine. "Where did you want to eat?"

I shrugged. "Pizza is good."

He laughed. "You always want pizza."

"It's good," I argued.

"Whatever you want, baby." He grabbed my hand and pulled me toward the door. His phone vibrated in his pocket so he pulled it out and checked it. Then he shoved it back inside.

I grabbed my coat then we walked down the stairs.

He sighed then pulled out his phone when it vibrated again. He looked at it with a sigh then put it back in his pocket. As soon as he returned it, it vibrated again.

"Someone is popular."

He rolled his eyes. "Slade has called me five times in a row."

My heart skipped a beat. I knew why he was calling.

"Damn, what does he want?" He pulled the phone out again.

I snatched it away. "He probably wants you to head to a strip club with him or something."

He cocked an eyebrow. "There're no strip clubs around here."

"That we know of. But Slade would." It kept vibrating in my hand.

"I'll just tell him to stop calling." He held out his hand and waited for me to pass it to him.

Uh…I took the call instead. "Cayson's busy. Stop calling."

"You didn't tell him, did you?" Annoyance was in his voice.

Cayson stared at me with a suspicious look on his face.

"He'll call you later," I said.

"You had all day to tell him and it's obvious you aren't going to. Now hand him the damn phone."

"Okay, talk to you later." I hung up and put the phone in my pocket.

Cayson eyed me with a raised eyebrow. "What's going on, Skye?"

"I'm just making sure you don't get a headache." I walked to his car, feeling the phone vibrate in my pocket again and again.

Cayson knew something was up. "Is there something you need to tell me?" He walked behind me then cornered me into the door of his car. He put his hands on either side of me, caging me in. A dark look came into his eyes.

I stared up at him, seeing his breath escape as vapor. "No…"

"We've known each other for a long time, Skye. I know when you're lying. You can fool everyone else but you can't fool me." He brushed his lips passed mine, his mouth warm in the freezing night.

I cupped his face and gave him a warm kiss. "I want to wait until after dinner."

"Why?" He stepped closer to me, pinning me against the car door.

"I'm hungry."

"You're always hungry." His teasing nature was gone, replaced by seriousness.

"Well, I'm really hungry."

"And I'm really curious."

I sighed, knowing he wouldn't let up. "I'm not telling you until after dinner. And it's not even that big of a deal. So drop it."

He studied my face, seeing the determination in my eyes. He lowered his hands. "Fine."

"Thank you."

He stepped back. "You better make this worth my while."

"I always do."

Cayson opened the door for me then helped me inside before he got into the driver's seat. He was about to start the car when a vehicle slammed to a stop behind us and blocked us in.

"What the...?" Cayson looked in the rearview mirror.

I looked in the side mirror and my heart fell. Slade's car had boxed us in. *God, he was annoying.*

"What the hell is he doing?" Cayson got out and slammed the door.

I rolled my eyes then left the car, joining Cayson in the rear.

Slade left his car, the engine still on.

Cayson's eyes were wide. "Dude, what's going on?"

Slade gave me a long glare before he looked at Cayson again. "Your precious girlfriend refrained from telling you an important piece of information. And since she isn't going to admit it, I have to say something."

"Slade, stay out of our relationship," I snapped.

"You had all day to tell him but you never did. He has the right to know! And not tomorrow or a week from now. He needs to know right this second."

"I was going to tell him after dinner," I hissed.

"Sure..." Slade wasn't buying it. He looked back at Cayson. "So this is the story—"

Cayson held up his hand. "I want to hear it from Skye."

Slade shut his mouth then looked at me.

Cayson turned his eyes on me, and he didn't look happy. "What is it?"

I wanted to slap Slade right then. "Trinity and I were in the library this afternoon when Zack stopped by. He's pissed I'm dating you and he wanted an apology. Trinity kicked him a few times then Zack pinned her down. Slade came in then and chased him off."

Cayson's face was unreadable. He stared me down, his jaw clenched tight.

"It wasn't even a big deal. It was just annoying." I crossed my arms over my chest. "I was going to tell you but I wanted to wait until after dinner. It's not even worth discussing."

"Not worth discussing?" Slade snapped. "He's bothered you twice now. And he held Trinity down. That shit's not okay in my book."

"Slade, go home." Cayson didn't look at him when he said it.

Slade sighed then walked off. His footsteps were loud against the cold pavement. His engine revved as he hit the gas and drove away. When the sound of his tires was gone, I knew we were alone.

Cayson hadn't blinked once. "Why didn't you call me?"

"There wasn't any time. And Slade was there."

"What does that matter?" His voice was low and calm, but the ferocity was evident in his tone. "I'm your boyfriend, not Slade."

I rolled my eyes. "Don't overreact."

"Don't. Roll. Your. Eyes." He stared me down, his anger flashing.

The world suddenly became silent. The snow fell around us, masking us in a winter wonderland.

"Skye, I was annoyed that Zack bothered you before. But the fact he's done it again makes me uneasy. Really uneasy."

"He's annoying but not dangerous."

"It doesn't seem like it. Holding Trinity down is unacceptable."

"I'm not saying what he did was right. But he wouldn't actually hurt me or Trinity."

"You don't know that," he snapped.

"In a few weeks, he'll be over it and move on."

"And I'm just supposed to patiently wait until he's ready to move on?" he snapped.

"There's no other option. It's not like I can call the police. What would I even say? What evidence do I have?"

"We don't need the police," he snarled. "We need someone with the power to get rid of someone—no questions asked."

I knew what he was implying. "Don't you dare tell my father."

"I'm running out of options, Skye. I'd gladly kill him with my bare hands but I have a feeling you wouldn't like that very much."

"No one is going to kill anybody," I snapped. "Why is that the first thing you think of?"

"Because it's the best option."

"No, it's not! Zack isn't a threat. I can handle him."

"And what would you have done if Slade hadn't showed up?" Cayson asked.

"I was about to slam my ethics book right on his skull. I'm sure that would have knocked him out."

He ran his fingers through his hair, flustered.

"Leave my father out of this. I mean it, Cayson."

He stared into the distance.

"Cayson."

He turned his gaze back on me. "I'm not letting you out of my sight. I don't care if it pisses you off. If he thinks he can harass you again, he's in for a surprise."

This was the reaction I expected so I guess I couldn't be upset. "Fine."

"I'm glad we're on the same page." His jaw was still clenched.

"Cayson, I can take care of myself."

"I know you can. But you don't have to."

I kept my arms across my chest. "Now what?"

"I'm not in the mood to sit in a restaurant and pretend I'm fine. Let's order in." He walked toward the apartment.

I stayed in my spot before I trailed behind him and walked up the stairs.

When he reached the door he held out his hand. "Can I have my phone back?"

I handed it to him.

"Just for the record, I don't like hearing this shit from my friends. I want to hear it from you." Anger still lingered in his voice.

"I wanted to wait until after dinner. I already said that."

He walked inside then pulled off his coat. "I think that's more important than a meal."

"I just didn't want to watch you brood all night long."

"That's too damn bad. You're everything to me, Skye. I'm not going to let some guy harass you. The fact you're my girlfriend is irrelevant. I will not let some jackass treat you that way."

"Like I said, I can handle him."

Cayson was struggling to still his emotion. He turned away from me then headed to the couch, his shoulders stiff with tension.

I opened the drawer of take-out menus then found my favorite pizza place. I pulled out my phone and made the call. When I was done, the silence stretched in my apartment. Cayson still sat on the couch, staring at the blank TV screen.

I didn't want to spend our night like this. Cayson wasn't angry very often, and I hated feeling his fury linger in the air like the moisture after a heavy rain. I sat beside him on the couch then scooted close to him. I hooked my arm around his stomach and leaned close to him. My lips brushed his neck before I planted a kiss on the warm skin. Cayson didn't react to my touch. I continued to kiss him, tasting him. When my hand moved up his chest, I guided him against the back of the couch, forcing him to relax. He sighed but didn't push me away.

I moved into his lap then straddled his hips. I flipped my hair over one shoulder as I undid my scarf.

Anger still thudded in his eyes.

I pressed my chest against his then sought his neck with my lips, kissing him the way he liked.

He leaned his head back and closed his eyes. But his hands were idle by his sides, not touching me.

My hands massaged his shoulders and I gave him my best moves. I knew it would take awhile to loosen him up. When a quiet moan, almost unnoticeable, came from his lips, I knew I was getting somewhere.

I leaned back then pulled my sweater over my head. I wore a burgundy bra covered in lace. It showed the color of my skin but hid the most intimate parts.

He took me in. Desire burned in his eyes but the resentment still lingered behind.

I unclasped my bra and let it fall.

He swallowed the lump in his throat. "I admit you're beautiful, Skye. But this isn't going to make me forget how upset I am—"

I grabbed my chest with both hands and massaged my breasts, squeezing and rubbing them while I stared into his eyes.

He swallowed the lump in his throat again while he stared at my moving hands. Quickly, he was forgetting the heated conversation we just had. The Cayson I knew and loved was in there, coming back.

I stood up then pulled off my boots and jeans. I left my thong on before I moved back to his lap.

Cayson eyed my body without shame, his thoughts as easy to read as an open book.

I straddled his lap again, my hands moving to his shoulders. My breasts were in his face, and I felt his warm breath fall on my nipples.

Cayson's hands moved to my hips.

I had him.

His hands moved up the skin around my ribs. Then they moved to my chest, groping them. He leaned forward then pressed his lips against mine, giving me a gentle kiss. "I know I come off a little strong sometimes, but it's only because I love you like crazy, Skye Preston."

I stared into his eyes, feeling the emotion leak from every pore in his body. Of all the years I'd known Cayson, he never gave anyone the look he was giving me. And he never said those words, at least not like that. "I love you too, Cayson."

He hooked an arm around my waist then rolled me to the couch, shifting on top of me. His lips found mine and he kissed me gently, moving his mouth against mine purposefully. He breathed into my mouth, making me hot everywhere. I hooked my legs around his waist and pulled him closer to me, wanting more than he could give.

I gripped his shirt and yanked it off, wanting to feel his muscled chest against me. Then I moved to his jeans, getting them off. I took the boxers too, wanting all of him. He grabbed my thong and yanked it off, practically tearing it.

I wrapped my legs around his waist again, feeling his cock against my folds. I'd been thinking about being with him for a long time. We'd been together for months, longer in terms of our friendship, and I didn't want to wait anymore. He was mine and I was his.

Cayson gave me one last kiss before he pulled away and looked into my eyes. It was clear he was thinking the same thing I was. He breathed hard then brushed his lips against mine.

I moved one hand down his back until I reached his hip. I tugged him toward me, telling him what I wanted.

Understanding filled his eyes. He adjusted himself then pressed his mouth against mine. Then he pointed himself at my entrance, ready to enter me. I dug my nails into his skin, anticipating the pleasure I was about to feel. I had decent sex throughout my life but I knew Cayson would be different. It would be beautiful and wonderful. My soul would touch his, and his mine.

A knock on the door interrupted us.

We both flinched, startled by the sound.

Cayson broke our kiss and glanced toward the door.

"Forget it. It's probably a girl scout." I grabbed his neck and crushed his lips to mine.

The knock sounded again.

Cayson pulled away. "It's the pizza guy."

"Who cares about pizza?" I wanted Cayson, not food.

He smirked. "Skye, I have to get that." He left the couch then quickly pulled on his clothes.

I sighed then pulled the blanket over me, hiding my body.

Cayson answered the door and took the pizza. After he paid the guy, he set it on the kitchen table.

The magical moment was ruined.

Cayson placed the pizza on two plates then he brought me one.

I sighed then took the plate, feeling my stomach rumble. I was more than disappointed. I was totally crestfallen.

Cayson leaned toward me and kissed me on the cheek. "We have the rest of our lives, baby."

I sighed then took a bite of my pizza. "You're right."

He rubbed his nose against mine then took a bite of his pizza. "*I Love Lucy*?"

"Sure."

He leaned back against the couch then pulled me next to him. We watched TV together, like we used to when we were just friends, but now everything was different. He was the best thing that ever happened to me.

Chapter Eleven

Slade

My life was turned upside down.

After I slept with Trinity, I couldn't stop thinking about it. She was drunk and I was drunk. We were both out of our minds. We fucked against a wall in the snow like animals. I had a lot of wild sex but I have to say that was the wildest. I didn't even wear a condom.

And it was Trinity.

If anyone found out, it would ruin me. It would get back to Uncle Mike and I'd be as good as dead. My dad was easy-going and pretty much cool with everything, but I don't think he would be too happy about this. My mom would probably slap me. I'd been a jerk to everyone I knew, but I was never a jerk to my family. I crossed a line I could never uncross.

But one thing made it worse. She was the best sex I ever had.

Maybe I remembered history in a different way than it really happened. Since I was drunk and disoriented, maybe I thought it was better than it really was. What if it was sluggish and awkward? How long did it even last?

The guilt was eating me alive.

Trinity and I talked about it and we settled our differences. I was grateful she wasn't in love with me like Cayson was with Skye. That would just give me more problems. I didn't want a relationship, especially with her. I wasn't a one-woman type of guy. She knew that. Shit, everyone knew that.

But I couldn't stop thinking about it. Every time someone asked me about her, I felt like they were shining a light in my eye. Did they know? Did they hear something? I had a small panic attack every time.

Since Cayson was my best friend, it was hard to keep him in the dark. I told him everything, even if he didn't always want to hear about all my sexual conquests. And he told me everything he did with Skye. The decent thing would be to reciprocate with what I did with Trinity.

But I couldn't tell anyone about that—not a soul.

I was going through women quicker than usual. I picked them up left and right and had my way with them. But nothing hit the spot. They either just lay there and did nothing, or they just weren't good in bed—period.

I kept comparing them to my night with Trinity. Even though most of it was a blur, I still knew it was awesome. I would never admit it to Trinity. I'd take it to the grave rather than say it out loud. But I was definitely thinking it.

I ran into Roland in the hallway. "Going to Trinity's tonight?"

"What? Why? I'm not seeing her," I blurted.

He cocked an eyebrow. "She's having people over for game night. I just assumed you were going."

"Oh…yeah. Totally." *Totally? I've said that word twice in my entire life.*

Roland eyed me for a long time. "You okay, man?"

"I'm groovy." I walked away before he could ask me another question.

***

When I arrived at Trinity's house, I set the beer on the counter.

Everyone was seated on the couch, talking and watching TV. Trinity wore a burgundy dress with a pink scarf. The color looked good on her fair skin tone, and her blonde hair contrasted against it perfectly. The fabric clung to her hourglass figure and her perky breasts. She was thin and tall, but she was all curves in all the right places. She kept brushing loose strands from her face but they fell every time. Her fingernails were the same color as her dress. Black tights were on her legs slightly see-through and lacy. Black heels were on her feet, making her calf muscles more prominent. She dressed in a classy but elegant way.

Why was I noticing every little damn detail?

I put the bottles in the refrigerator and kept one for myself. I used my lighter to pop open the cap.

"I have a bottle opener."

I turned to see Trinity. Up close, I could see the light make up on her face. Gray eye shadow was over her eyes and black eye liner really made them noticeable. Her lips were red and shiny. "This works too."

"Yeah…but I don't want you to set off the fire alarm."

"This is the cool way to open it."

"And the dangerous way," she added.

I leaned against the counter and drank my beer. "Are you asking me to stop?"

"No. I'm just offering a better solution."

Our eyes met and a moment passed between us. I thought about our night fucking against a wall and I was pretty sure she did too. "Are you doing okay?"

"Why wouldn't I be okay?"

"Zack held you down in a library…that couldn't have felt good."

"Oh, that." She rolled her eyes. "I wasn't scared then and I'm not scared now."

"Has he bothered you or anything?" *If he did, I'd kill him.*

"No. But I usually wear heels so I'll give him a good kick in the nuts next time I see him."

"Leave him to me. I'll kill him instead."

"I'm sure Cayson will beat you to the punch."

I eyed Cayson and Skye on the couch. They were close and cuddly. Just as in love as ever. "I guess he got over it."

"I'm sure she did something with her titties and Cayson completely forgot."

I glanced at Trinity's breasts then looked away.

"Did you just check out my chest?"

She caught me? "No…"

"Slade, I saw you."

"I didn't."

"I was looking at you when you did it."

"Wow, you're conceited."

"I'm not conceited," she argued. "I know what I saw."

"You're absolutely hideous."

"It didn't seem that way when you were fucking my brains out," she snarled.

I glanced at everyone in the living room then turned back to her. "Shh! Keep your voice down."

She rolled her eyes. "They aren't listening to us."

"You better hope not."

"I'm the one who has something to be embarrassed about. So just chill out."

"See?" I said. "Conceited."

"I just know my value."

"If you did, you wouldn't let me screw you next to a dumpster."

"Maybe I like being screwed by a dumpster."

My cock hardened and twitched. What the fuck was wrong with me? "You've done it before?"

"Just because I don't talk about every sexual experience doesn't mean I don't have plenty."

"Sounds like you're a whore."

"Sounds like you're a sexist pig," she countered. Trinity was the only woman who argued with me like this. All the other women in my life listened to what I said and let me get my way. She called me out on my shit and told me off more times than I could count. I didn't realize it until that moment.

I finished my beer then grabbed another.

She held out the bottle opener.

Being defiant, I took out the lighter and burned the lid.

"You don't even smoke. It makes more sense to carry around a bottle opener instead of a lighter."

"Not really. You can do a lot with a lighter."

"Like burn down trees?" she said sarcastically.

"You're such an annoying brat."

"And you're a jerk. What's new?"

I stared her down, feeling annoyed all over again. "I'm going to walk away before I slap you across that pretty face."

"You think I have a pretty face?" she challenged.

I walked away before I did something stupid. I sat beside Cayson on the couch.

Cayson eyed me, seeing the annoyed look on my face. "So you and Trinity are back to normal?"

"Something like that." I drank my beer with a clenched jaw.

"Twister!" Trinity pulled out the box and set it up. "Let's do it."

"We aren't five," Conrad said.

"Come on," Trinity said. "It'll be fun."

"Let's do it." Silke straightened out the game on the floor.

"Whatever." Conrad rolled his eyes. "But then we're playing UNO."

They started the game but I didn't participate. Trinity put her hands and feet on the right dots. As much as I tried not to look at specific parts of her body, I couldn't help it. When her ass was directly in my face, I stared at it, remembering how good it felt in my hands.

They played a few rounds before we moved on to UNO. I stayed far away from Trinity and tried not to look at her. She was distracting and it was really getting under my skin.

Skye won three rounds in a row.

"God, you're annoying," Roland said.

"It's not my fault you suck," she countered.

Cayson gave her a fond look then rubbed his nose against hers.

"None of that," Conrad said. "It's gross."

"You're gross," Silke said. "Cayson and Skye are adorable."

Conrad rolled his eyes. "Girls…"

When we were tired of the board games, we watched TV. I leaned back in the chair and didn't finish my third beer. I didn't eat enough and they were going to my head. The last time I was around Trinity when I was drunk, it was a disaster.

My phone rang in my pocket and I saw the name on the screen. It was my dad. Why was he calling me? I walked out the backdoor and stood in Trinity's back yard. Then I took the call. "Yo."

"Yo," he said back. "What's going on?"

"You tell me. You called."

"I haven't talked to you in a while. Wanted to see what you were up to."

"You never check up on me," I countered.

"I know. I'm a horrible father," he said with a laugh.

"No. You're an awesome father."

My dad didn't have a response to that.

"Why are you calling so late?"

"Late? Aren't you a night owl?" my dad asked.

"Yeah." He had a point.

"So, what's new?"

"Nothing. Just school."

"There's got to be something else," he pressed.

"I've been getting pretty good with the guitar. I should drop out of school and join a band."

"Your mother would love that," he said sarcastically.

"And my artwork is getting better. I drew this piece of a tiger moving through stalks of grass. I want you to ink it on me."

"I'll take a look at it when you come down for a visit."

"So, what's new with you, Dad?"

"Nothing. The shop is doing well. Your mother has been busy with work, but that's not surprising."

"Why don't you guys retire?" I asked. "You're like a hundred."

"Do hundred-year-old guys get hit on left and right?"

"Rich ones do."

"Well, I'm not rich. So it's obviously just my looks and sex appeal."

"I'm going to tell Mom you said that."

He laughed. "You think she doesn't know this already?"

"I guess you're right," I said with a laugh.

"Well, I'll let you go. I'm sure you're up to no good and I'm interrupting."

I smirked. "You know me so well, Dad."

"I do," he said. "I'll talk to you later."

"Okay."

"I love you, kid."

"I love you too."

He hung up.

I put my phone back in my pocket then stepped inside.

Everyone was gone. Empty beer bottles were on the coffee tables and counters. The games were piled on the floor. Snacks and plates were littered everywhere.

How long was I on the phone?

I closed the door and stepped inside.

Trinity was piling garbage into a bag. "You're still here?"

"I was talking to my dad," I explained.

"What's he up to?"

"Nothing new." I watched her bend over and grab an empty beer bottle. "Everyone left?"

"You think they're all in the bathroom?" she said sarcastically.

"You know, I'm a jerk to you because you're a bitch to me."

She laughed. "Cut the shit, Slade." She threw the plates and napkins away then left the bag against the wall. "Well, thanks for coming over."

"Sure..."

She put her hands on her hips and stared at me.

"I guess I should go..." It was awkward being alone with her...in a house...with a bed.

"Yeah." She walked toward the door and I followed her.

She opened it. "I'll see you around."

"Yeah." I stopped and looked at her. "Thanks for having me over..." I wasn't sure why I said that. I was never polite.

Surprise moved into her eyes but she didn't say anything.

I didn't cross the threshold. I stayed on this side of the door, unsure what was keeping me there. I kept thinking about her long legs under her dress. When they were wrapped around my waist, it felt so good. I remembered how good it felt to be inside her. All the girls I'd been screwing didn't compare to her—at all.

She studied my face, her eyes guarded.

I needed to leave…

Trinity said nothing, just waiting.

Whatever. I was horny and I was going for it.

I pushed her against the wall then sealed my mouth over hers. The door was still open and the nighttime air came in but I ignored it. I gripped her hips then moved my lips against hers aggressively.

She didn't respond initially. Her mouth was immobile. She was probably in shock, unsure what was going on.

I kept kissing her, hoping for the best. I pressed my body against hers, my erection noticeable in my jeans. I felt her breasts against my chest and I wanted to feel them again. I wanted to taste them this time.

Then she kissed me back. Her lips sought mine like she was desperate for me. Her hands moved into my hair, fisting it while she deepened the embrace. She was an amazing kisser, one of the best I ever had. She knew when to use her tongue and when to pull away. Sometimes her lips would brush past mine, teasing me, and then she would kiss me again. Her hands moved down my shoulders and to my arms, squeezing the muscle. She breathed into my mouth, panting.

I used my foot to kick the door closed. It slammed so hard it shook the walls of the house. Neither one of us noticed. I'd never been in her bedroom but I knew it was down the hall. Still kissing her, I guided her through the living room and around the couch.

She suddenly gripped my shoulders then jumped up, wrapping her legs around my waist. Like I could read her mind, I caught her ass and held her. Then I kissed her again while I walked down the hallway. I spotted a bed with a yellow bedspread with pink and purple pillows. White dressers were arranged in the room. I knew this was her bedroom.

I walked inside then laid her on the bed. I looked down at her, seeing the same desire in her eyes that burned in mine. My hands moved up her dress then yanked down her leggings. I got them off then tossed her shoes across the room.

Trinity undid my jeans while I grabbed the bottom of her dress and pulled it up. Like we'd done it a hundred times, we pulled each other's clothes away. I was desperate to see her, needed to see her.

When I was naked, I stood in front of her, my cock throbbing.

She eyed my chest, seeing all the tattoos that covered my arms and stomach. I had everything you could possibly imagine. I was a walking canvas. I was quickly running out of room and would have to add ink down below.

Trinity leaned forward, her face close to my waist. Then she parted her lips slightly and pressed a kiss to the head of my cock.

Oh my fucking god.

She grabbed the shaft then licked my tip like it was a lollipop. Her warm and wet tongue felt so good across my skin. Her breath fell on my cock, exciting me even more. Then she took me into her mouth—all the way in—and moved up and down.

I could hardly get girls to go down on me. And whenever I brought it up, they always acted like it was a chore. Trinity sucked me off like she liked it. A moan escaped her lips while she did it and I thought I'd come right there.

She pulled me out slightly then moved her tongue across the tip, giving it a kiss goodbye.

I was breathing so hard I thought I just ran a marathon. That was the best two minutes of my life. My cock twitched, wanting more. Now I wanted to be inside her. My level of desire had increased by tenfold.

At the speed of light, I pulled the rest of her clothes off then yanked her yellow thong off. I stared at her naked body, my cock getting harder with every passing second. I thought I might explode. I picked her up then moved her further up the bed. Then I separated her legs and pressed my face right in between.

She immediately moaned and fisted my hair.

I hated going down on chicks. It was the worst. But with her, I didn't mind. She made me feel unbelievably good and I wanted to make her feel the same way. I used my tongue to circle her clit then I slipped it inside her, making her cry out. My thumb rubbed her nub in a circular motion. Soon, she was panting for me, wanting me as much as I wanted her.

I moved up her body and separated her legs with mine. When she positioned her legs practically behind her head, my eyes widened. I had no idea she was so flexible. I was caught off guard, just staring at her.

She grabbed my neck and pulled my lips to hers. My cock moved past her folds, feeling the wetness and warmth. I was shaking because I was so excited to be inside her, and without a condom. I never knew bare pussy felt so good.

Trinity dug her nails into my back then gripped my ass with her other hand. Then she pulled me inside her, moaning the entire time.

Shit, she felt good.

I slid inside her slowly until I was completely buried. She felt even better than last time. She was warm and tight, creating just the right amount of friction. As soon as I started to move, I moaned. Sex had never felt this good in my life.

Her breasts shook while I rocked into her, and seeing her legs by her head was only making it more enjoyable. Quiet moans escaped her mouth. She bit her lip while she watched me pound into her. "God, you feel so good..."

I rocked into her harder, giving her all of me. I was moving so fast sweat was accumulating on my chest. I held my weight on my arms and used my hips to thrust inside her hard and fast.

"Slade...fuck me just like that."

"Fuck, you're killing me." When she talked like that, I wanted to come.

She gripped my ass with both hands and pulled me into her harder. "God, yes! Yes!" She was practically screaming, coming hard.

I gave it to her as hard as I could.

"Harder!"

"This is as fast as I go!" My cock was sliding in and out of her quicker than I could see.

Her head rolled back and she moaned, breathing hard. Then she spiraled down, releasing her nails from my ass. "That was nice…so nice."

Seeing the redness flood her face and the look of pure satisfaction in her eyes made me want to come. The idea sounded so good.

Trinity gripped me then rolled me to my back, still keeping me inside her. My head hit the pillow and I looked up at her. She kept her knees on either side of my hips and she rode me hard, using her thighs and ass to bounce up and down, not forward and backward. She took me over and over, her hands resting on my chest.

Watching her bounce on my dick shattered my inhibitions. I wanted to make this last as long as possible. I normally wanted to finish quickly but this felt so good. Every time I slid inside her, it was heaven. Fucking heaven.

"Come for me."

I was never into dirty talk but Trinity knew how to do it right. I felt my body tensing as the orgasm was about to happen. Trinity seemed to know because she increased her pace, riding my dick like a cowgirl.

I gripped her hips as the unbelievable sensation struck me. I moaned and bit my lip, and then I came inside her, filling her.

"Fuck…" I breathed hard as she kept riding me, making it last as long as possible. I closed my eyes as the sensation lingered for a second. Then it drifted away, making me feel tender.

Trinity rested on my hips, leaving me inside her.

I caught my breath, feeling winded. She did the same.

Then she moved off me then lay at my side.

I stared at the ceiling, still in my post-orgasm high.

Trinity got under the covers then sighed happily, obviously satisfied.

When the sensation started to wear off, I realized what just happened. I fucked her—again. And this time, I wasn't drunk and neither was she. We both knew what we were doing. The fact it was decided by free will disturbed me even more.

Fuck. Now what?

Trinity lay beside me and didn't say anything.

I couldn't look at her. I wasn't sure why. Was I awkward? Was I embarrassed? Was I angry? I couldn't tell.

Trinity sighed. "Let's just not talk about it."

I cocked an eyebrow and looked at her. "Just not say anything?"

"Yeah." She set her alarm then adjusted her pillow. "Good night, Slade."

That was the last thing I expected her to say. I figured we would have the conversation all women wanted to have. *Where was this going? Did that mean we were in a relationship*? But she didn't ask any of that. It didn't seem like she cared—at all. "Good night, Trinity."

Chapter Twelve

Trinity

What have I done?

Slade threw himself at me and I just couldn't stop him. And honestly, I didn't want to. I hadn't had good sex in so long I couldn't even remember it. And Slade definitely knew what he was doing. It was nice to be with a guy who knew where everything went.

But the fact he was a friend—in a way—complicated things.

What did it mean? I knew Slade only felt lust. There was nothing else there. And I felt the same way. I guess it wasn't a big deal. Neither one of us wanted anything more. As long as we didn't tell anybody, our secret would be safe.

This time, we didn't avoid each other. I saw him in the library and around campus often. But we never spoke to each other. Sometimes I caught him looking at me but he quickly turned away when I saw him. We weren't fighting anymore, and that didn't go unnoticed.

"What's going on with you now?" Skye asked from across the table.

"What are you talking about?" I asked while I flipped through a magazine.

"You and Slade. You guys aren't fighting anymore."

I felt my skin prickle. Did she know something was up? "I guess we ran out of ammunition. I thought you and everyone else would be relieved."

"It's just weird how quiet it is…" She eyed me for another second before she turned back to her textbook.

I guess I'd have to pick a fight with Slade next time I saw him to keep up pretenses.

***

"Ugh, I suck at bowling." I picked up the lightest ball I could find then headed to the lane. I aimed the ball but it sped into the gutter—like usual.

"You suck at life so it isn't that surprising." Conrad grabbed his ball then came up next.

"Shut up." I walked past him and sat down.

Slade was sitting beside me, sipping a soda.

We were both quiet, having nothing to say to one another.

"Baby, you're the best bowler I've ever seen." Cayson nuzzled Skye's neck while she sat in his lap.

"You don't even watch me," she said. "You just stare at my ass."

"It is a lovely ass." Cayson rubbed his nose against hers.

"You're going to make me gag," Slade said.

"Ditto," I added.

"Wow," Roland said. "You guys actually agreed on something for once."

I flinched at the accusation. "Slade could die for all I care."

"Dumb bitch," Slade muttered, half assed.

We still didn't look at each other.

They finally backed off and returned to the game.

Phew.

Slade's turn was up. He grabbed the ball and rolled a perfect strike. His thick arms were covered in bright and beautiful tattoos. I was never attracted to them before but know I couldn't stop staring. His shoulders were broad and strong, and his back was tightly packed with muscle. I remembered how he looked naked…it was a nice sight. And his package was pretty nice too.

Cayson tickled Skye while she sat on his lap.

"Stop," she said with a giggle. "You're going to make me pee."

"Please don't," Roland said with a cringe. He stood up and bowled his turn. He got a spare then sat down again.

"Come on, baby." Cayson slapped her ass. "Show us up."

She smirked at him then retrieved her ball.

"You fucked her yet?" Slade blurted.

Cayson glared at him.

"You do see me, right?" Roland asked. "Her brother? Her flesh and blood?"

Slade rolled his eyes. "You thought your sister was a blushing virgin?"

Cayson never answered. He ignored Slade.

"So that's a no," Slade said.

"I'm not having this conversation right now," Cayson whispered.

Slade rolled his eyes. "Ro, you care if Cayson sleeps with your sister?"

Roland left the table. "I'm going to take a piss…"

Cayson gave him a hard look. "He might be my brother-in-law someday. I'd prefer it if he liked me."

"He already likes you," Slade said. "Everyone does. And your life would be a lot simpler if you didn't give a damn what people thought of you to begin with."

Cayson stared at Skye while she bowled.

"Dude, what are you waiting for?" Slade asked. "Do the deed already."

"I will…soon. Now let's stop talking about this," Cayson said.

"Skye really wants to do it," I added. "Like, *really*."

Cayson's face flushed red and he ignored my look.

Skye came back and sat on his lap. "Did you see that? I hit one pin!"

"Good job, baby." He kissed her.

"Wow," Slade said. "You're worse than Trinity. I didn't think that was possible."

I wasn't sure if he wanted to pick a fight or if he was just doing it to keep people from being suspicious. I couldn't tell what was going on anymore. I decided to go along with it. "You suck at everything."

He gave me a glare but it didn't look genuine. "You're ugly."

"Likewise."

"There they are," Conrad said sarcastically.

We finished the game, and Cayson was the victor.

"When did you get good at everything?" Skye asked.

He smirked. "I used to let you win. You still haven't figured that out?"

"What?" Skye look shocked. "Then why did you stop?"

"I already have you. I don't have to do anything." He smirked at the appalled look on her face.

Roland nodded. "Good. My sister is too much of a brat anyway."

We turned in our equipment to the counter then walked to our cars. Slade walked close to me, his hands in his pockets.

Roland and Conrad got into the truck then drove away, waving. Skye and Cayson left in his car, just leaving him and I. Instead of walking to his car, Slade walked with me.

This was weird.

I stopped when I reached my car. "What?"

He leaned against the side and crossed his arms over his chest. He stared across the parking lot for a long time before he spoke. "What's going on between us? Like, what is this?"

"Slade, why are you acting like a girl?"

He rolled his eyes. "I'm not asking if we're in a relationship. Just...what is this? Like, are we going to keep doing it? Or...just at random times? Shouldn't we talk about this? Or should we stop?"

I shrugged. "I guess."

"What? That we should talk about this or stop doing it?"

"I don't know...what do you want to do? I didn't think we'd do it again after the first time but then you jumped my bones."

"Don't act like you didn't want it."

"You came on to me, remember?"

"And you sucked my dick then rode me like a damn cowgirl," he snapped. "Let's not play the blame game. You wouldn't have fucked me so easily unless you had thought about it before. And you didn't drink at all that night so you were totally sober."

I didn't have an argument against that. "Well, what do you want to do?"

He shrugged. "What do you want to do?"

It seemed like neither one of us wanted to put our cards on the table.

He stared at me, waiting for me to respond.

I held his gaze and said nothing.

He sighed. "Fine. I'll go first." He paused for a long time, running his fingers through his hair. "Honestly, sex with you is pretty fucking fantastic. Of course I want to keep doing it."

"I like it too…" I crossed my arms over my chest, still acting indifferent.

"If we keep doing this, we should have some sort of system so we don't get caught. You agree?" he asked.

I nodded.

"Okay. I really don't want anyone to find out about us."

"That makes two of us," I agreed.

"So…this is a booty call situation, right?"

"That's fine."

"Alright. We'll text in code just in case someone sees the messages."

"What kind of code would this be?"

He shrugged. "'A' means come over. 'B' means can I come over?"

I shook my head. "And you don't think that would be suspicious if someone read it? Like Cayson?"

"Then what's your idea, genius?" he snapped.

"'Go to hell' means come over. 'I hope you die' means can I come over? That sounds a lot more believable coming from us."

"What if I want to call you?" he asked.

"Just call, idiot."

He rolled his eyes. "Do we have any rules?"

"What kind of rules?"

"Are we exclusive?"

"I assumed we weren't." I wouldn't stop dating and looking for Mr. Right just because I was fooling around with a jerk.

"That's fine with me. But are…we going to keep doing it…without wearing anything?"

"As long as you're clean, I don't care. It feels better anyway."

"Are you clean?" he demanded.

I glared at him. "I'm going to pretend you didn't ask that."

"Do you normally not wear anything with guys?" he asked.

I glared at him.

"Hey, I'm sleeping with you. I have the right to ask this."

"Never."

"Then why didn't you make me wear anything?"

"I don't know. There wasn't time. It all happened so fast. And since you didn't wear anything the first time, if you had something, I was already screwed. So why wear something a second time?"

"Well, I'm anal about my sexual health so don't worry about that."

"Do you always wear something?"

"Fuck yeah," he snapped. "I don't want to catch something or knock up some girl. They might say they're on the pill even if they aren't just to trick you."

"How do you know I'm not tricking you?" I questioned.

He gave me a look that clearly said, "Shut the hell up."

"Okay. So, we always wear something with other people. We only text in code. What else?"

"What about our friendship?" he asked.

"What about it?" I questioned. "We were never friends to begin with."

He smirked. "I guess that's true. But what about when one of us wants to end it?"

"Then we walk away. End of story."

"Just like that?" he asked incredulously. "You aren't going to start crying or beg me to stay?"

I cocked an eyebrow. "Slade, you're the kind of guy I like to sleep with, not *go* to sleep with. Believe me, we won't have a problem."

"Good, because I don't do the relationship thing and I never will."

"Shocking," I said sarcastically.

"I'm serious. Don't expect me to change for you."

"I don't," I said firmly. "I would never want something more with you—ever."

He seemed to believe me. "I'm glad we got that settled."

"Alright. Are we done here?" I was eager to go home and take a bath.

"Yeah." He moved away from my car and put his hands in his pockets.

"I'll see you later." I opened the car door then got inside.

He drifted away and found his car on the other side of the parking lot.

I couldn't believe I just had that conversation with Slade. We were fuck buddies now. Never in a million years did I think that would happen. I should have just said no, but I liked good sex. And Slade was at least good at that.

My phone vibrated so I looked at the screen.

It was Slade. *I hope you die.*

I smirked and stared at the screen. *See you soon.*

Chapter Thirteen

Cayson

I dropped the subject of Zack but that didn't mean I stopped thinking about it. The fact he bugged Skye twice got under my skin. He obviously planned it when I wasn't around. That meant he was watching her. That made me extremely uncomfortable.

What did he want from her? What was he trying to do? What was he trying to gain? I couldn't find an answer just and that made me panic. It seemed like he wanted revenge.

Maybe I was overreacting, but when it came to Skye, I was always like that. If it were any of the girls in my family, I'd be on edge. Harassment wasn't okay in my book. But since Skye was at a different level than every other person on the planet, that just made me more concerned about the situation.

What were my options? I could kick his ass but what would that accomplish? He would just come back, even more pissed off. I could kill him but I'd have to live with the guilt forever. Plus, I had to do it and not get caught. And I would be a prime suspect in the investigation. I could try to have an adult conversation with him and make him see reason, but Zack didn't strike me as a reasonable guy. I could walk Skye to every class and never leave her side, which was fine, but she wouldn't live that way forever. Knowing Skye, she would quickly get irritated by the constant watch. She would lash out at me and that would put a strain on our relationship.

I had to tell her father.

I knew she would be pissed but I didn't care. He was the only person who could make something like this disappear. He had the money and the resources to get away with pretty much anything. Skye would be pissed if she knew but I had to do it. I had to.

***

The bar was quiet tonight. Only a few guys hung around and watched a recap of a game from earlier that day. My beer sat in front of me but I didn't touch it. I just wasn't in the mood for alcohol, or anything. Skye thought I was playing ball with Slade. It seemed to be the most convincing excuse.

The door opened and a tall man in a suit walked inside. He headed to my place by the bar, walking with perfect posture. When he reached me, he unbuttoned his jacket then slid onto the stool. He looked at me with his menacing blue eyes but didn't say anything.

Uncle Sean never greeted me this way. It was always with a warm hug and a smile. But I knew he was on edge. My phone call didn't exactly make him happy.

"What's this about?" he asked quietly. He glanced around the bar discreetly, making sure no one was near us.

"Skye."

He tensed up noticeably and his eyes became more threatening. "Is my daughter okay?" He kept his voice low but his tone conveyed his concern. And his protectiveness was obvious.

"She's fine. She's sitting at home watching *I Love Lucy*."

He relaxed slightly. "Then what is it, Cayson?"

The bartender approached and gave him a beer.

Uncle Sean didn't drink it.

There was no going back. "Zack. He won't leave her alone."

He stared at me, his eyes guarded and his jaw clenched tightly.

"I kicked his ass the first time, broke his nose and unhinged his jaw. The second time Slade gave him a good pounding. But he won't stay away. He waits until Skye is alone then he harasses her. He keeps asking for an apology. Skye claims he isn't dangerous but I don't believe that. He sounds like a fucking psychopath to me."

He didn't react. He hardly moved. It was almost like he hadn't heard me at all. His Rolex shined on his wrist, and his wedding band reflected the dim lighting in the bar. "I'll take care of it."

"What are you going to do?"

"Kill him." He said it plainly, like he was discussing the weather.

"Skye is going to know it was you. I don't think that's a good idea."

He processed my words for a while. "I'll make sure he doesn't bother her, Cayson."

"What are you going to do?"

"I'll hire someone to give him a good scare. He'll shit his pants. Then I'll have a few guys tail him everywhere he goes, and they won't make their presence unknown. Zack will know he can't do anything without my knowledge. If he knows what's good for him, he'll knock it off and never speak to her again."

That was good enough for me. "Okay."

He finally sipped his beer, his eyes dark.

"Please don't tell Skye I told you."

He wouldn't look at me. "She should have told me herself."

"She thinks she can handle everything on her own. For the most part, that's true. But in this case…I'd rather not take the chance."

"I'll keep your secret, Cayson."

"Thank you." I could tell he was still in a bad mood. "I can take care of her myself. I haven't let her out of my sight. I just thought you would want to know—"

"I know you can take care of her, Cayson. I never doubted that."

"Okay. Because even now, Slade is sitting in his car in front of her apartment while I'm here."

Uncle Sean looked at me with approval in his eyes. "You have my respect. You've always had it. And keep in mind that most men don't. I have no doubt you're the right man for my daughter."

That meant the world to me. "Thanks."

He patted my shoulder then tossed some cash on the table. "I need to hit the road. My wife is waiting for me."

"I should get home too."

This time he hugged me and held it for a while. "Thank you for telling me. I only wish my daughter would turn to me more often."

"She knows how you get."

"I get that way for a reason—because I love my daughter more than anything." He pulled away then gave me a firm look. "I'll see you later."

"Bye."

He walked out and disappeared.

I stayed at the bar and finished my beer.

***

When I got out of my car, Slade got out of his. He rubbed his hands together and vapor escaped his lips.

"About damn time." He cupped his hands to his face and blew his hot breath on them. He was wearing a t-shirt and jeans even though it was snowing outside. "I've been freezing my ass off."

"Then turn on the heater."

"And waste the gas? I'm not rich, man."

"Then wear a jacket," I argued.

"Then you can't see my tatts."

"Were you expecting to run into someone while you sat in your car for an hour?" I asked sarcastically.

He shrugged. "It could happen."

I rolled my eyes then stuffed my keys into my pocket. "Did he come by?"

"No. He probably never will. I'm sure he knows you're hanging around like a bat in a cave."

I cocked an eyebrow. "What kind of comparison is that?"

"What? Don't bats always stay in one spot?"

"Because they have to be in the dark," I argued. "That makes no sense at all."

"Whatever. Fine. Zack knew you would be hanging around like a...shark."

"A shark?" I asked. "They are fish so they have to swim around. By definition, they can't linger in one spot."

He rolled his eyes. "Fine, like a sand fish. You know, those things that hide under the sand in the ocean and become camouflaged. Then they—"

"Okay. Just stop. I get your point."

"About time." He rubbed his hands together again. "So, what were we saying?"

"Zack didn't come by."

"Yeah, no sign of him. How was Uncle Sean? Was he pissed? Did he turn into the Incredible Hulk?"

"He was pissed but he didn't freak out."

"Is he going to kill Zack?"

"No. He's going to scare him off and have guys follow him everywhere he goes."

Slade nodded his head in approval. "Uncle Sean…the badass."

"I don't think he's a badass…he just cares about his daughter."

"Same difference." He leaned against the car door. "So, are you going to get laid tonight?"

Did he ever talk about anything else? "Why do you care?"

"You're my boy. You've been dating her for months. You deserve some action."

"I get plenty of action from her," I argued.

"Unless it's pussy, it's not the same thing."

I raised my hand. "Look, you can talk about the other girls I've been with like that, but not Skye. It's different with her. I mean it."

He rolled his eyes. "Whatever, Romeo. So, are you going to get it on or what?"

I leaned against my car door and faced him. "We almost did last week."

His jaw dropped. "What the hell stopped you?"

"The pizza guy knocked on the door."

"I'm not following… Why didn't you just take the pizza, slam the door, and then slip it inside her?"

"That's not exactly romantic."

"So?" He shrugged. "Sex isn't supposed to be romantic. It's sex."

"You've obviously never been in love with anyone before."

"What gave you that idea?" he said sarcastically.

"I just want it to be perfect, you know? This is the woman I'm going to spend the rest of my life with."

Slade gave me an incredulous look. "Aren't you jumping the gun?"

"You even said the same thing."

"Nothing is set in stone," he argued.

"Well, it's going to happen. I know it is."

"Then you have the rest of your life to make it romantic. Now get your dick wet," Slade said. He rubbed his arms to fight the chill.

"What did I just say?" I snapped.

"You're no fun anymore."

"And you need to grow up."

He crossed his arms over his chest and eyed her apartment. "Have you seen Jasmine since?"

"No…I feel bad."

He shrugged. "Whatever. You told her you were with Skye. It shouldn't be surprising."

"But Skye was all over me, practically rubbing Jasmine's nose in it." I ran my fingers through my hair. "I hated the pained look on her face. I felt like such a jackass."

"Hurting her will probably make it easier for her to move on."

"She's such a nice girl…she deserves someone really great."

"Well…do you mind if I get in on that action?"

I gave him a threatening look. "Don't even think about it."

"What?" He raised his hands in innocence. "If you aren't tapping her, somebody should. Ever since she said you fucked her on the dryer in your apartment building, I've been intrigued."

"I mean it, Slade. She's off limits."

He rolled his eyes. "Greedy…"

"Slade, do I have your word?"

He sighed. "Fine. Whatever."

"Thank you." I moved to my feet. "I should get inside." I eyed his pale skin. "And you should go home before you get hypothermia."

"I don't need to be told twice." He turned to his car.

"And get a jacket."

"No. I got these sleeves for a reason."

"Fine. Die for all I care."

"I'll see you in hell then." He shut the door and started the car.

I shook my head then walked up the stairs to her apartment. I used my spare key to get inside.

Skye was sitting on the couch with a bowl of popcorn in her lap. "How was hanging out with Slade?"

"Fine."

"Who won?"

"Who won what?" I asked.

"The game." She raised an eyebrow. "Didn't you play basketball together?"

Oh yeah. "I won," I blurted. "He was a big baby about it."

"Slade's a big baby about everything."

I moved to the couch beside her and grabbed a handful of popcorn. Then I shoved it into my mouth. "What have you been doing?"

"Just watching TV." She wore a t-shirt with her flannel bottoms. Even when she was wearing her pajamas, she still looked beautiful.

"I'm surprised you aren't studying for a test or something."

"I can only read a textbook for so long." She munched on the popcorn until it was gone. "I'm exhausted..."

"Why?"

"I don't know." She yawned. "I went on a jog earlier. I guess I'm really out of shape."

I stilled. "You went on a jog—alone?"

"It was only for a few miles."

"Skye, I told you not to leave my sight." My voice became full of anger.

"Well, I don't do whatever you tell me," she argued.

I knew where this was going. "I'm not trying to boss you around. With Zack giving you a hard time, I would prefer it if you didn't go around by yourself, especially at night."

"I'm not scared of him and I refuse to live my life that way."

"It's only temporary. Then you can go back to doing whatever you want. If you go on a jog, I'm more than happy to go with you."

She gave me a hard look. "You've known me your entire life, Cayson. You know what kind of girl I am. I'm not going to let that fly."

I knew I had to be firmer with her. "We can do this the easy way or the hard way. Your choice."

Her eyes narrowed. "Excuse me?"

I sighed. "I'm sorry, Skye. I hate to be this way. You know it's not in my nature. I just care about you and I need to look after you…until I know he'll really leave you alone. Please don't make this harder for me."

She spotted the unease on my face. "Fine. But it's only temporary."

I sighed in relief then kissed her forehead. "Thank you."

She stood up then set the bowl on the table. "I'm going to bed. Are you coming?"

"Duh." I turned off the TV and followed her into the bedroom. I was more aggressive with Skye than I used to be. Now when I wanted something from her, I just took it. Judging the moans that escaped her lips and the way her fingernails dug into my skin, she liked it. I pulled her top off then unclasped her bra with lightning speed. I groped her breasts, loving how warm they felt in my hands. I loved her chest and now I wasn't afraid to admit it. She let me suck them and kiss them whenever I wanted…among other things.

I really wanted to take our relationship to the next level. I was ready and I knew she was too. But tonight didn't feel right. Since I just went and spoke to her father, something she specifically asked me not to do, I felt guilty. Another night of fooling around would have to suffice—for now.

Chapter Fourteen

Skye

"If Cayson thinks he's going to boss me around, he's got another thing coming." Zack tried to do the same thing, much more aggressively, and I wasn't a push over. I was a strong, independent woman. It was my way or no way.

Trinity smirked at me then sipped her coffee. "Honestly, Skye...I'm with him on this one."

We were sitting in a coffee shop right off campus. Students littered the tables and jazz music played overhead. I got a blueberry muffin but I only ate half of it. I stared at her incredulously. "Sorry, did I hear you right?"

"If Cayson just brushed off Zack's behavior, I would be worried. You can't blame him for wanting to look after you. I wish I had a guy that was so concerned for my well-being."

"I'm glad he's concerned. I just don't want to be bossed around. There's a big difference."

"He just asked you not to jog in the dark alone." She stared at me like I was crazy. "It's really not a big deal."

Trinity had been my best friend since we could speak. She had my back for everything—except for this. "What happened to my sassy best friend?"

"She's just telling you how it is. It's not like Cayson is like that all the time. He just wants to wait until Zack stops obsessing over you."

"You know how hard it was for me to come to coffee with you?" I asked. "Without him?"

"Because you miss him?"

"No," I snapped. "Because he almost didn't let me come alone."

She shrugged. "I like Cayson. I wouldn't mind if he came."

I rolled my eyes. "That's not the point. I can hang out with my best friend whenever I want."

"And if Zack appears?"

"We'll kick his ass."

"Last time we tried that, he sat on me like a log."

"I had him," I hissed. "I was going to break his skull with my textbook."

"I still think it's better to avoid Zack than go head-to-head with him again. You must see the logic in that." She rested her elbows on the table while she stared me down.

"I guess..."

"Now cut Cayson some slack. He's the sweetest guy in the world. He would never boss you around. He recognizes your independence and it's one of the reasons he's so attracted to you. Just humor him for a few weeks."

I knew she was right. I was being too stubborn about this. "Okay. Fine."

"Good. Now invite him to coffee with us."

"No, I want to have girl talk with you."

"I'll say anything to Cayson that I say to you," Trinity said.

"It's still a lot more fun when it's just us."

"Well, of course," she said with a laugh. She sipped her coffee then flipped her hair over her shoulder. "Please tell me you've taken a ride on his cock."

"Trinity!" I pressed my finger over my lip. "Shh!" I glanced around the nearby tables to see if anyone had heard.

"Grow up, Skye. No one cares."

It seemed like no harm had been done.

"You better say yes," she pressed.

"No…it hasn't happened yet."

"What the hell is wrong with you guys?" She stared at me like I was crazy.

"It was going to happen the other night but the damn pizza guy ruined it."

"How did he ruin it?"

"He came to the door."

"So? Wasn't he only there for a minute?"

"But it ruined the moment," I said with a sigh.

"Ruined the moment?" she asked incredulously. "Wasn't he still hard? That's enough to keep going."

I laughed lightly. "Cayson wants it to be special."

"Well, if he keeps wanting it to be special, you're never going to have sex at all."

I laughed again. "I know, right?"

"You must be going crazy. It's been months."

I gave her a firm look. "I am going crazy. We fool around but I want everything."

"He satisfies you, right?"

"Oh yeah," I said immediately. "That's not a problem. But I want him, not his hand or his mouth."

"I hear you, girl."

I pulled my tea bag out of my cup then set it on a napkin. "Any men in your life?"

She looked down at her cup and blew the steam away. "No."

"How long have you been single?"

Trinity thought for a moment. Her gold earrings reflected the light, and her lip gloss was shiny. She had perfect features, and her make up only highlighted her stunning appearance. I definitely felt dwarfed by her beauty. "Almost a year."

"When's the last time you had sex?"

She sipped her coffee. "Uh…I can't remember. It's been a while though."

"We should go out so you can pick up someone."

She smirked. "It'll happen when it happens. No need to rush."

"I feel like we haven't gone out in so long." I felt guilty. Since Cayson and I got together, I hadn't been the closest friend to Trinity.

"We're going out now."

"It's not the same. We should hit a club." I didn't really have any interest in that. Now that I had a serious boyfriend, the idea of going out to a noisy club where a bunch of men would stare at my rack and Trinity's legs didn't exactly sound fun.

"We'll see." She looked out the window and watched people go by. Her eyes lost their light for a moment, seeming to disappear. Her lips pressed tightly together like she was thinking.

"Everything okay, Trinity?" I asked.

She turned back to me. "Yeah. I've just got a lot of homework and stuff..."

It still seemed like something was off but I didn't press her on it.

***

Cayson was leaning against my car when I walked outside the coffee shop. He was staring at his phone, hitting his thumb against the screen like he was playing a game. He wore dark jeans and a gray t-shirt. His muscled arms were noticeable under the winter sun. Hair started to come in around his chin, thick and brown. I loved it when he shaved but I also loved it when he didn't. I eyed his body for a moment, remembering how he looked naked on my bed. I wanted to run my tongue all over his body and taste him.

I shook my head and made the thoughts escape. Then I walked over to him. "Hey you."

He put his phone down then turned his gaze on me. His blue eyes suddenly looked brighter when he took me in. A grin stretched his lips. "I'm glad you're happy to see me, not pissed."

"Trinity talked me down."

"I've always liked her." He put his phone in his pocket then embraced me. One hand moved into my hair while he kissed me, making my lips burn. He always moved his lips against mine in just the right way. He clearly knew what he was doing. He steered me against the car door and pressed his body against mine while he continued the embrace.

Then he pulled away slowly. "I think this is getting out of hand..."

"A little." I glanced at his lips then returned my look to his eyes.

"Have a good time with Trinity?"

"Yeah."

"What did you guys do?"

"Talked."

"About?" he asked. "You guys always talk."

"Boys, sex, music…stuff like that."

"Did I come up?" he pressed.

"You always come up."

"Oooh…I hope good things were said."

"They were." I gave him a flirtatious smile.

"And I hope it wasn't just about my…size." A tint came into his cheeks.

"No." I started to blush too.

He stared at me for a moment before he moved his hands to my hips. "Have plans tonight?"

"With you, I assume."

"Can I take you to dinner?"

"You can take me anywhere."

"Good answer." He leaned in and kissed me. "I'll pick you up at seven."

"Okay."

"You want to sleep at my place tonight?"

Why did it matter? He never asked that. "Sure."

"Okay." He opened my door and helped me get inside. "I'll see you then."

"Okay."

He gave me another kiss. "Wear something nice." He shut the door and walked back to his car.

***

I wore a backless black dress with silver heels. A matching bracelet was on my wrist and diamond earrings were in my lobes. My pea coat was hanging over the chair. I wanted Cayson to see my dress before I put it on, just to see his reaction. I thought I looked pretty decent. Hopefully he liked the way I looked.

A knock on the door announced his presence.

"Come in," I called.

He stepped inside, wearing slacks and a button up shirt.

I whistled. "Someone looks like a million bucks."

He eyed my waist and legs. "I can say the same about you." He hooked one arm around my waist and rested his hand on my bare back. His fingers trailed down the skin. "I like this…"

"You do?" I was pleased by his words.

"I like your skin." He moved behind me then pulled my hair over one shoulder. Then he pressed a kiss between my shoulder blades, making heat move through my body.

"I like your lips."

He came back around me, his hand moving to my chin. "You look lovely tonight." His eyes moved down to my chest then back to my eyes. "But you're missing something."

"What?" I blurted. I checked everything.

He pulled a box out of his pocket then opened it.

Inside was a white gold bracelet. On the chain were moons and clouds. I stared at it for a moment before I picked it up. It was light and smooth in my hands. I turned it over and saw the engraving.

A billion stars in the Skye. Only one you.

My heart swelled at the sight. I looked back at him, at a loss for words. "Cayson…"

"Shh." He grabbed the bracelet then clasped it onto my wrist. He removed the one that was already there. "You don't need to say anything. I just want you to have it." His fingers stroked the skin of my wrist before he placed a gentle kiss there. "Now you're perfect."

My eyes watered. "I'm perfect with you."

Affection moved into his eyes then he stepped closer to me. "That's the truest thing I've ever heard you say." He cupped my neck and placed a gentle kiss on my forehead.

I rested my face against his chest, treasuring the moment. Cayson's sweetness always caught me by surprise. He did everything and anything to make me happy. "I'm sorry I was being a brat before…"

"It's water under the bridge." He kissed my lips gently then pulled away. "Are you hungry?"

"Have we just met?" I countered.

He gave me a fond look before he grabbed my coat and put it over my shoulders. "Ready?"

I nodded.

We left the apartment then headed to the restaurant. When we pulled up to the front, I realized it was an Italian place.

"I know how much you love pizza," he said. "This was my way of taking you to a nice place but giving you what you really want."

I smirked. "Genius idea."

We walked inside then moved to the table near the window. Like always, Cayson pulled out the chair for me and allowed me to sit down before he sat across from me. He handed a menu to me before he looked at his own.

"I don't know if I should get the eighteen inch or sixteen inch pizza…" I stared at the menu while I tried to decide.

He smirked at me. "Get the twenty inch and take the leftovers home. I know you like to munch in the middle of the night."

"So, you won't judge me?"

"Have I ever?" He looked at his menu again. "I'm getting the tortellini."

"Pizza is better," I blurted.

"You never order anything else." He said it in a condescending way but affection was in his eyes.

"Because it's good."

The waiter came to our table and took our order. The bottle Cayson ordered when we arrived was poured.

"This is a fancy evening," I said.

"I wanted it to be special." He looked into my eyes as he said it.

Then it hit me. When we went back to his place tonight, we wouldn't fool around and go to sleep. What I've been looking forward to was finally going to happen. I tried to hide my excitement but I had a feeling my face was giving it away.

We made small talk about school and our family. Our voices were low while we talked over the clanking glasses and moving plates. We drank our wine until the bottle was empty then ate our meals when they arrived. I would normally eat half of my pizza but tonight I didn't want my stomach to be too full. So, I just ate a few slices. Cayson didn't eat as much as he normally did. Perhaps he was nervous.

When the check came, he slipped the cash inside.

"Can I get the tip?" I asked.

"Nope." He pushed the tab away then placed the remainder of my pizza in the to-go box.

"You need to let me pay sometime."

"Nope," he said again. He stood up then pulled out my chair for me. "Let's get this pizza in the fridge." His arm moved around my waist and he led me out of the restaurant. Knowing what we were going to do when we got to his place made my heart race. I was excited and warm. My nerves were firing off and I was eager to feel him. I daydreamed about our rendezvous for the entire ride home, imagining how he would feel when he was finally inside me. By the time we pulled into the parking lot, I was wet.

After we walked inside, he put the pizza box in the refrigerator then came back to me. "Thank you for having dinner with me."

"Thanks for feeding me."

Silence.

He stared at me, his hands by his sides.

I met his gaze, suddenly feeling sweat on my palms. I was nervous, but not in a bad way.

Cayson moved his hands to my hips then bunched up my dress lightly. He eyed my body for a moment, his eyes lingering on my chest, and then he met my gaze. Desire was in his eyes, shining bright.

My lips parted on their own, my need guiding me. I pressed my chest to his then leaned my face near his. His warm breath fell on my cheek. Since I knew where this was going, it felt different. It was like the first time all over again.

Cayson stared at me until he finally closed the distance and kissed me. His embrace was gentle and purposeful. He took his time, not rushing. His hand moved up my stomach and my chest until he reached my neck. His fingers dug into my hair while he deepened the kiss. His tongue slipped into my mouth, lightly touching mine.

I was lost to him immediately. His kiss always swept me off my feet. The way his tongue felt against mine was unlike any experience I ever had. He was the best kisser I've ever been with, hands down. He put every other guy I dated to shame. My relationship with Cayson was different. It was beautiful, pure.

Cayson slowly led me down the hallway, stopping every few feet to give me a passionate kiss. He pressed me into the wall while his hands moved over my body. He would grip me tightly, like he never wanted to let go. Then he led me down the hallway again, heading for his room.

When we walked inside, there was a gentle glow from dozens of white candles. They flickered as we passed. He continued to kiss me as he led me to his bed. When I felt the frame behind me, I stopped.

Cayson stared into my eyes while he found the zipper at my side. He pulled it down, never looking at his hand. Once it was loose, he pulled it down, revealing my bare chest. I couldn't wear a bra with the dress so nothing was covering me. He got it off then picked me up and placed me on the bed. He grabbed each foot and slipped my heels off. Then he kissed my calves and knees, moving to my inner thighs. When he was between my legs, he grabbed my thong and pulled it off.

I lay back on the bed and felt a lump. I reached behind me and pulled out a candy bar. Rose petals and bite size candies were across the bed. "Candy bars?" I asked with a smirk.

"I know what my baby likes."

My heart swelled and I cupped his face. "I love you so much, Cayson."

His eyes filled with emotion. "And I you." He placed a gentle kiss on my lips before he moved down my body and to the area between my legs. His mouth moved over my folds and his tongue did wonderful things. He always touched me the right way, like he could read my mind. He pushed me to the edge but wouldn't let me fall over.

I leaned up and unbuttoned his shirt. I was eager for him so my fingers worked furiously. They shook slightly, my need obvious.

"Don't rush. Make it last." He kept his voice low while he stared at me.

My hands slowed down as I finished. I couldn't contain my excitement. I'd been waiting for this my whole life. When every button was undone, I pushed the shirt over his shoulders and let it fall to the floor. Then I pressed my lips to the skin over his heart, giving him a gentle kiss. His hand moved into my hair, a quiet moan that was almost inaudible coming from his lips.

My hands undid his jeans then pulled them down. I took his boxers too. Cayson kicked out of his shoes then tore off his socks. When he was naked, I stared at him for a second, taking in all his glory.

Cayson stared back at me before he scooped me up and moved me further up his bed, resting my head on one of his pillows. A few candy bars got in the way so we pushed them aside.

I wrapped my legs around his waist then dug my hands into his hair. His lips sought mine in the dim glow and he breathed hard into my mouth, setting it on fire. His hard cock lay against my stomach. It was thick and long, definitely impressive. I was eager to feel him. I knew it would be an experience I'd never forget.

Cayson opened his nightstand and pulled out a foil wrapper. Then he tore it open like he'd done it a hundred times.

I snatched it from his hands then threw it on the floor. "I don't want you to wear one." I always practiced safe sex but Cayson was different. I didn't want to be separated by latex for our first time.

"Are you on the pill?" he whispered.

"Yes."

"Good. I didn't want to wear one either." He moved back over me and separated my legs with his.

My hands moved to his arms, feeling the muscle, and then around to his back. I was shaking with excitement and I wasn't sure how to hold on. Cayson grabbed my legs then moved his arms behind my knees. We were as close as possible. His head was pressed to mine and then I felt his tip at my entrance. My hands moved to his arms and I squeezed them in anticipation.

Cayson slowly moved inside me, stretching me the second he entered me. I was wet so it was easy for him to slide through. He stared into my eyes as he inserted himself further, going until he was completely sheathed.

Damn, he felt good.

I breathed hard while he stretched me. My body took a moment to acclimate to his large size. My fingers dug into his skin of their own accord. I stared into his eyes, seeing the desire and love shine back at me.

Then he started to move, sliding in and out without shaking the bed. Every movement was precise, hitting me in the right spot. He didn't kiss me. Instead, he watched my face and locked his eyes with mine. He took his time, going slow.

My hands moved up his neck and into his hair. He already felt so amazing and I didn't want it to end. I enjoyed him in a way I never enjoyed another guy before.

Cayson continued to move and a moan escaped his lips. "Fuck, you feel good, Skye."

"You feel better." Sweat formed on my upper lip.

He leaned in and kissed me gently, using his tongue to tantalize mine. He moved at that pace for a long time, not in a hurry to reach the finish line. Then he pulled away and started to move faster. Sweat formed on his chest and I touched it with my hand, feeling the heat.

"Cayson..."

He moved harder and faster, pushing me into the bed with his strength.

I felt the distant burn in my stomach as his desire grew to a crescendo. My legs started to shake and I moaned incoherently. My nails dug into his skin, about to make him bleed. Then it hit me like a slab of bricks. My head rolled back as the explosion reached every part of my body, making my fingers and toes tingle.

"You're so beautiful," he said through his heavy breathing.

It lasted for almost a full minute, the longest orgasm I've ever experienced. The area between my legs grew tender as he continued to slide in and out. Even though I had already climaxed, it still felt good.

Cayson pressed his lips to mine then breathed hard. He started to tense up as he moved into me harder. A deep moan from the back of his throat escaped his lips then he tensed again, starting to fill me. "Skye..." He moaned again as he finished.

I moved my hands through his hair, feeling the sweat.

He stayed over me, still inside me. When he recovered from his moment, he looked into my eyes. An instant passed between us, unspoken but still acknowledged. I knew what it meant on his part, and I knew what it meant on mine.

Cayson kissed my forehead before he pulled out of me then lay in the bed beside me. He was hot and sweaty but he still hooked his arm around my waist and cuddled with me. "How was that for you?"

I rolled him to his back then leaned over him. "Wow…just wow."

He smirked with fondness in his eyes.

"I want to do it again," I blurted.

He laughed slightly. "I'd love to. Just give me a few minutes."

I kissed his chest and stomach. "You're really good at that. I can't believe we waited so long."

His hands moved through my hair. "It was worth the wait."

"I want to do it all the time," I blurted again.

"Can I get that in writing?"

I laughed then rubbed my nose against his. "Cayson, you're the perfect man. I was stupid for not realizing it before, but now that I do, you're mine forever. I'm never letting you go."

Fondness moved into his eyes. He stared at me for a long time. "The feeling is mutual."

"Good. Because you're stuck with me."

"And there's no one else I'd rather be stuck with."

We lay in the dark, touching each other and sharing quiet kisses. Silence stretched as our hands did all the talking. He moved his fingers through my hair then across my skin. I felt his chest, noting the feel of his muscles.

When an hour had passed, I crawled on top of him. "Round two."

A grin stretched his face. "Yes, ma'am."

Chapter Fifteen

Slade

When I saw Cayson on campus, he had a stupid grin on his face. "Why do you look like an idiot?"

He shrugged, the ridiculous grin still there. "It's a beautiful day."

I cocked an eyebrow. "A beautiful day? Are you a poet now?"

"You asked what I'm grinning about and I told you."

I studied his face, not believing him. Then it hit me. "You fucked Skye!"

"Keep your voice down," he hissed. He looked around the hall to make sure no one had heard. "I mean it. I don't want everyone knowing my business."

"I can't believe this. How was she?"

"Why do you think I'm grinning?" he countered.

I clapped him on the shoulder. "You're finally a man."

"I've been a man for a long time, actually."

"You aren't a real man until you've had Skye Preston, man."

I cringed. "Dude, for the last time, she's your cousin."

He ignored my words. "So, what position?"

"I'm not going into detail with you."

"Was she on top?"

"How lazy do you think I am?" I snapped.

"Was she ever on top?"

"Why does it matter?" I asked.

He shrugged. "If this is the girl you're going to spend the rest of your life with, you got to make sure she's not selfish in bed."

He rolled his eyes. "Well, we're good there."

"Did you buy her dinner first?"

"Yeah," he said. "And I had candles and rose petals in the bedroom."

"Cliché," I blurted.

"And candy bars," he added. "You know Skye has a sweet tooth."

"Okay…that's pretty cool," I agreed. "Wait until everyone hears about this."

"Slade, this stays between us. I don't want Roland to know."

Cayson could be annoying sometimes. "Dude, you've known Roland your whole life. He's never been the protective brother type. He doesn't care what Skye does."

"I still don't think he wants to hear about me having sex with her," he snapped.

"Whatever."

"Don't say anything to anyone."

"What about Trinity?"

"What? Why would you talk to her at all?"

Oh yeah. We hated each other. That's right. "I just meant in passing."

"I'm sure she knows anyway. Skye tells her everything."

"That's what normal friends do," I snapped.

Cayson looked at his watch. "I have to get to class. I'll see you later."

"Basketball tonight?"

"Sure." He disappeared down the hallway.

***

I went to a local bar and scouted the talent. Sipping my beer at the counter, I searched the crowd and tried to find a winner. A lot of cute girls lingered around. They were in packs, wearing short dresses with sparkly rhinestones. When it came to women, I was particularly attracted to long legs. I'd always been that way. A nice rack and ass were important too but I usually searched for legs.

I zoned in on one blonde in particular. She had a curvy waist and bright blue eyes. When she laughed, a full set of perfect teeth were noticeable. She was really cute. I wouldn't mind watching her breasts jiggle while I fucked her on my bed.

When I fast-forwarded through our evening together, I realized I'd have to wear a condom, a thick slab of latex that blocked the best sensations from my cock. Then she would want to snuggle and I'd have to push her away. Then I'd have to kick her out and she would call me a dick. It sounded like a lot of work.

My phone vibrated and I looked at the screen.

It was Trinity. *Go to hell.*

I smirked when I read the message. I was in the middle of catching tail, but Trinity was a good lay. I didn't have to wear a condom with her, I didn't have to pretend to care, I didn't have to kick her out, and I could be myself.

She was the clear winner.

I abandoned the blonde in the corner and drove to Trinity's house a few miles away. The lights shone through her windows and snow littered her lawn. I parked in her driveway then headed to her front door. After I knocked, she answered.

"You came quick."

"I was down the street," I answered.

She walked away and let me come inside.

I shut the door and locked it behind me. "Did you know Skye and Cayson finally fucked?"

"Yeah, she told me." Trinity walked into her bedroom. "About time. If she wasn't going to fuck Cayson, I was going to do it for her."

I followed her then saw her pull her shirt off. "You have a thing for Cayson?"

"Of course not. But I'm not stupid. He's clearly a catch."

"You think I'm a catch too?" I winked at her.

She rolled her eyes. "Sure, Slade." She unbuttoned her jeans then pushed them down. She stood in a purple bra and matching thong. Her long legs traveled for days. I eyed them for a long moment, excited to feel them wrapped around my waist.

I came closer to her then pulled my shirt off.

Trinity stared at the tattoos that marked my chest and arms. Her hand moved to my sternum while she stared at the artwork.

"I always knew you were into ink."

"It is pretty hot."

Wow, she actually paid me a compliment.

"Now, are we going to talk all night or get to the good stuff?"

Her forwardness surprised me. "I don't need to be told twice."

I lay beside her, trying to catch my breath. I never expected Trinity to be so good in bed. She knew exactly what she was doing and how to rock my world. Every kiss and every touch electrified me.

She pulled her pillow closer to her then sighed in satisfaction.

I stared at her, watching her face. "You know what's weird?"

"Hmm?" She didn't open her eyes.

"This isn't weird."

"Why would it be weird? It's just sex. It's like two friends going for a jog together. It's just an activity like any other."

"I've never had a fuck buddy relationship like this."

"Really?" She opened her eyes and seemed surprised.

"Yeah. They always want more."

"Well, I think since we despise each other so much, we don't have to worry about that." She laughed lightly.

"Man, having sex without a rubber is heaven. I was going to pick up this girl tonight but the thought of wearing one made my hard-on disappear."

"It's that different?" she asked.

"Just take my word for it." I rested my hands behind my head and stared at the ceiling. Normally, I would leave a girl's house as quickly as possible but I didn't feel rushed. Trinity knew my visit didn't mean anything. "Meet anybody lately?" I wasn't jealous, just curious.

"No." She sighed sadly. "I'm not even bothering to look anymore."

"What do you mean?" I grabbed my beer from the nightstand and took a sip.

"All guys are jerks. I'm sick of expecting them to be anything more than that."

"I'm not a jerk."

She gave me a look that clearly said, "You've got to be kidding, right?"

"I'm not Prince Charming, obviously," I blurted. "But I'm not a liar or a cheat. With me, you know exactly what you're getting."

"Which isn't much," she said sarcastically.

"The guys that lie and treat you like you actually mean something to them then run around with other girls and spit out lies more than truths are the real assholes. I don't like hurting people so I avoid it. I get this reputation for being a jackass when all I am is honest. It gets old."

She processed my words for a moment. "I guess you have a point."

"Damn right I do." I took another drink.

She turned on her lamp and then grabbed a book from her nightstand. She sat up and began to read it.

"What are you reading?" I asked.

"One Flew Over the Cuckoo's Nest."

"Are you reading it for class?"

"No." She continued to read through the words. "I like to read."

I eyed her bookshelf in the corner and saw all the books piled high. "That's an interesting choice for a girl."

She cocked an eyebrow and looked at me. "What's that supposed to mean?"

"I just don't think most girls would like to read that."

"And what should I be reading?" she demanded. "Jane Eyre?"

"No, I'm just surprised. That's all."

She closed the book and looked at the cover. "It's my dad's favorite book. He let me borrow it."

"Uncle Mike knows how to read?" I said with a laugh.

"He reads a lot, actually. He started a few years ago. We have our own father-daughter book club."

"That's actually really cute."

"Cute?" She looked at me like I was crazy. "I've never heard you use that word before."

"Doesn't mean I don't know it," I snapped. "I did get into Harvard after all."

"And how is still a mystery…" She opened her book again.

I rolled my eyes and let her comment go unchallenged. I eyed the window and watched the snow fall. Trinity kept her house particularly clean. You could eat soup off the carpet if you really wanted to. She always had flowers on every table, and candles were lit in the kitchen, her room, and the bathroom. It was peaceful and warm. "I'm too tired to go home."

She flipped the page and kept reading.

"Do you mind if I sleep here?"

"I don't care." She pulled her knees to her chest and rested the book on her thighs. "Just don't get in my way in the morning."

"I can do that." I took out my phone and played a game. "What's your favorite book of all time?"

She sighed and put her book down. "You aren't going to let me read, are you?"

"Let's be real; my company is far more entertaining than a psych ward full of weirdos and a murderous nurse."

"That's debatable." She put the book on her nightstand.

"You don't have a bookmark?"

"No."

"Then how do you know where you left off?"

"I remember it," she said with an attitude. She turned off the lamp then got comfortable under the covers.

I turned on my side and faced her, the comforter up to my shoulder. "So, what's your favorite book?"

"*The Odyssey.*" She said it without hesitation.

I didn't expect her to say that. "Isn't that the epic Greek novel that's a million pages long?"

"It is."

Trinity caught me by surprise. I never thought she was stupid but I didn't think she was smart either. "Why?"

"I like that it's a story that takes place over years and years. It's chronological and shows a man's life over time. I think that's how a story should be. Not every chapter is a synopsis of the good stuff. It tells everything, the good and the bad."

I processed her words for a moment. "Do you have any other favorites?"

"By definition, you can only have one."

"Then what are others you like?"

"Why do you care?" she snapped.

"It's the first time I've spoken to you and haven't hated you. I think we're making progress. Now answer the damn question, you annoying brat."

She smirked. "*Harry Potter*."

"Wow...those books couldn't be more different."

"*American Psycho* is another favorite. My dad recommended it."

"About the guy who kills prostitutes?" I blurted.

"Yep. I'm guessing you've only seen the movie. Believe me, the book is a lot better."

"Your dad has interesting and violent tastes in literature."

She shrugged. "My dad can be a bit of a brute sometimes."

"So, are you going to ask me what my favorite book is?"

She laughed. "You know how to read?"

I narrowed my eyes at her. "Yes, I know how to read. Now ask me."

She stopped laughing. "Fine. What's your favorite book?"

"*Schindler's List*."

She gave me an incredulous look. "About the holocaust?"

"I'm a history major. It shouldn't be that surprising."

"But that's...so depressing."

"And your favorites aren't?" I asked. "I like it because it's real. What could be more terrifying, more meaningful, than something that horrific happening less than a hundred years ago? Isn't it weird to think about it like that?"

"I suppose." She stared at me while she thought about it. "And it's weird that slavery wasn't really that long ago."

"Right?" I asked. "It's really weird. That's why I like to read about it because nothing like that would ever happen now—thankfully."

"If you want to ink, why didn't you major in art?" she asked.

"I already know how to draw. I'd rather learn something new that I'm interested in."

She nodded. "I guess that makes sense."

"A lot, actually. Why are you majoring in business if you hate it?"

"I don't hate it."

I gave her a look that clearly said, "Cut the shit."

"Okay, I loathe it," she admitted. "I told my dad how I felt and he said I could pursue fashion if that's what I wanted."

"He wasn't mad?"

She shook her head.

"Wow. That's really cool. Then why are you still here?"

She shrugged. "I'm almost done with my degree. I may as well finish it."

"True. I can't deny the logic in that."

"So, you're really going to ink then? That's set in stone?"

"And I'm going to play in a band."

She smirked. "What band?"

"I don't know yet. But I'll find them."

"I've never heard you play guitar."

"I'm pretty damn good," I said.

"Cocky." She gave me a grin.

"I know I'm good. Why does admitting that make me cocky?"

"You could say it in a better way."

"How?"

"Like, 'I've been playing for a long time and I know all the chords.'"

"But that's pretty much what I said."

"But in a nicer way," she said.

I shook my head. "No. I'm blunt and honest and I'll never change."

"Fine. Be hated by everyone you meet."

"I'd rather be hated for who I am than loved for who I'm not. Besides, you hate me but you're sleeping with me."

She stared at me for a long time. "Slade, I don't hate you…"

"You don't? Because I hate you."

She hit my arm lightly. "No, you don't. I know you don't."

I avoided eye contact and stared at her comforter.

"I think there's more to you than you let on, Slade. But don't worry, I won't tell anyone. You can pretend to be shallow and rude all you want."

"I *am* shallow and rude."

"No. You just try to be. You can fool everyone else but you can't fool me."

"What makes you say that?" I asked.

"You've saved me twice now. And I didn't even ask you to."

"I would have done it for any girl."

"But I don't think you would have beaten the shit out of those guys for just any girl."

I guess she had a point.

"And you even said you couldn't stand the thought of something bad happening to me."

"Well…yeah. You're family."

"See?" She gave me a victorious look. "You are a good guy."

"A guy that uses his friend as a fuck buddy?"

"It's mutual. I'm using you as much as you're using me."

"Let me ask you something," I said.

"What?"

"You can have any guy you want. So why are you settling for this arrangement?"

Her eyes widened when she looked at me. "Did you just give me a compliment?"

"No. Not at all." *Did I? I'm pretty sure I didn't.*

"You just said I could have any guy I wanted."

"That's not a compliment," I argued.

"Yes, it is. It means you think I'm pretty. And not hideous."

"If you were hideous, I wouldn't be fucking you," I said.

She smirked. "Slade thinks I'm pretty." She said it in a high-pitched sing-song voice.

"No, I don't!"

"You think I'm pretty! You like my hair and my face. You like my body and my legs. You like my—"

I sealed my mouth over hers and gave her a hard kiss. My hand dug into her hair, gripping her tightly. I breathed hard into her mouth and she reciprocated that. Our lips crashed together and our tongues danced. Then I pulled away. "Stop talking."

The redness moved into her face and she kept her mouth shut.

"That's better." I settled down under the covers and got ready for bed. The room was dark and warm. Her bed was a million times more comfortable than mine.

She remained quiet on her side of the bed, her breathing even. She never answered my question and I didn't ask her again.

***

When I woke up the following morning, our bodies were tangled together. Her head was resting on my chest and my arm was around her shoulder. Her leg was hooked around mine and it felt smooth against my skin. When I realized what we were doing, I slipped away and got dressed without waking her. Then I left without looking back.

Chapter Sixteen

Trinity

Slade still annoyed me but he didn't irritate me as much as he did before. But the friendship and bond forming between us was creating a huge problem. When we were around the others, we didn't fight as much. We had to force it.

Slade looked at me, and his eyes darted back and forth while he was thinking. "I hate you."

Everyone looked up from their food. We were having dinner at a burger place down the street.

"That was random…" Roland eyed him suspiciously.

It sounded forced and unnatural. I could tell Slade was trying too hard. I decided to take the lead. "Cayson told me he beat you at basketball the other day. I knew you sucked."

"I don't suck," he snapped. "You suck."

I gave him a look that said, "I suck your dick alright."

"I mean, you're lame." He picked at his French fries.

"That was the weirdest fight I've ever seen the two of you have," Conrad said. "That was totally out of nowhere."

"Well, I'll always hate her and I never want her to forget it," Slade said.

We really needed to get better at this.

"Why don't you just try to get along?" Conrad asked. "Wouldn't that make everything easier?"

Slade shook his head. "Never."

I finished my fries and ignored him.

"So…I bet you guys are anxious to get home." Conrad gave Skye and Cayson a playful look.

Cayson glanced at Slade and gave him a merciless glare. "I don't know what you're talking about."

"Come on," Conrad said. "We all know you guys finally did the deed."

"Slade, I'm going to kill you," Cayson snapped.

"It wasn't me!" Slade said immediately.

"Who else would have said anything?" Cayson demanded.

"Uh…I did," I said. "Skye told me."

"Oh." Cayson looked apologetic.

"Are you mad I told her?" Skye asked fearfully.

"No, of course not." Cayson put his arm around her shoulders.

"Excuse me?" Slade demanded. "Don't I get an apology?"

"For what?" Cayson asked.

"For being called a liar." He pushed his food away, finished with it.

"Nah." Cayson turned back to Skye and rubbed his nose against hers.

Slade brooded from his seat. "Jackass…"

***

A few days later, I was in the library reading a book. It'd become a pastime that I loved almost more than anything else. Fashion was always my number one choice. But it was nice to get lost in a story that was different from my lame and boring life.

Slade pulled out the chair across from me then sat down. "Yo."

"Hi." I didn't look at him.

He was eating a sandwich, chewing loudly. "What are you reading now?"

"Same book."

He set his sandwich down then opened his backpack. "I got you something."

"If it's a sandwich, I don't want it." All he cared about was food and sex.

"No, it's not that." He placed a book in front of me. It was *Schindler's List*.

"Why are you giving this to me?" I examined the hardcover and the wear and tear along the pages.

"I want you to read it. I'll read The *Odyssey*."

What? "Are we in a book club now?"

He shrugged. "I just thought it would be cool. You can understand why I liked this book so much and I can try to understand why you like yours so much." He examined my open book. "And it looks like you're almost done with that one."

This was weird. Slade and I never did anything together except screw. "Seriously?"

"Yeah. Why not? Can you only be in a book club with one person?"

I guess there was no harm. "Okay. Come over tonight and I'll give you *The Odyssey*."

"We're going to have sex too, right?" he blurted.

I rolled my eyes. "If I'm in the mood."

He laughed. "You're always in the mood."

"Then maybe you should do a better job of keeping me satisfied," I jabbed.

"Hey, I always make you come!"

"Shh!" I narrowed my eyes at him.

He closed his mouth and fell silent just as Skye took a seat at the table.

"Hey," she said.

"Hi." I smiled at her.

"Yo." He grabbed his sandwich and kept eating.

Skye eyed our books. "Were you both reading?"

Uh… "No, these are both mine." I scooped them up and put them in my bag.

"*Schindler's List*?" Skye asked incredulously. "That doesn't sound like something you'd want to read."

"I'm trying new things," I blurted.

Slade kept his eyes glued to his sandwich.

"What's going on with you?" I tried to change the subject.

"Just school," she said. "And Cayson." A smile lit up her face.

"He's good in bed?" I asked.

"Like you wouldn't believe." Skye kept smiling.

"I taught him everything he knows." Slade said it while chewing a mouthful of food.

"I doubt that for some reason," Skye said.

Actually, I didn't. Slade really knew his way around the bedroom. I was never left unsatisfied. It was a nice change to be with a guy that could rock your world and give you exactly what you wanted without having to ask for it. Unfortunately, he was a jerk covered in tattoos and had a horrible attitude. So, the package wasn't pretty but the gift inside was exquisite.

"And if you think his dick is big, you should see mine." Slade shoved the rest of his sandwich into his mouth.

"How would you know unless you've seen his?" Skye argued.

"You look at Cayson's package?" I asked Slade.

"I just know, alright?" Slade said, annoyed.

"I think someone is into Cayson," Skye teased.

"Am not," Slade argued. "He's my best friend. I know everything about him."

"Yeah…everything." I loved teasing Slade. He would get so mad.

He rolled his eyes then crinkled up his wrapper. "I'm out of here."

"Thank god," I blurted.

"Shut up, Trinity." He left the table and put his backpack over his shoulder. Then he walked off.

Skye looked at her textbook then eyed me. "That's weird."

"What?" I asked.

"Slade's favorite book is *Schindler's List*."

How did she know that? "Why do you say that?"

"He mentioned it to me once."

"Oh." *What else was I supposed to say?*

"Did he give it to you?" she asked.

I felt like she was cornering me. Sweat started to form on my palms. "No. It's mine."

She finally backed off and looked at her textbook.

Phew. I stared across the library and tried to gather my bearings while Skye wasn't looking. Sneaking around was becoming more stressful than I realized. I was never good at keeping secrets and I was a horrible liar.

While I stared across the library, I saw a familiar face. "Code red. Zack is in the building."

Skye sighed and slammed her textbook closed. "I'm going to beat him over the head with this if he comes over here."

Zack was approaching our side of the library. A book was under his arm and he was typing on his phone. When he looked up, he spotted Skye. Like he was scared, his eyes widened and he immediately turned around, practically running out of the library.

"No running!" the librarian yelled at him.

Skye turned to me, her eyebrows raised. "What the hell was that?"

"I don't know. It was like he was scared of you."

"But why would he be scared of me?"

I shrugged. "I wouldn't have believed that happened unless I'd seen it myself."

"That was...bizarre." She was quiet for a long time. "Zack would never be scared of me. The only person I know who can possibly make a grown man scared is..." She stopped in midsentence. Her eyes were wide. "My father."

I watched her face, seeing the emotion and anger come through.

Skye slammed her book down then packed her bag. Judging by her quick movements and the anger burning in her eyes, she was pissed.

"What?"

"Cayson told my father—even though I specifically asked him not to." She put her bag over one shoulder and stormed off.

Shit, I felt bad for Cayson.

***

I just took dinner out of the oven when I got the message.

Go to hell.

Slade texted me four times that week to hook up. I didn't mind. My mind wasn't used to having four amazing orgasms in a week but my body could get used to it.

Sure.

I finished preparing the vegetables and rice just as the doorbell rang.

"It's open," I yelled.

Slade walked inside. "I could be a murderer."

"I doubt criminals ring the doorbell before they rob someone."

He shut the door then joined me in the kitchen. He wasn't wearing a jacket, just jeans and a t-shirt. "You should still be smarter about it."

"I unlocked it because I knew you were coming."

"It takes two seconds to unlock the door and let me in. You better do it next time."

"If you want to get laid, I suggest you not be a dick to me."

"I've been worse and you still spread your legs," he countered.

I eyed his arms. "You really should wear a jacket."

"I'm fine," he growled.

I felt his arm and was surprised by the heat.

"Told you." He pulled his arm away from my grasp. He walked through the kitchen then sniffed the air. "Something smells good."

"Chicken, broccoli, and rice," I answered. "Would you like to join me?"

"Free food?" He sat down at the table. "Hell yeah."

I served the food on plates then put them on the table.

Slade cut into his food and stuffed it into his mouth. "Wow, this is good."

"Thank you."

"I wasn't complimenting you," he said quickly.

"Well, I did make it."

"I'm still not flattering you." He ate everything off his plate then moaned. "Even the green stuff was good."

"Again, thank you."

"Again, no compliment." He leaned back in his chair while he waited for me to finish. "Do you cook a lot?"

"About five times a week."

"How do you have time for that?"

"I make time," I answered. "Eating healthy is important."

"No wonder you have such a nice body."

I smirked. "You're giving me compliments left and right."

He shook his head slightly. "Don't let it go to your head."

"Too late." I finished my food then put my dish in the sink. "Since I cooked, you should clean."

He laughed. "Yeah right."

Why did I expect anything else? I put hot water in the sink then placed the dishes inside to soak.

"You got dessert too?"

"I wouldn't have a nice body if I ate junk all the time," I countered.

"I know there's a little fat girl deep inside."

A lot of fat girls, actually. I opened the freezer and revealed a Ben and Jerry's pint of chocolate ice cream.

He winked. "Now that's hot."

I grabbed two spoons then sat beside him at the table. We ate out of the same carton, our metal spoons tapping together as we tried to get to the large chunks of chocolate before the other.

"That shit was good." Slade left his spoon on the table. "If you cook every night, I'm coming over more often."

"I'll make sure the door is locked," I said sarcastically. I shoved the empty pint into the garbage can then walked into my bedroom. "Are we going to do this or what?"

"Right to the chase, huh?" He followed behind me, stripping his shirt off as he went.

When we were in my room, I turned around and looked at him. I never had a thing for guys with ink and it was something I never expected to find attractive. But seeing them on Slade made me hotter for him. His body was thick and toned with muscle, and that just highlighted the appearance of the different colors on his skin. He was a collage of different art, a canvas that was beautiful in a chaotic way. I'd had sex with Slade dozens of times, and every time we were together it was better.

I found new ways of appreciating him, of understanding him. He could be the biggest dick I knew, but when we were alone, he lowered his walls. He was a much different person. There were layers unseen to the naked eye. He had more depth than he was willing to reveal. And in a complicated way, that made me like him more than I did before. It seemed like this odd relationship made us better friends, unexpectedly.

He crossed the room then pulled my shirt off, eager to see my naked body. He was aggressive with me, doing exactly what he wanted when he wanted. My previous partners were hesitant and slow. There was no heat in their eyes, not the way Slade had at least. He removed the rest of my clothes, practically ripping them. "I've been thinking about this all day."

"It didn't seem that way."

"Well, I was."

I kissed his chest. "How do you want me?" We'd done it in every position imaginable. It surprised me that they were all enjoyable. Only Slade could pull that off.

He smirked. "I like it when you give me the control. But I like it when you take it too. Most girls don't."

"You didn't answer my question." I sucked his bottom lip. Every time I touched him, I was lit on fire. The desire I had for him was paramount. I'd never wanted someone in such a sexual way before. Perhaps it was because there were no emotional feelings to dilute it. It was carnal, animal-like.

His hand moved down my back to my ass. "How about anal?"

"Okay," I said without hesitation.

His eyes widened. "You like that?"

"Yeah. Why are you surprised?"

"I just didn't expect you to have done it before."

I smirked. "I'm not sure what I did to give you the impression I was a good girl. Believe me, I'm not."

He took a deep breath and desire burned in his eyes. "You're good at hiding it."

"Just because I don't talk about my sex life like you do, doesn't mean I don't have one."

"Apparently." He squeezed my ass with his hand. "Man, we should have been doing this a long time ago."

"Yeah, we should have." I lowered myself to my knees and sucked him off.

He fisted his hands into my hair and moaned while he stared down at me. A moan escaped his lips every few seconds. Then I moved to the bed and got on all fours.

"What are you waiting for?" I asked with a sexy voice.

After Slade was lubed and ready, he was inside me faster than I could process.

***

"Oh my fucking god, that was good." Slade caught his breath beside me. "Best anal I've ever had."

"It was pretty good, huh?"

"Hell yeah, it was." He ran his fingers through his hair then sighed.

I lay on my side of the bed then got comfortable. Whenever I had a huge climax, like the one Slade gave me, I was exhausted and relaxed. My mind just wanted to drift in and out of reality. I almost felt high.

Slade stared at the ceiling, his chest still rising and falling with a quick pace.

I was in the mood for a bath. I liked to take them in the wintertime to stay warm. Candles lit the room. I closed my eyes and let my worries escape the surface of my skin. That's what I was planning on doing tonight before he came over. Since Slade would fall asleep soon, I decided to get up and head to the bathroom.

I drew the bath and added bubbles. Then I lit a few candles and got a stack of magazines to read. The mirrors on the wall started to fog from the humidity. When everything was ready, I slipped inside and felt my body relax as the heat surrounded me. I closed my eyes and thought about nothing in particular.

Slade walked in some time later. I wasn't sure when. My mind was on a different planet at the time. He lifted the toilet lid then took a piss.

"Do you mind?" I asked. "There are two other bathrooms in this house."

"Too far away." He held himself with two hands and filled the bowl.

I shook my head and ignored him. When he was finished, he flushed the toilet then came to the bathtub.

"What are you doing?" he asked.

I rested my head on a towel. "Taking a bath. What does it look like I'm doing? And did you wash your hands?"

He rolled his eyes then washed his hands in the sink. "There. Are you happy?"

"Much. Although, I'm concerned for your overall hygiene."

He eyed me in the water. "So, you're just sitting there in your own filth?"

"How dirty do you think I am?" I countered.

He sat on the corner of the tub. "I've never taken a bath before."

"Not even as a kid?"

"Well, not as an adult at least."

"They're wonderful."

He shrugged. "I prefer the shower. You can't have sex in a tub."

"Yeah, you can."

He eyed me for a moment, amusement in his eyes. "Really?"

I nodded.

"So, you've done it?"

I nodded again.

"You really are a whore."

"Hey." I gave him a firm look. "Just because I enjoy sex doesn't make me a whore. I don't sleep with married men, I don't cheat, and I don't accept money as payment. Don't ever call me that again. It's sexist and offensive."

He seemed to understand he shouldn't push me on this. For the first time, he backed off. "I'm sorry. I take it back."

Whoa...did Slade just apologize? "I've never heard you say that before."

"What?"

"That you're sorry."

"Because I only say it when I really mean it. And when your voice gets all firm like that, I know you aren't kidding around. You were actually hurt by what I said."

Maybe Slade knew me better than I thought. "Well, I appreciate it."

"Yeah…" He scooped up the suds with his hands then blew them back into the water. "That's some girly shit."

"It's really nice. Join me."

"It'll be a tight fit."

"Bend your knees," I said.

"Fine." He stood up then came to the rear of the tub. I scooted forward so he could move in behind me. When he was settled, I leaned back against his chest. It was cramped but we were both covered by the water. He leaned his head against the towel pillow I made.

"It's nice, huh?" I asked.

"It's not bad." Both of his hands hooked around my waist and he anchored me to his chest. He never held me like that before. It was something I wasn't used to. I didn't say anything and just let it play out. "What do you do when you're in here?"

"Read magazines. Think." I played with the bubbles on the surface, cupping them into my hand.

"Think about what?" he asked.

I shrugged. "My life. What I want to change. Where I'm going in life."

"And what have you decided?"

"One of the best parts of life is its wonderful unpredictability. So, I really don't know where I'm going."

"Where would you like to go?" he asked quietly.

"I just know I love fashion and I'd like to be a part of it."

"Be a model," he blurted.

I smirked. "I could get used to these compliments."

He chuckled. "I guess you aren't totally hideous."

I leaned my head back and looked up at him. "Just admit it. You think I'm pretty."

He stared into my face, and his eyes became darker. The change was so sudden it was hard to notice. He kept staring, like he was trying to find something. "I think you're beautiful."

I stopped breathing for a second because his response caught me off guard. That was the last thing I expected Slade to ever say, especially to me. No smartass comment came to mind. I couldn't think of a response.

It didn't seem like Slade wanted one. He leaned down and pressed a kiss to my shoulder where it emerged from the water. Then he leaned back and rested his head against the towel.

Did that just happen?

His hands were still wrapped around my waist, holding me to his chest. "Since you're so into fashion and appearances, I never expected you to be such a book worm. I didn't think you were so intelligent and witty. You continue to surprise me the more I get to know you. It's weird. I've known you my whole life but I never really knew anything about you."

"Yeah, me too. I feel like we're actually friends now."

He chuckled. "Yeah, I never expected that to happen."

"Me neither."

"I mean, you're still annoying and all that, but I definitely have a new respect for you."

"Me too." I felt his chest rise and fall, noting its power and strength.

"We have to start doing a better job of arguing in front of the others," he said. "I think we're losing our touch."

I laughed. "Yeah, it's getting hard. We could just get along and let them get used to it."

"No," he said immediately. "They'll know something is up, especially Cayson. That damn psychologist can analyze me like a bug under a microscope."

That reminded me of what Skye said that afternoon. "She knows Cayson told her father about Zack. And she was really mad."

He sighed. "Poor Cayson. It's going to be a long night for him..."

"I don't blame him for protecting her, but I understand why Skye is mad. She isn't going to just let this go. She's always been really obsessed about proving her independence to her father. I think this is the worst thing Cayson could have done to piss her off."

"She needs to get over it. Cayson did the right thing. I have his back on this one."

"Well, I'm not on anyone's side. I just want them to be together, to be happy."

"Yeah..." He moved his fingers against the skin of my stomach. "I was pissed that Cayson stopped spending as much time with me because of Skye, but I definitely want him to be happy. And that little brunette with a huge rack really makes him giddy."

I cringed. "Slade, she's your cousin."

"But I'm not blind to her most attractive feature."

"I don't think anyone is."

He adjusted himself in the tub then sighed. "This is nice."

"Told you."

"I guess sitting in your own dirt isn't so bad."

"It's not like I'm a gardener that just got off work," I snapped.

His hand moved down to my belly button piercing. "I really like this."

"You do?"

"It's hot." He touched it again before he pulled his hand away.

I touched his arm. "I like your tattoos. They're hot."

"Well, duh."

I chuckled. "Don't be cocky."

He moved his lips to my ear. "I'm glad you like them."

I felt my spine shiver when his lips touched the shell of my ear.

Slade massaged my thigh. "You're doing okay? I didn't hurt you, right?"

"No, definitely not."

"Good. Sometimes I'm afraid I'm too rough with you."

"If you are, I'll tell you."

"Thank you." He rubbed my shoulder. "I don't want this to end so I don't want to give you a reason to leave."

"I don't want this to end either."

He held me in the tub for several minutes, not speaking. His hand glided over my skin, making me feel warm and comfortable. I'd always taken baths alone, but I didn't realize how enjoyable they could be with another person. It was nice to cuddle under the water. It was an intimacy I never shared with another person. I'd had sex with countless guys but no one had ever held me this way, like they cared.

"Last week, I asked you a question and you never answered it."

I didn't know what he was talking about. "Refresh my memory."

"You can have any guy you want. So why do you settle for this type of arrangement?" He stared at the side of my face as he waited for me to answer.

This wasn't a conversation I ever had with anyone. But I guess I could have it with Slade since I was sleeping with him. "Ever since I was a little girl, my dad told me that I'd end up with a really great guy that would treat me like a princess. And he told me to never settle for anyone unless he was absolutely perfect. He would open every door for me, listen to my every thought, and always take care of me, even if he hurt himself in the process. And for the longest time, I believed that.

"My father has always been a great role model to me. He's smart, loyal, strong, and he treats my mom like he loves her as much as the day he married her. It's like he lives and breathes for her. I guess, in a twisted way, I've always compared every guy to my father. Does he open every door for me? Does he treat me right? Would he die for me?

"Then I grew up. With every date I went on and every guy I met, I realized none of them gave a damn about me. Some were better than others, but it was pretty clear they just wanted sex or a short-term commitment. And the ones who did want to be with me didn't treat me right. My only somewhat serious boyfriend cheated on me with a friend from high school. Men are all the same. I keep waiting to meet a guy who's different, who's right. I know Cayson isn't perfect, but when it comes to Skye, he is. I've quickly realized I'm wasting my time searching for that perfect guy, someone I can actually introduce to my father and not feel a single doubt. So, I stopped searching.

"I don't need a man in my life to be happy. I can take care of myself and do everything on my own. I refuse to settle for someone who can't give me everything I want, so I'm not going to do it. But I need sex. I love sex even if it's meaningless. Which is why this relationship with you is so perfect."

Slade said nothing. Time stretched for a long time. I didn't expect him to say anything, but the quiet echoes in the bathroom were awkward. I spilled my deepest secret to him and now I wasn't sure why. Then he cleared his throat. "Trinity, I care about you—a lot."

I sighed. "It's okay, Slade. I know you're just using me and it doesn't bother me at all. I don't think less of you."

"But I really do care about you, Trinity. I do give a damn. I know I've been an ass to you a lot in the past—"

"A lot."

He smirked. "But you're important to me. And you do mean something to me."

They were just empty words but I didn't want to argue about it anymore.

"Trinity, you're one of the most beautiful women I've ever seen, on the outside as well as the inside. You're a strong woman who's too intelligent for her own good, and you're fun to be around. I know the right guy is out there, just waiting for you. And when he finally has you, he'll ask himself how he got so lucky. And when you compare him to your father, you'll realize he's better."

His words echoed in my mind long after he said them. Slade hardly said anything without a curse word in it, and I've never heard him say anything so heartfelt in my life. It pulled at my heartstrings and made me feel a twinge of hope. "Thanks…"

He held me close to his chest. "I'm right. I promise you."

"How can you make a promise like that?"

"I just can."

Chapter Seventeen

Cayson

I just got out of the shower when I heard someone ramming into my door like they were trying to break it down.

"Cayson! Open up!" It was Skye.

I panicked at the urgency in her voice. Was she okay? Did something happen? Just wearing a towel, I ran to the door then opened it. "Baby, what's going on?" I immediately looked outside and made sure there was no danger.

"What's going on?" Anger was heavy in her voice. *"What's going on?"*

What was she so mad about?

She pushed herself inside, forcing me back. "I specifically told you not to tell my father about Zack. I trusted you not to tell him. You even promised. And then a second later, you went behind my back and did it anyway!"

"I didn't promise anything," I said immediately. "When you asked me not to tell him, I didn't say anything."

That just pissed her off even more. "Seriously, you're trying to get out of this on a technicality?"

"I'm not trying to get out of anything," I snapped. "I know what I did and I take full responsibility for it. You may not always like the decisions I make, but that's too bad. I had to protect you. So if you're upset about it, fine. I would do it again in a heartbeat."

Skye looked like she might explode. "Cayson, if there's one thing you should know about me, it's how strongly I value my independence. I've spent my entire adult life proving to my father that I don't need his money, his protection, or his concern. I'm perfectly capable of taking care of myself. And you sabotaged that by snitching on me to him."

"I didn't snitch—"

"Shut up! I'm talking."

I pressed my lips together and clenched my jaw.

"I don't need a man to take care of me, whether that be my father or you. Alright? Do you understand that? I chose to go out with Zack and I got myself in this mess. I admit my mistakes and my poor judgment, but I will get out of this situation without my father or you. If you don't understand that, understand how important that is to me, then we shouldn't even be together."

Her words echoed in my mind long after she said them.

"I'm sick of my father constantly hovering over me. He did it all through my life. As a result, he never let me handle anything on my own. As soon as I got into trouble, he fixed it for me. But when it came to Roland, my dad turned his back and forced him to figure out everything on his own. As a result, Roland is stronger and more self-sufficient. I don't want to be babied anymore. I'm sick of it."

I tried to keep my anger back so I wouldn't push her over the edge. "I agree with you—for the most part. But Zack is a fucking psychopath. You claim he wouldn't hurt you but you don't know that for sure. And I'm sorry, Skye, but he's a guy twice your size and height. If he wants to hurt you, he will. You will never be strong enough to match him. I had to do what was right to protect you."

"Fuck you, Cayson."

My eyes widened. "Don't talk to me like that."

"Don't go behind my back and betray my trust!"

"It's not the same thing and you know it. If you don't want to be treated like a brat then don't act like one!"

Her eyes were smoldering in rage. "I can't believe you..."

"I stand by what I did and I won't apologize for it." I stood my ground and didn't back down. "Zack has left you alone ever since and I know he won't bother you again. I can sleep at night and so can your father. Now if you want to go for a damn jog in the middle of the night, you can. You have your independence back."

She gripped her hair in frustration. "I've never been so angry in my life!"

I said nothing, staring her down.

"I can't be with someone I can't trust, Cayson. I just can't."

My heart skipped a beat. "What did you just say?"

"You heard me, Cayson. I can't do this relationship anymore. Without trust, there is no relationship."

Now I was pissed. I marched to her so fast she almost tripped. I slammed her against the door with my body. "Take that back. Now."

Fear filled her eyes while she was pinned down.

"Don't you ever say that to me again." Spit was flying out of my mouth because I was so angry. "You're being a pain in the ass about this, Skye. I love you more than anything on this damn planet and I will do whatever it takes to keep you safe. If that means you can't trust me, fine. You'll just have to deal with that. You can throw a hissy fit and play the victim all you want, but I know without a doubt that if the situation were reversed, you would do the same for me. And honestly, I would judge you if you didn't.

"Now let's get something straight here. Do not ever treat me like this again. I've been the perfect damn boyfriend of the year to you. I do everything for you and break my back just to make you smile. You do not have the right to say that to me. You do not have the right to get upset with me. Now shut up and deal with it."

She stared at me, breathing hard. Her eyes started to water.

I stepped back and gave her space. "Now get out of my apartment." I turned my back on her and walked into my bedroom. Then I slammed the door so hard it broke off the hinges.

***

Slade held the door while I used my screwdriver to put the door back into place. "So...you guys had a fight?"

I was still fuming about it. Skye and I hadn't spoken since the night before. She didn't call me and I didn't call her. I didn't go by the library during the day like I usually did. She owed me an apology and I wasn't going to do anything until I got it. "Something like that..."

"You guys didn't break up, right?" Fear was in his voice.

"No." I wouldn't let her go without a fight.

He nodded. "Is there something I can do to help?"

I shifted the door then drilled the hinge back into the case. "Just hold the door steady."

"I *am* holding it steady."

"Then keep doing it."

Slade fell silent while he waited for me to finish.

When I was done, I opened the door then closed it again. It didn't creak or shake. "It works."

"You ripped the door off like the Incredible Hulk or what?"

"No. I just slammed it too hard."

Slade kept staring at me like I might snap. "Damn…how hard did you slam it?"

"Pretty damn hard," I snapped.

Slade was usually full of jokes but today he kept them to himself. He knew I wasn't in the mood. "It's probably not the best time to bring this up but…"

"What?" *What more could possibly go wrong in my life?*

"My dad called and said the family is getting together at the ski lodge in Connecticut. We're staying at Sean's ski Chalet. Since it's a four day weekend coming up, they want to go then."

I really didn't want to deal with any of that right now. "Great."

"I think it'll be fun. I love snowboarding. None of that pretentious skiing bullshit."

I didn't give a damn about whether he preferred skiing or snowboarding. "I'm surprised my dad hasn't called me."

"I'm sure he will."

"Well, thanks."

"Yeah." He nodded then headed to the front door. "Cay, you want my advice?"

"Not even a little bit," I blurted.

"You're going to get it anyway," he said. "Chicks are always wrong. But always let them think they're right." He walked out and shut the door behind him.

I thought about his words for a long time after he left. Maybe he understood women more than I gave him credit for. I tested my bedroom door again when my father called.

"Hey, Son."

"Hey, Dad."

He knew something was off. "Everything okay?"

I didn't want to talk about Skye right now. "I just fixed my bedroom door and I'm a little tired from it."

"What happened?"

"Since you're a computer geek, you wouldn't understand."

"Very funny," he said sarcastically. "So, how's school?"

"Boring."

"And your lovely girlfriend?"

"She's lovely—like usual."

"Give her a kiss for me, please—on the cheek. None of that face-sucking stuff."

"Sure, Dad." I just wanted to get off the phone.

"We're skiing this weekend. Everyone is going. You're coming, right? Your mother and I would love to spend time with you."

Since Skye and I were going through a hard time, I didn't want the added pressure of family. But I couldn't think of a way to wiggle out of this one. "Sure."

"Great. We'll see you on Friday."

"Sounds like a plan."

"Okay, kid. I'll talk to you later."

"Bye, Dad."

"Bye, Son. I love you."

"I love you too." I quickly hung up then shoved the phone into my pocket. Then I sat down on the couch and stared at the blank TV screen. I wanted Skye to call me but she never did. I guess I would have to keep waiting.

Chapter Eighteen

Skye

Five days had passed without speaking or seeing Cayson. I was starting to go through withdrawals. I missed my best friend. I missed looking at his ridiculously perfect face. His lips were unbelievably tasty. His hands fit my hips perfectly. I missed talking to him. Did he miss me?

But I was still so pissed at him.

I couldn't believe he deliberately went behind my back and pulled that stunt. And to make it worse, he wasn't even going to tell me about it. If he didn't get caught, I never would have known. I knew I was headstrong and stubborn, but I was particularly passionate about this subject.

We were going skiing in a few days with my family, and with the drama going on with Cayson, I knew I wouldn't have a good time. How would we act? Would we tell everyone we were fighting? Or would we pretend that nothing was going on?

Every time I was in the library, I hoped Cayson would stop by. He never did. Clearly, he was as pissed as I was. When I was home in the evenings, I always listened for a knock on my door. It never came. And my hand was glued to my phone, waiting for it to ring. It never did.

"Just talk to him," Trinity said. "You're being a big fat baby over this."

"Big fat baby?" I asked.

"Yes." She gave me a hard look. "It would be different if Cayson was trying to purposely hurt you but he's not. He was just looking out for you."

"He of all people should know how I feel about this."

"Which only proves how much he loves you," she snapped. "He was willing to piss you off in order to keep you safe. That's the most selfless thing I've ever heard."

"Trinity, just stay out of it."

"If you lose him, I will beat you up, Skye."

I gave her an incredulous look.

"I mean it. He's my family too, Skye. Just because we're related by blood, doesn't make me more loyal to you. If you hurt Cayson, I'll hurt you."

"I can't believe you're taking his side."

"I can't believe you aren't." She grabbed her bag and stormed off. "Pull your head out of your ass, Skye."

I growled then tried to focus on my textbook. But that was pretty much impossible.

Slade dropped into the seat across from me.

"Go away. I'm not in the mood to even look at you."

He had a serious look on his face. "Then I'll make this quick."

The last thing I wanted to do was talk to Cayson's best friend. "What?"

His eyes appeared lifeless and dull. He seemed sad and torn apart. "I just wanted to give you a heads up. I told Cayson I wouldn't say anything but I'm going to."

What was he talking about?

"Cayson doesn't think this relationship is going to work. He says he loves you like crazy but you're too headstrong for him. He understands you don't want anyone to take care of you, but he hates how difficult it is. He thinks it's best if he ends it now before it gets worse…and you can't be friends again."

My hands started to shake and I felt my heart fall into my stomach. It was a deathblow. I couldn't live without him. I just couldn't. When I suggested breaking up a few days ago, I didn't mean it. Cayson was the best damn thing that ever happened to me. I couldn't let him go.

Slade stood up again. "Since you're my cousin, I wanted to make sure you were prepared." He walked away without another word.

Fuck, I had to talk to Cayson.

I left the library then walked outside. When I looked at the time, I realized he just finished his class. He normally went to the library, but since he wasn't going there, he was probably going to his apartment. Or he would be with Slade but he clearly wasn't. I walked over there as fast as my short legs would carry me.

I was still pissed off at him for what he did, but I could let it go as long as I got to keep him. There was so much goodness to our relationship. Nothing was worth losing that bliss. He made me happier than I ever thought I could be. The idea of him being with someone else was sickening. It would be torture.

I arrived at his apartment and slammed my fist into the door, impatient. He opened it a moment later, his eyes guarded and his jaw clenched tight. He didn't speak, just staring me down like he loathed me.

Tears sprang from my eyes and I moved into his chest, wrapping my arms around him. "I'm sorry… I'm so sorry." I squeezed him hard, never wanting to let go.

Cayson pulled me inside the apartment then shut the door. Then his hands were on me. He rested his chin on my head then moved his fingers through my hair. He stood there, just holding me.

"I'm sorry about everything. Please don't leave me. Please don't go."

"Shh," he whispered in my ear. "I'm not going anywhere."

I clutched him harder. "I know I can be stubborn and annoying but I'll work on it. I know in my heart you were just trying to do the right thing for me. I know…"

"It's alright, Skye." His voice was gentle. His fingers soothed me, making me feel calm.

"Please don't go. I'll beg if I have to."

"Skye, I would never leave you."

I pulled away then looked into his eyes.

He used the pad of his thumb to wipe away my tears. "Ever."

"But Slade told me…"

His eyes narrowed. "Told you what?"

"That you were going to leave me…because you were sick of putting up with me."

Realization came into his eyes then he sighed. "I never said that, Skye. Slade must have said that to get us back together."

Now I felt like an idiot. But I was so relieved Cayson wasn't leaving me that I didn't care about my premature apology. "That jackass."

He smirked. "He's spent the week with me and he knew how upset I was. I'm sure he was just eager to get us back together."

"That's really sweet…but pisses me off at the same time." I wiped my tears away then chuckled.

"He's a jerk but he has a heart of gold."

"Apparently…"

He looked down at me. "Does that mean you're going to walk out again?"

"No…I miss you."

He sighed. "God, I miss you too."

"I'm sorry, Cayson. I just don't want to get my father involved in anything. It's really important to me."

"I know, baby. I never would have done it if I didn't have to."

I was scared to ask my next question. "What did he do to Zack?"

"He just scared him a little bit then had two guys tail him everywhere he went. I'm sure Zack is scared to death to be seen within a hundred feet of you. He won't bother you anymore, Skye."

That kind of protection was excessive but at least they didn't hurt Zack. And I didn't have to deal with him anymore. "Okay."

He cupped my cheek. "So…are we okay?"

I nodded. "I'm sorry about everything I said."

His eyes turned serious. "I never want you to say that to me again. And if you say it, make sure you really mean it. Because there's nothing worse you can do to hurt me."

I felt lower than dirt. "I'm sorry. I was just angry."

"That's no excuse."

"I know…it won't happen again."

"Good."

I was feeling worse by the second. "I'm sorry I keep messing this up. I'm not doing it on purpose."

"It's okay." He kissed my forehead. "It's water under the bridge."

"You always say that."

"With you, it'll always be water under the bridge."

I held him close and cherished the moment. He was still mine. I didn't mess this up too badly.

"Are you going skiing this weekend?" he asked.

"Yeah. Are you?"

"Like my parents would let me say no," he said with a laugh.

"It should be fun."

"It'll be a lot more fun without us fighting."

"Well, there is one good thing about fighting…"

"What?" He held me close.

"Make up sex."

His eyes sparkled. "I do like sex—any sex—with you."

"Well, let me make up for my behavior."

"That sounds like a good idea."

***

We piled our belongings into my SUV.

"Trinity, why do you always need to pack so much shit?" Conrad snapped. He tried shoving her final bag into the pile but it wouldn't fit.

"Because we're going skiing for four whole days." She crossed her arms over her chest and glared at her brother. "I need clothes."

"If you donated your wardrobe to a charity, they would have enough clothes to wear a different outfit every day for a year." Conrad tried to push the bag in again. It still wouldn't fit. It kept falling off. He dropped it on the ground. "Trinity, it's not coming."

"Find a place for it," she snapped.

He looked at her like she was crazy. "It. Won't. Fit."

"Rearrange the bags," she said.

"*You* rearrange the fucking bags," Conrad snapped.

Cayson kept his arm around my waist. "This will be a fun trip…"

Slade sighed then approached the back of the SUV. He pulled all the bags out and dropped them on the ground then started to rearrange them like a puzzle.

I shared a shocked look with Trinity. Roland looked at Conrad like he just saw a snake with wings. Cayson stared at Slade like he's never seen him before.

Slade managed to fit in every single bag. Not an inch of space was unutilized. The luggage was packed so high Roland wouldn't be able to see in his rearview mirror but everything was there.

Slade wiped his hands on his jeans. "Now shut up so we can get on the road." He wore a t-shirt and jeans. His breath came out as vapor against the cold.

Trinity looked at Slade but didn't say anything. It seemed like a silent conversation passed between them.

Did I just see that?

I must be seeing things.

"I sincerely hope you brought a jacket," Roland said. "Remember, we're going skiing."

"Snowboarding," Slade snapped. "And I don't fall so I don't need a jacket."

I knew where this was going. I decided to stop the argument before it started. "Where's Silke?"

"She's riding with Theo and Thomas," Slade answered. "She had something to do this morning."

"Oh. I just saw her the other day and she didn't mention that," I said.

"Not my problem," Slade said. "Now let's get on the road before it gets dark. I don't trust Roland's driving."

"I'm a fantastic driver," Roland argued.

"In the snow, no one's a fantastic driver," Slade said. He walked to the side of the SUV then got in.

"Alright, let's head out," Conrad said.

Roland got behind the wheel and Conrad sat beside him.

I moved to the back seat and scooted over so Cayson could sit beside me. Trinity moved to the middle row and sat by the window. When Slade got inside, he glanced back and forth between the empty seats next to Cayson and Trinity.

I assumed he would sit next to Cayson because he despised Trinity. It was weird to watch him debate it.

"I don't want to watch you guys make out for the whole drive." Slade took the spot next to Trinity and faced forward.

Trinity looked at him then stared out the window.

That was not the choice I expected him to make.

Roland left the city then got onto the highway. He turned on the radio but kept it low. He and Conrad talked about sports and a few girls they met at a bar.

Cayson put his arm around my shoulder and moved closer to me, his leg touching mine. With his other hand, he grabbed mine and caressed my knuckles. "What should we do on the drive?"

I gave him a knowing look.

"Okay, not that," he blurted.

I smirked. "What do you want to do?"

"I brought a deck of cards."

"We can play that."

"Okay." Cayson dug into his bag and pulled out the deck.

I stared at the back of Slade's head, noticing his gaze pointed toward his lap. Trinity was doing the same, clearly reading something. I sat forward and looked over the seat. They were both reading books.

What the hell? "Slade, you read?"

He flinched at my words. "What's it to you?" Aggression was in his voice.

"You don't strike me as the reading type," I said.

"Well, I am." He turned his gaze back to his book. "Now mind your own business."

"You're one to talk. You lied to me and told me Cayson was going to leave me."

"You're welcome, by the way," Slade snapped. "I just saved you a month of fighting over something so stupid. If you ask me, Cayson should leave you. He's the best damn boyfriend on the planet. Maybe you should appreciate him once in a while."

"Word," Roland said from the driver's seat.

"Ditto," Trinity added.

"Yep," Conrad said.

I sighed in annoyance. "Don't gang up on me, alright?"

"You fuck with one of us, you fuck with all of us," Conrad said.

"I'm your cousin," I argued.

"Well, Cayson is my brother." Conrad looked out the window.

I hated being singled out. "Whatever…"

Slade read his book again.

I looked at the title. "*The Odyssey*?" I didn't expect Slade to read at all, let alone an epic Greek novel.

"What?" he snapped. "I'm a history major. It makes sense for me to read this." He sounded defensive.

"That's Greek mythology," I argued.

"Based on historical events," he snapped.

I turned to Trinity. "Isn't that your favorite book?"

She flipped a page in her book. "It's an odd coincidence…"

"Can you leave us the fuck alone now?" Slade snapped. "Give your boyfriend a handy in the backseat."

Roland swerved slightly. "Please don't."

I leaned back against the seat and ignored Slade.

Cayson passed out the cards. "Ready to lose?"

"How about we just make out instead?"

His eyes darkened at the idea.

Roland swerved again. "Please don't."

Cayson returned to the cards. "Let's just play instead."

I sighed then gathered my cards. "I'm going to beat you this time."

"I'll let you win a few times." He gave me a smirk then played the game.

***

"Is this it?" Conrad stared at the wooden cottage. Lights were bright in every window. Snow was piled on the roof and the road. The lawn was completely white, covered with powder.

"It's a fucking mansion," Roland said.

"Well, there will be twenty people staying there," Trinity said.

"Check the address again," Roland said.

Conrad looked at his phone. "They match."

I looked through the window. "I see my mom's car."

"Alright." Roland drove over the snow then found a spot to park.

Trinity stared out the window. "It's beautiful."

Slade stared out the window too but held his comment. No smartass words came out.

"How's this going to work?" I asked Cayson.

"What do you mean?" he asked.

"How are we going to sleep together?" I asked. "Are you going to sneak into my room?"

He stared at me like I was crazy. "Is that a joke?" he blurted. "I'm not sleeping with you when your dad is around. I don't need a pistol blowing my brains out."

I rolled my eyes. "My dad loves you, Cayson."

"A father's love for his daughter makes him blind to everything else."

"He's not stupid. He must know we sleep together."

"But I doubt he wants to think about that when he's staying in the same house."

"He'll still have sex with my mom," I argued.

"Who he's married to..." Cayson gave me an incredulous look. "Forget it, Skye. I'm not sleeping with you."

"But I can't sleep without you," I argued.

"Neither can I but I'll deal with it."

"Is this an episode of *The Young and The Restless*?" Slade snapped.

Cayson ignored his comment. "Forget it, okay?"

I gave him my best pout. "Please..."

"No." He gave me a firm look. "We have the rest of our lives. Your dad likes me and I want to keep it that way."

"He'll always like you no matter what happens between us," I said. "He's your godfather."

"When it comes to you, anything can change. Believe me." He got out of the SUV and helped me out.

I always got my way with Cayson but I knew it wasn't happening this time.

We grabbed our bags out of the back. Cayson carried my bags and his own inside. He refused to let me touch anything. He always carried my stuff but I knew he was insistent because my father was there.

We walked inside and saw our parents sitting in the expansive living room in front of an enormous fireplace. A fire burned inside, crackling and licking the wood.

"About time." Uncle Ryan got up first then went to Slade and hugged him. "I'm glad you made it here in one piece."

"Me too." Slade eyed Roland. "Daredevil over there managed to not drive over a cliff."

"Where did I get this reputation as a bad driver?" Roland said.

"You didn't," Slade said. "I just know you're stupid like your sister."

Roland shrugged. "My sister is stupid…"

Uncle Ryan came to me next and hugged me. He was my godfather so I knew he saw me as his own daughter. "Beautiful like always."

"Thanks, Uncle Ryan."

He pulled away and patted me on the shoulder. "Are you ready for that tramp stamp? My door is open anytime."

"Just because you're my brother-in-law, doesn't mean I won't break your neck," my dad threatened.

"My baby will avenge my death," Uncle Ryan said. "You know my wife. That girl is a fucking ninja."

The parents greeted their kids with long-winded conversations and hugs. When my dad looked at me, affection was in his eyes like it usually was. "You look more like your mother every time I see you."

"Thank you." To me, that was a compliment. My mom still turned heads whenever she went to the grocery store. She took care of herself over the years and worked out every morning. She was curvy but still in great shape.

He hugged me for a long time. "Every time I say good bye to you, my heart breaks a little. But when I see you again, I'm so happy."

I wanted to yell at him for interfering with my personal life and Zack but I didn't have the heart to do it then. He seemed so thrilled just to hold me. "I missed you too."

He pulled away then kissed my forehead. Then he looked down at my wrist, noticing the white gold bracelet I wore. He examined the moon and the stars. "Where did you get this?"

"Cayson gave it to me."

"It's nice." He nodded his head in approval.

I flipped it over and showed him the engraving.

He nodded again. "Very nice." He swallowed the lump in his throat like he was moved.

"What's wrong?"

His face immediately returned to normal. "I'm just happy my daughter is taken care of even when I'm not around. It's every father's dream come true." He stepped away so my mother could embrace me. Then he headed to Roland.

"I'm so happy you're here." My mom gave me a big smile then hugged me.

My mom was my favorite person in the world. She had a warmth about her that couldn't match anyone else. I loved my father just as much, but we were so similar that we butted heads constantly. I always wanted to be more like my mother, with the grace to forgive anyone for anything. To love and never hate. Like my father, I was headstrong and aggressive. My mom was the only person I knew who never let her emotions dictate her actions. "I missed you."

"I always miss you, honey." She pulled away then gave me an affectionate look. "You didn't kill each other on the drive?"

I shook my head. "We survived somehow. But Cayson beat me at every round of poker."

"Well, Uncle Mike taught him how to play. You never stood a chance, honey."

I laughed. "I guess not."

"I'll show you to your room."

"Am I sharing with Trinity?"

"No. You guys can have your own room."

"Cool," I said.

My dad grabbed my bags and carried them to my bedroom. Roland carried his own things.

It was small with just a twin bed. A window overlooked the back of the house. Tall trees were covered with patches of snow. Several blankets covered the bed. There was a closet and a single dresser.

"There's a bathroom down the hall," my dad said.

I made a face. "I have to share it with the boys?"

My mom laughed. "I'm sorry, dear."

"Ugh. I have a feeling I'm going to throw up at some point on this trip," I said.

"We're having dinner in an hour," my dad said.

"Ooooh…what are we having?" I asked.

"Pizza." My dad gave me a fond look. "Your favorite."

"Yes!" I rubbed my hands together greedily.

My dad chuckled. "My girls are so much alike."

My mom shrugged. "She has good taste."

"I know she does." My dad put his arm around her. "Let's let her get settled. We'll be downstairs."

"Okay."

They closed the door and disappeared.

I stared at my tiny bed and the hardwood floor. Sleeping alone would be lonely and cold. I wished Cayson was more of a daredevil like Slade and would just sneak in during the night. But he was too good for that.

My door opened and Cayson appeared. He stared at the small bed then at me. "My room is pretty small too."

"At least we don't have to share."

Cayson sat beside me on the bed. "I heard we're having pizza."

"Me too." I patted my stomach. "I'm starving."

"Like always," he teased.

"Where's your room?"

He stared at me suspiciously. "I don't think I should tell you…"

I hit his arm playfully. "Just tell me."

"Last door on the left."

"Where are the old people staying?" I asked.

"The third floor."

My eyes widened. "This place has three stories?"

He laughed. "Apparently."

I snuggled close to him. "Then they'll never know…"

He scooted away. "Don't even think about it, Skye."

"Come on. We've barely had any sex this week."

"Whose fault is that?" he asked.

I gave him my best puppy eyes.

"Forget it, Skye."

"Well, I'll just sneak into your room…"

"Don't even think about it. I'll throw you out on your ass so fast."

I rolled my eyes. "Why can't you be more like Slade?"

"I can't believe you just said that," he said with a laugh.

"I guess my hormones are doing all the talking."

"I can tell." A smirk was on his lips.

"Let's go down to dinner. I'm about to eat your lips if I don't get something in my stomach."

"Then let's go. I need these bad boys to kiss you."

Chapter Nineteen

Slade

Dinner was served at the long table. Ten boxes of pizza were ordered to feed everyone. Skye probably ate half of that herself because she's a fatty. My aunt Scarlet came in second place. I wasn't sure where they put all those calories because it didn't show.

Trinity and I didn't speak to one another. It was easier just to avoid each other. Just reading at the same time in the car sent out red flags. People were constantly watching us, finding any interaction between us to be abnormal. I never knew sleeping around with someone would be so difficult. If she weren't the best lay I ever had, I wouldn't bother.

At the end of the night, people drifted to their bedrooms. I was a night owl so I preferred staying up until the distant rays of the sun crested the horizon. My dad was the same way. He usually went to bed when my mom did, but I knew it was only to get laid. When she fell asleep, he got up and watched TV and drank beer. He'd been that way all through my childhood. Sometimes I wondered if he was an insomniac.

I poured myself a brandy then sat in the comfy armchair by the fire. My dad sat on the other couch, his glass in his hand.

"You excited for tomorrow?" he asked.

"Hell yeah. It's been too long since I've hit the slopes."

"Me too. Are you going to try to ski for once?"

"Duh. Only annoying, pretentious people ski."

He smirked. "I couldn't agree more." He drank his glass then refilled it. He rested his legs on the table, something he would never do if my mom were around.

"How's the shop?" I asked.

"Good. I'm thinking about opening another one in Times Square."

"Seriously?" I knew my dad was doing well, but damn.

"Tourists get crazy when they come to New York. They want it to be thrilling and exciting. It's a tourist trap."

"How are you going to work at two places at once?"

He gave me a serious look. "I figured I'd have my son run one of them."

My heart hammered in my chest. "Are you shitting me?"

"You're graduating soon. If it's still what you want to do, it's yours."

I sat up, my glass still in my hand. "That would be fucking awesome." My dad didn't care if I cursed. Actually, he was worse than I was.

"Are you sure it's what you want to do? You could pursue something with your degree, even continue your education."

I shook my head vigorously. "Inking is what I was meant to do. Why are you trying so hard to dissuade me from it?"

My dad drank from his glass then rested it on his knee. "It's not as glamorous as you think. There isn't a lot of respect for the institution. I love what I do but I've always felt like I wasn't good enough for your mom, an educated woman who works for a huge publishing house."

"Well, I don't care what people think. I never have."

Affection was in his eyes. "You have more wisdom than I give you credit for."

"I'm a genius but no one ever recognizes it." I rolled my eyes and put my feet on the table.

"You are a genius. But you get that from your mom."

"You're smart too."

He shrugged. "I have street smarts. Your mom is a bit of an airhead about that stuff."

"I'm going to tell her you said that." I smirked.

"Go ahead," he said. "I'll say it to her face."

My parents fought a lot but I never feared they would break up. It was obvious how much they loved each other even though it grossed me out most of the time.

"I'm thinking about getting another tat." I pulled up my shirt and pointed to the area over my ribs.

"What are you thinking?" he asked.

"I don't know. Something green. I think it would look cool."

"What about a tree?" My dad started talking with his hands. "Like, going up and curving around your side. A few leaves could be falling."

I nodded my head. "That sounds sick."

He shrugged.

"Why don't you have any tats, Dad?"

"I have this one." He held up his left hand. Around his ring finger was a tattoo of a black ring.

"Yeah, but that one is lame."

"Lame?" he asked with a laugh. "The fact I'm so committed to your mother that I permanently marked my skin so I can never remove it—even when death takes me? I think it's romantic as hell. So does your mother."

"I guess I don't do romance so it's not impressive to me."

"Still having fun I take it?"

"I told you, Dad. I'm a terminal bachelor."

"I said the same thing until I turned twenty-nine."

I raised an eyebrow. "What happened when you turned twenty-nine?"

"Your mother walked into my apartment." He finished his glass then poured another. He held his alcohol well, another reason why I looked up to him so much. He was a badass.

"And you just knew she was the one?" I asked incredulously. "I think that whole love at first sight thing is bullshit."

"I didn't say it was love at first sight," he said immediately. "The only things I noticed were her long legs and awesome rack. Don't get me wrong, all I wanted to do was fuck her."

I cringed. "I don't mind talking about my sex life, but I don't want to hear about yours…well, at least when it's about Mom. The others are okay."

He ignored my comment. "As soon as I got to know her, I was smitten. She was the best lay I ever had and I didn't want to have sex with anyone else. That's how I knew."

"You still feel that way? Twenty years later?"

He smirked. "Your mom has only gotten better with age."

I cringed again. "Anyway…I don't see me settling down for anybody."

"That will change."

"Nope." I finished my glass and poured another.

"All your uncles went through the same thing. And they all seem pretty happy."

"That's debatable…"

"Who are you juggling now?" he asked.

I usually had several girls at once. "Actually, just one." I'd never tell him it was Trinity. He wasn't just my dad, but my closest friend. But I knew how close he was to Trinity's father, Mike, and I wasn't stupid. My dad would beat the shit out of me if he knew what I was doing with her.

He cocked an eyebrow. "Just one?" Surprise was in his voice.

"She turned out to be pretty good in the sack. And she doesn't care that I'm just using her. Actually, she's using me just as much. And I don't have to make excuses to get away from her. I can be myself, and I don't have to worry about leading her on. She doesn't want a relationship any more than I do."

My dad processed my words for a long time. "How long has this been going on?"

I shrugged. "Over a month."

"And you haven't slept with anyone else?" he asked incredulously.

"No. Every time I think about it, I remember I have to wear a damn rubber. With this girl, I don't have to."

Alarm moved into his eyes. "Slade, don't fuck around like that. She could trick you into getting her pregnant."

"Believe me, she's not like that. I'm pretty sure she never wants to have kids—ever."

He calmed down slightly. "Still, be careful."

"I've known this girl for awhile. I trust her."

"Trust?" He stared me down. "You never trust people."

Was I making it obvious it was Trinity? "Well, I've known her all through college because we've had classes together. I know she's cool." *Did that cover my tracks?*

"And you only like having sex with her?"

"Well, she's really good and why would I go somewhere else when I know it's going to suck in comparison?"

My dad smirked at me, a knowing look in his eyes.

"What?"

"Nothing." He sipped his brandy and looked at the fire.

"I saw that look," I pressed.

"I think your bachelor days are almost over."

"No," I blurted. "Absolutely not. It's not what you think. Don't get your hopes up."

He shrugged. "I heard what I heard."

"Just because I'm sleeping with her now, doesn't mean I won't get tired of her and move on to someone else. I guarantee that will happen."

"You just said sex with anyone else wouldn't compare."

"For now."

He shook his head. "The definition of a monogamous relationship is when two partners only hook up with each other. And you've never been monogamous before..."

"I never said we were monogamous. We aren't. I just haven't slept with anyone. Big difference."

"Has she?"

"No."

"Would it bother you if she did?"

"I don't give a shit what she does," I blurted.

"Right..."

"What? I don't."

"Whatever you say, Son."

"I'm not lying," I argued.

My dad smirked but fell silent.

"You're a jackass."

"You're a cunt," he snapped.

I narrowed my eyes at him. "Go to hell."

"I'll see you there."

I leaned back in my chair and brooded.

"If you want that shop, you better be nicer to me."

"If you don't want me to tell Mom you drink like a camel, you better be nice to me."

He gave me a knowing look. "Your mother knows everything about me. I have no secrets from her."

"And she approves of you drowning your liver in alcohol?"

"She doesn't tell me what to do. Love is about accepting each other, not controlling each other. If I tried bossing her around, she'd slap me across the face."

"I know. I've seen it countless times."

My dad stared into the fire.

"You guys fight all the time…" The realization hit me hard.

"Yeah." He sounded bored.

"But…you guys still like to be around each other all the time." *Were Trinity and I like that?*

"Every relationship is different. But your mother and I are both headstrong and passionate. We fight a lot because we care so much. There are lines we never cross but we always speak our mind. Some people find it dysfunctional, and that's true, but it works for us. Believe me, even though I scream in her face, I love her more than I could ever put into words."

I processed his words for a moment. Then I sipped my drink. Trinity and I fought like we were going to battle. If we had guns, we would have blown each other to smithereens. We had no problem saying the most hurtful things to each other. But our sex was off the charts. *Did that mean something?*

"What are you thinking?" my father whispered.

My thoughts were shattered. I sipped my drink again and looked at the fire. "Nothing."

***

When I got back to my room, I texted Trinity. *Are you awake?*

Now I am.

Can I come over?

Our parents are upstairs.

Whatever. They aren't going to know.

It's risky…

Come on. I'm horny.

Slade, it's three in the morning. We're getting up in three hours.

Like I give a damn. I waited for her to respond. When she didn't, I texted her again. *I'll do that thing you like.*

There are a lot of things I like.

I'll do them all.

Fine. Make sure you aren't seen.

See you soon. I put my phone in my pocket then walked into the hallway. Just as I stepped out, I saw Skye step out in just a nightshirt. I froze, panicking. When she turned around, she saw me. Her eyes widened but she didn't say anything.

Fuck. Fuck. Fuck. *Why would I be up in the middle of the night?*

She stared at me then crossed her arms over her chest. "What are you doing?"

"What are *you* doing?" I countered.

"Um…"

I realized she was in front of Cayson's door. Then it hit me. "A midnight fuck?" I grinned at her.

"Shut up, Slade. Don't say anything."

"Maybe I will…maybe I won't."

"And what are *you* doing?" she demanded.

I went with the first excuse that came to mind. "Going to the bathroom."

She seemed to accept that. "Keep this to yourself."

"Then be nice to me."

"Go to hell." She walked into her bedroom then shut the door.

I stayed in the hallway, making sure she didn't come out again. Then I dashed into Trinity's room and shut the door quickly. The lights were off and I could barely see her. The outside light filtered through her window and allowed me to see her outline.

Wordlessly, I undressed then got into the bed with her.

"Be quiet," she said. "I share a wall with my brother."

"If he hears anything, just tell him you were fingering yourself."

"What makes you think I'm the loud one?" she demanded. "You're always the one moaning like you haven't had sex before."

"Shut up. Fucking bare pussy is totally different than regular sex."

She sighed. "Let's stop arguing and just screw already."

"Fine by me. I hate listening to you talk anyway."

"That makes two of us."

I moved on top of her then pulled her close to me. I slipped inside her without any problems. "You're already soaked."

She dug her nails into my back but didn't make a sound.

"I guess you wanted me more than you let on."

"Just shut up and fuck me."

Her words made my spine shiver. I pressed my face closer to hers and kissed her while I rocked into her. She breathed into my mouth while I breathed into hers.

Her pussy was the best damn thing in the world. It felt so good that I wanted to explode the moment we started. Her long legs wrapped around my waist, only arousing me more. I loved her legs more than any other feature. I loved how smooth and toned they were.

I moved in and out without shaking her bed. We were both deadly silent. She moved under me slightly, clearly enjoying it. When she tensed around me, I knew she was hitting her climax. I crushed my mouth against hers and tried to keep her moans down. She was particularly loud during an orgasm. I usually didn't mind because we were alone, but I definitely didn't want her brother to hear it. When she was finished, her breathing returned to normal and I let myself go. I didn't try to make it last longer because of our situation. I just wanted to get off and go to bed.

I rolled off her then lay beside her. We both breathed hard, catching our breath. Trinity sighed loudly, the sound she usually made when she was satisfied. We didn't speak, having nothing to say. I stared at the ceiling then felt my eyes grow heavy. Then I fell asleep.

***

A knock on the door made my eyes snap open.

"Trinity, are you awake?" It was her dad.

Fuck. Fuck. Fuck.

Trinity and I were snuggling so close together we were practically one person. Her body was wrapped around mine and my arms formed a solid cage around her. I quickly sat up then kicked the blanket away.

Trinity sat up and pulled the sheet over her. She looked at me with fear in her eyes. Too scared to speak and be overheard, we just spoke with our eyes.

She pointed underneath the bed. "Hide," she mouthed.

I got down then moved under the bed, pulling my clothes with me.

Fuck, I was a dead man.

Trinity quickly pulled a shirt on. "Come in, Dad."

The door opened and he stepped inside. I could see his feet as he moved across the hardwood floor. I prayed he didn't see me. He would strangle me then crack my skull open with his gorilla hands. My dad wouldn't be able to protect me. Shit, my mom wouldn't even be able to. She'd probably help him.

He sat on the edge of the bed, the mattress sinking under his weight.

I took a deep breath, trying not to be heard. My heart was pounding so fast I heard it in my ears.

"Morning, honey." He spoke with a gentle voice I never heard before. He was always so stern and deep all the time. He joked around a lot but there was always a threat in his eyes. He was the kind of guy I wouldn't want to see in a dark alley. He was generous and compassionate, but he was also murderous. But he didn't act that way at all with Trinity.

"Hey, Dad."

"Sleep well?"

"Yeah. It's peaceful up here." She also spoke in a tone I'd never heard before. It was quiet, almost submissive. Whenever she spoke to me or anyone else in our group, there was a fire in her voice. And there was always an attitude. But her father didn't get that tone from her.

"Your mom has always liked the snow. Whenever it falls at home, she never wants me to shovel it off the driveway…even though it makes it nearly impossible for me to get to work."

She chuckled lightly. "But she always gets her way."

"And so do you."

What the hell? I didn't realize they were so close.

"You ready to go skiing today?" he asked.

"I'm excited. But I really want a cup of hot cocoa from the lodge. It's my favorite."

"We'll get one together. How about that?"

"We can't break tradition, right?"

"Never," he said. "Are you hungry?"

"A little."

"You want me to bring you something?"

"No, it's okay. I'll go down there after I get ready."

"Okay, Honey."

I heard him kiss her on the cheek or forehead.

"I'll see you soon."

"Okay, Dad."

He got up and walked to the door. "I'm excited to spend time with you this weekend."

"Me too."

He shut the door.

I waited until I couldn't hear his footsteps anymore.

Trinity got up then locked the door.

I slid from under the bed then got dressed as quickly as possible. "Shit, that was close."

She rounded on me like she might kill me. "Why did you sleep here?"

"I don't know. I always sleep with you."

"What kind of argument is that?" she hissed.

"What? I was tired and fell asleep. Get off my case."

"*Get off your case*?" she snapped. "We almost got caught, you stupid idiot."

"Shut up, daddy's girl."

"Is that supposed to be offensive?" she asked incredulously.

"If you weren't such a daddy's girl, he wouldn't have come in here."

"Don't blame him for saying good morning to me! You should have been out of my room as soon as we were done."

"Just calm down, alright? We didn't get caught so shut the hell up."

"You shut up!" She slapped me across the face.

I took the hit then clenched my jaw. For some reason, inexplicably, it turned me on. I grabbed her face then shoved her against the wall. Even though neither one of us had brushed our teeth, I didn't care. I kissed her hard, and to no surprise, she kissed me back.

A knock on the door made us break apart.

Then they tried the doorknob. "Trinity, why is the door locked?" It was Skye.

Both of our eyes expanded to the size of orbs. Since I was right next to the closet, I got inside then she shut the door quickly.

Trinity opened the door. "I'm getting ready. What do you want?"

"Wow…talk about attitude. Not a morning person, huh?"

"Skye, what do you want?" she asked firmly.

"Have you seen Slade? His dad can't find him."

"Why would I know where he is?" She said it a little too quickly and a little too defensively.

"I'm just wondering. They can't find him anywhere."

"Well, I don't know where he is, alright?" She shut the door quickly then locked it again.

Fuck, could this day get any worse?

Trinity opened the closet and looked like she might murder me right on the spot.

"I'll go out the window and pretend I was playing in the snow," I blurted.

"But you're wearing what you wore yesterday." She sounded hysterical.

"It's me," I said quickly. "No one will question it."

She ran her hands through her hair in a panic. "If we get through this, I'm going to kill you."

"Well, if we don't get through this, your dad is going to kill me. So I'm dead either way."

"Good," she snapped.

I opened the window then peeked around. No one was out and about.

"Duck under all the windows so no one sees you," she whispered. "Just walk through the front door."

"You act like I've never escaped out of a girl's bedroom before."

"We're on the second story, Sherlock."

"I've had worse, trust me."

"Shut up and go." She slapped my ass.

"Did you just slap my ass?"

"Just go, Slade!"

I put one foot through then looked back at her. "I'm coming over tonight, right?"

Fire burned in her eyes. "That better be a fucking joke."

"So yes? Great. See you then." I crawled out and shut the window before she could scream at me.

I ducked as I moved around the roof, making sure no one could see me. Then I moved to the edge and peeked at the ground. It didn't seem like anyone was around. I slid down a pipe then landed in the snow.

I stood up and brushed it off, proud of myself for not getting caught.

"What are you doing?"

I stilled when I recognized my dad's voice. *Oh shit.* I turned around and smirked. "Practicing my parkour. What else would I be doing?" I tried to act as normal as possible.

"On the roof?" he asked incredulously.

"You know me, I like a challenge."

He stared at me like I was crazy. "At six in the morning?"

"When else would I have time to do it?"

My dad seemed to accept my story. "Sometimes I wonder if your mother drank when she was pregnant with you."

"I wouldn't put it past her. Or maybe your sperm was soaked in brandy and that's where the problem started."

He shook his head slightly.

"So, you wanted to see me?"

He cocked an eyebrow. "How did you know that?"

Fuck. Fuck. Fuck. "Why else would you be outside? You must have seen me practicing." *Please buy it.*

He did. "I wanted to order our gear before we got to the resort. What size are you?"

Seriously? I jumped off a roof just because he wanted to know what size shoe I wore? "Eleven." I tried not to let my anger come out.

'Thanks." He took out his phone then made the call.

I rolled my eyes and walked inside.

Everyone was sitting at the table eating breakfast. When Trinity saw me, she glanced at me then looked to her food. I sat at the end of the table and piled food onto my plate. No one questioned where I was. And I ate like I didn't just almost die.

***

We got our equipment from the front then stood in a circle.

"Baby, Slade and I are heading to a black diamond." He kissed my mom quickly then pulled away.

"Be careful, Ryan." My mom gave him a look like she would kill him if he didn't come back alive.

"Mom, we'll be fine," I said. "We know what we're doing. Have fun on those sticks you call skis."

"Skis are a lot harder than snowboarding," Silke argued.

"No, they aren't. A two-year-old could ride on those," I snapped.

"Let's go before the kids pull each other's hair," my dad said.

"Good idea," my mom said. She wore a green beanie and her long blonde hair stuck out underneath.

"Be careful," he said to her.

"Dad, they'll be on the bunny hill. They'll be just fine," I said.

My dad held his board with one arm. "Let's go."

Everyone else was sticking with their parents. My dad and I were the only ones who preferred snowboarding over skiing. We were cool like that. We moved to the chair lift then let it take us to the very top of the mountain.

"You want to race?" I asked.

"Not really."

"Scared?" I teased.

"I just don't want to hurt your feelings. I know how sensitive you are."

I slugged him in the arm.

"Was that supposed to hurt?" he said sarcastically.

"Go to hell, Dad."

We reached the slope far in the back then finally got off the lift. Like pros, we moved off the lift easily then rode our boards out of the way of other people. We stopped when we reached a good part to drop in at. It was almost a cliff face. I smirked in excitement.

"I can't believe you aren't wearing a jacket."

"It's not even cold. It's sunny as hell."

"You should still wear one."

"Then how will anyone see my tats?" I argued.

"Maybe you should put them on your face if that's all you care about," he snapped.

I shrugged. "I guess that would be cool."

He rolled his eyes then buckled himself in. "Ready?"

I checked my boots then strapped myself in. "Let's do this."

"You first."

"Dad, you don't have to trail behind me. I'm a big boy."

"I like to know where you are. There's no reception up here."

"Whatever, Dad." I moved forward then pushed my weight into the dive. I picked up speed as soon as I took off. Like I'd done it a million times, I cut through the snow, shredding the fresh powder. My dad was close behind me. I could see him in my peripheral vision. He was pretty good, just as good as I was. There's no one I'd rather go with than my dad. He was the only one who could keep up with me.

I was going fast down the slope, faster than I ever had. It made me feel alive, exhilarated. When I cut through the snow, I felt like I could do anything. I didn't think about school or life. I just thought about the moment I was in. Personally, that's how I thought life should be lived.

When I reached hard snow that was practically slush, I lost control then slipped down the mountain. I was going so fast that I couldn't stop. I dug my board in to slow down but it was too hard. It must be an area where it melted overnight and refroze as ice. There was no friction so I kept going. I dug my hand into the snow so I would stop. My skin burned from scraping against the ice.

When I flew off the trail and into the trees, I started to panic. I'd never done that before.

Fuck. Fuck. Fuck.

When I was about to hit a tree, I managed to swerve out of the way.

Shit, that was close.

"Slade, I'm right behind you!"

My dad was there. *Thank god.* "I can't stop!"

"Dig your board into the snow!"

"What do you think I'm doing?" I screamed.

"Slade! Stop! Cliff!"

Shit, did he just say cliff?

Fuck. I tried to grab onto anything.

All of a sudden, I felt something heavy land on top of me. I was pulled to an immediate halt. I felt hands grip both of my arms.

"Son, are you alright?"

I looked up and my dad was looking down at me with concern in his eyes. His nose was bloody.

"Yeah…I'm fine." I sat up then rubbed my head. "What happened?"

"I landed on you." He said it like it was no big deal.

"How did you manage that?"'

"I don't know. I wasn't thinking. There's a cliff fifty feet away. If I didn't do something, you were going to fall."

Holy shit.

He wiped the blood from his nose then caught his breath.

"Thanks…"

"Yeah. Be a little more careful next time."

"I don't know what happened. I just hit an ice patch."

Then I heard a sound that made me even more terrified than I've ever been in my life.

A bear roared.

My father and I both moved to our feet with a quickness that belied our ability. Twenty feet away was an enormous grizzly bear. He was on his hind legs and didn't look happy to see us.

Could this get any worse?

"Give me your lighter." My dad said it calmly.

"Why?"

"JUST DO IT!"

I dug my hand into my pocket then threw it at him. "What the fuck are you going to do with it?"

My dad cracked a branch off a tree then held the lighter to it. It caught flame in a few seconds. Then my dad marched to the bear with the stick raised. The bear started to back away. My dad swung it at the beast, the heat searing its fur. Then it turned around and ran away.

My dad turned around then dropped the branch in the snow. "Let's get back to the slopes. Now."

I didn't need to be told twice. I grabbed my board then walked alongside my father, looking around to make sure we were alone. When we made it back to the main lift area, I started to breathe again.

I looked at my dad. "We almost died. Twice."

"Say a word to your mother and I will kill you."

"Your secret is safe with me."

"Good." He ran his fingers through his hair but he still seemed calm. My dad saved my ass twice and he didn't even freak out over it. It was like nothing phased him.

"Dad, you're a badass."

He looked at me, his eyes dark. "No. But I would give my life for my son. It's called being a parent." Seriousness was in his voice.

We stood there, saying nothing. No other riders were on the slope. We were there alone, listening to the silence.

"Want to hit the bunny hill?" I asked.

He laughed. "I thought you'd never ask."

Chapter Twenty

Trinity

We spent the entire day skiing. My brother was pretty good and so was my father. My dad grew up skiing so he was practically a pro. My mom had never skied before she met my dad, so she and I sucked equally.

My ass was sore from falling down more often than standing up. Every time I fell, my dad waited for me to get back on my feet. I would slide down a few feet before my face was in the snow again. My dad showed me a few tricks but I could never grasp it. By the time we went to the lodge and had lunch and cocoa, I was exhausted. My brother and I didn't even argue because we were so tired. I needed a nice nap right then.

When the sun went down, we finally returned to the house. Everyone else was already back, probably passed out on the couch or asleep in their beds. The first thing I did was take a shower to warm up. Then I went downstairs and shoveled twice as much food as I normally would onto my plate. I sat down on the couch and ate quietly, too exhausted to talk to my family.

A lot of people were in the other living room, watching TV. But I sat on the couches in front of the fireplace, enjoying the silence. I could practically hear my muscles screaming because they were so exhausted.

My dad sat in the seat next to me, his plate in his hand. "You doing okay?"

"Just exhausted."

He nodded. "Skiing is harder than it looks."

"But I think I'm more tired from falling than actually skiing." I laughed at my own comment.

"You'll get better."

I noticed my dad always teased everyone else mercilessly. He was particularly harsh with his own brother. But when it came to me, he treated me in a different way. He never teased me when I failed at something. He always tried to make me feel better. He wasn't that way with Conrad, just me. "Dad, it's okay to say it. I know I suck."

"I never said you didn't. But you will get better."

At least he didn't lie to me. I ate my potato salad then moved on to my chicken.

"How's school going?"

"It's okay."

He ate quietly and slowly. "Have you decided what you want to do yet?" He stared at his plate while he said it.

"I want to go into fashion. There's no doubt about that."

"Then are you going to drop out?"

"No," I said with a sigh. "I'm almost done. I'd rather finish."

"Honey, do whatever you want. Don't worry about pissing me off."

"You spent so much money on my—"

"And you know I don't care about that. Don't let money be a factor."

"But I might be able to use my business degree for what I want to do."

"Which is?"

"Running my own clothing line."

He nodded. "It will be helpful. And your old man has a lot of experience to help you." He gave me a smile before turning his attention back to his food.

"Not according to Uncle Sean," I teased.

"Well, that guy is an idiot. Don't listen to him."

I finished my food then left the plate on the table.

"There's pie. Do you want me to get you a piece?" he asked.

"No. As odd as this sounds, I'm too tired to eat."

He chuckled. "You need to exercise more often."

"I jog."

"Not the same. You need to do some weight training."

"I don't even know the difference between a bench press and a squat."

"I can show you," my dad offered.

"Nah. I'll stick to running on a treadmill."

My dad finished his food. "Did you finish that book I gave you?"

"I did."

"Did you like it?"

"Actually, I did."

He crossed his foot at the ankle. "We should watch the movie sometime. It's a classic."

"Sure." I settled into the couch and pulled my knees to my chest.

My dad grabbed a blanket then placed it over me, tucking me in like he used to when I was a child.

"Thanks."

"Yeah." He stared at the fire while he rested his hands in his lap. "Anything new in your life?"

I immediately thought of Slade. I spent a lot of time with him, more than I expected to. "No, not really. Skye and Cayson bring a lot of drama to the group but that's not surprising."

"Well, Skye is Sean's daughter," he teased.

I laughed. "She can be too stubborn sometimes."

"Just like her dad."

"But they're good together," I said. "I know they're going to last forever."

"You think?" he asked.

"I know." I was jealous when I thought about it. Skye had a guy that loved her more than life itself.

"You're going to find that someday too." It was like my dad could read my mind.

"You think?" I was already twenty-two and I hadn't found anyone who came close.

"I know. You're a beautiful girl who's smart and fun. Believe me, you have admirers even if you don't know it."

The only admirer I had was a tattooed bad boy that just wanted to have sex. "Maybe."

"No, not maybe." He said it firmly.

I decided not to argue with him.

"I finished your book," he said.

"How did you like *The Count of Monte Cristo*?"

"It was good. Too many characters to keep track of but good."

"Totally different than the movie, huh?" I asked.

"Yeah. But I like the ending in the movie more."

I gave him a smile. "I did too. I'm a sucker for happy endings."

"I guess I am too." His hand moved through my hair for a second before he dropped it.

Companionable silence stretched between us. We could spend hours sitting together without saying anything. It wasn't awkward at all. Skye and I did the same thing countless times. My dad was my dad, he always would be, but he was also my friend. I knew he babied me a lot. When it came to Conrad, my dad was strict and firm. He pushed him a lot more than he pushed me simply because Conrad was a man. Sometimes I wished he didn't do it, but there were times when I absolutely loved it. My dad had unique and special relationships with each of us. I never felt like he loved me more or less than my brother.

My eyes were growing heavy and I couldn't keep them open anymore. "I'm sorry, Dad. I'm so tired…"

"It's okay, honey. Go to sleep."

***

My phone vibrated on my nightstand and woke me up. I was tucked in my bed. I was wearing what I wore earlier except my shoes were gone. My dad must have carried me up and put me to bed. That wasn't surprising.

I squinted at the clock and realized it was three in the morning. Then I looked at my phone.

Are you awake? It was Slade.

Stop waking me up in the middle of the night! I'm tired.

And I'm horny. Cry me a river.

Good night, Slade. Leave me alone. I turned off my phone so he wouldn't wake me up again.

Just as I fell asleep, my bedroom door opened.

Ugh.

Slade took off his clothes then got into bed beside me. "Hey," he whispered.

"We have to wake up in three hours. I'd rather go to sleep than have sex."

"I didn't come here to have sex. I want to talk."

Did I hear him right? "What?"

"You'll never guess what happened to my dad and I today. We almost died—twice."

I sat up. "What?"

Slade told me he almost fell off a cliff but his dad saved him. And then a bear almost ate them but his dad used his lighter to scare it off.

It was almost too ridiculous to believe. "Are you making this up?"

"No! Don't tell my mom. My dad doesn't want her to know."

"But...that's crazy."

"I know! I almost died twice in one day. It was so awesome."

"Awesome?" I asked incredulously.

"How many people can say something like that?"

"How many people *want* to say something like that?"

"I just had to tell you."

"Me? Why me?"

"Because..." He seemed to be at a loss for words. "I don't know. I just wanted to tell you."

Silence stretched between us but it was a little tense.

"How was your day?" he asked.

Slade never asked me stuff like that. I turned on my side and faced him in the darkness. His hand rested on my hip. "It was okay. I suck at skiing."

"What's new?"

I hit his arm lightly.

He chuckled. "It's okay. I can teach you if you want."

"No, it's fine. My dad shows me but I just don't get it. I've fallen on my face so many times that it's sore as hell."

"Your face?" he asked incredulously. "Is it even possible for it to be sore?"

"Yes, it is," I said firmly. "I just found that out. And my ass is killing me."

"That's sore too?" he asked.

"Yeah."

Slade undid my jeans and pulled them off.

"What are you doing?"

"Who the hell sleeps in jeans?"

"Who the hell doesn't wear a jacket in the snow?" I countered.

His hand moved to my ass and he started to massage it.

I winced in pain then it started to feel amazing. I moaned quietly and closed my eyes.

"Your ass is really tense."

"I'm not surprised," I said with a sigh.

He rubbed the other cheek then moved down to my thighs.

"You're good at that. You should be a masseuse."

"I know the female body pretty well." He gave me a cocky wink.

"Shut up, Slade."

He chuckled then kept rubbing me. "Other than that, how was your day?"

"Well, it wasn't as exciting as running away from a grizzly bear and almost falling off a cliff."

"Well, your day will never be as exciting as mine was," he said with a laugh.

"The highlight of my day was when my father and I got hot cocoa and discussed the books we just finished reading."

"Wow…that's lame."

I hit him in the arm.

"You want me to stop rubbing you?" he snapped.

I quickly rubbed his arm. "Please don't stop."

He smirked. "I've heard you say that several times—but in a very different context."

"Go to hell, Slade."

He laughed then rubbed my calves.

"It's nice to talk about stuff like that with my dad. We discuss politics and economics, and we talk about fictitious characters and storylines. I can't have those kinds of conversations with anyone else but him."

Slade stared at me for a long time. "You guys are really close."

"Yeah…"

"It's actually really cute."

"Cute?" That was the second time he used that word.

"Yeah. I've known Uncle Mike my whole life and he's always been fun and aggressive. He tells more jokes than my dad. He's the life of the party but he can be a brute like a gorilla. But when he's alone with you...he's totally different. He's gentle, quiet, and thoughtful. He treats you like....like a princess."

"Pretty much," I whispered.

"And you're different around him too, a completely different person."

"You mean I'm myself?"

"Is that the real you?" he asked. "Because I've never seen it before. You're always so sarcastic and have a hot-headed attitude."

"Well, I know my dad would never hurt me. It's totally different. He would never make fun of me for saying something stupid. I can say anything and he won't judge me."

He stopped rubbing me. "You can say anything to me... We talk about books and stuff."

I eyed him, unsure of his meaning. "What are you saying?"

He was quiet for a long time. "I'm not sure what I'm saying, actually."

I didn't either.

"I guess...I feel like I could tell you anything." He didn't look at me when he said it. His hands rubbed me again, removing the aches and sores.

When I thought about it in retrospect, I realized I told Slade a lot more than I told anyone else. Perhaps this arrangement brought us closer together as friends. I was close to everyone in my circle, especially Skye who was my best friend, but I never told her any of that. "I could tell you anything too."

He looked into my eyes. "Wow…I never thought this would happen."

"What?"

"You're like…a really good friend to me. Cayson has always been my best friend but…I don't tell him every thought that runs through my head. With you, I do."

"Are you saying I'm your best friend?" I asked.

"I guess. Isn't that what a best friend is?" he asked. "Someone you can say anything to? You can be yourself without any fear of judgment or repercussion?"

"Yeah…" That's exactly how I described my relationship with my father.

He shrugged. "I guess sleeping together was the best decision we ever made."

My hand moved to his bicep, the muscle I grabbed more often than not. Slade had a particular smell to him, cologne mixed with his natural scent. I recognized it so well that I could tell where he sat on a couch even after he left the room. I'd grown accustomed to his company. We spent over half the week in the same bed. Now I was used to his morning routines before we left for school. He always made toast in the toaster then left new bread inside so all I had to do was turn it on. I hated him for the longest time but…now I really cared about him. "I think you're right."

Chapter Twenty-One

Skye

I hadn't cornered my dad about the episode with Zack. We were having a lovely weekend hitting the slopes and bundling up to stay warm. There was never a good time to unleash my rage.

After spending most of the day on the hill, we headed to the ski resort for lunch. We grabbed our trays and piled them with food. Naturally, my tray had the most items.

My brother eyed it. "You're such a fat ass."

"No, I'm not," I argued. "I've been running around all day."

"Maybe your ass will get smaller then." He walked to a table near the fire and sat down.

I held my tongue and imagined ripping his eyes out.

"He teases you because he loves you." My mom stood behind me while my dad pulled out his wallet and paid for the meal.

"Mom, I know you're right about a lot of stuff…but this time you aren't."

She smirked. "Your uncle Ryan and I are the same way."

"You guys tease each other in a completely different way."

My mom laughed. "Actually, we don't."

We took a seat at the table. Roland was already eating his pizza and fries.

My dad had a salad, like usual, and my mom was eating a burrito.

I ordered a hot cocoa because it was freezing outside. The sun was out most of the day but then the sky became hazy with clouds. A few snowflakes sprinkled the ground.

My dad eyed my mom. "You like your food, baby?"

She already ate half of it. "It's delicious. How's your…salad?" She smirked while she stared at it.

He grinned. "It's…decent."

She laughed. "You look like a man but you eat like a rabbit."

"But you like the way I look, right?" he asked. "And I don't want you to run off anywhere…"

"Like she would," Roland said. "You'd put a bullet in her new man's head."

I knew my brother wasn't joking. That honestly sounded like something Dad would do.

My dad gave him a dark look. "Don't joke about stuff like that."

"Because you're afraid Mom will cheat on you?" he asked.

"No." My dad remained calm. "Guns aren't a good subject over lunch."

"And you talking about having sex with Mom is?" Roland questioned.

"Shut up and eat your food, Roland Preston." My dad stared at him from across the table.

That shut my brother up.

"I don't want to go home," my mom said with a sigh.

"We can stay," my dad blurted. He'd do anything to make her happy.

"No," she said. "You need to get back to work. I'm more sad about the kids heading back to school."

I wasn't looking forward to it either. I loved spending time with my parents, even if they were a little annoying and overly affectionate sometimes.

"I hate school," Roland said. "The only good about it are the girls."

"But don't you prefer them married?" my dad jabbed.

Roland rolled his eyes. "I'm never going to live that one down…"

"Probably not," my dad said.

My mom shook her head slightly. "We all make mistakes as we age. But you better not repeat that one."

Roland shoved his pizza into his mouth and stayed quiet.

"Have you seen Cayson much this weekend?" my mom asked.

Just at night. "No. We've been busy with our families all day. But that's fine. I see him every day at school."

"So, everything is great between you two?" my mom asked. "Because your father and I really love Cayson."

"Who doesn't?" I blurted. "Yeah, we're great."

"When Skye isn't fucking it up left and right," Roland said with a mouthful of food.

I kicked him under the table.

"Argh!" He kicked me back.

"Fucking it up?" My dad raised an eyebrow while looking at me. "What's that mean, Skye?"

Great. My brother put me right on the spot. "We've had a few fights…nothing major."

"You almost dumped him," Roland said.

"Why don't you shut up and mind your own business?" I kicked him as hard as I could under the table.

"Bitch," he mumbled.

My dad's hand snatched his throat from across the table quicker than I could see. He pulled Roland toward him and lowered his voice. "Never talk to your sister like that again." He released him then leaned back.

Roland would normally argue but this time he didn't.

Awkwardness set in at the table.

My dad knew we teased each other often, but there were certain rules he had. We weren't allowed to say anything unforgiveable or hateful to one another. Everything else was fair game.

"Anyway…" My mom cleared her throat. "Skye, is that true? You almost dumped him?"

When I looked at my dad, I felt my anger come out. "Cayson betrayed my trust and tattled on me to Dad about Zack. I'm perfectly capable of taking care of myself and handling my own problems. But Cayson seemed to disagree. I told him I couldn't be with someone I didn't trust implicitly. We quickly made up and moved on."

"Such a stupid thing to get upset about," Roland mumbled. "He was just looking out for you."

My dad kept a stoic expression on his face. I couldn't tell what he was thinking. "He did the right thing coming to me. I wouldn't want him to be with you if he made any other judgment call."

"You and everyone else I know," I mumbled.

"I made sure Zack will never bother you again," my father said. "Now Cayson and I can both get some sleep at night."

"He was never a threat to me," I snapped.

"Cayson didn't agree. And I'd take Cayson's opinion over yours any day." His eyes narrowed while he stared me down.

When it came to this topic, my dad was aggressive and mean. He always pinned me down and wouldn't let me get the upper hand. Just like me, he was stubborn and argumentative. He would never let me win, no matter what, and he would put his foot down over and over. He had the patience of a sloth and the adrenaline of a coyote.

"Than your own daughter's?" I snapped.

"I admire your independence and intelligence. I really do." My dad's voice was calm the entire time. We were in a crowded room full of people so he acted normal, like we were discussing the lotto numbers that were announced the evening before. But his eyes gave his rage away. "I would never want you to be any different. Just like your mother, you're strong and understand your self-worth. But you're blind to your own safety and foolishly think you're invincible. You have no idea what this guy is thinking, and as strong as you might think you are, he's twice your size and could take you down with one throw of a fist.

"You know why I'm such a successful businessman?" He asked it like a question but I knew it was rhetorical. "How I grew a large company into an international empire? It's because I'm proactive, not reactive. I don't take chances when it comes to stuff like this. I'm always on the offense, not the defense. If this guy isn't leaving you alone and he held down Trinity—a fucking red flag—then I don't want him anywhere near you. Being angry with Cayson is immature and petty. You're lucky he loves you as much as he does to put up with your naivety. Not all men are like me, your uncles, your cousins, and Cayson. There are men who will rip you apart the first chance they get. It's a lesson I thought you already learned."

I looked away and stared at the fire in the stone hearth. My dad always got under my skin when he made speeches like this. He never got emotional, but he did get angry. He somehow reduced me to a shadow, stripping my confidence and my strength. He did it every time, leaving me defenseless and raw.

"Don't be so hard on her," my mother whispered.

"Baby, stay out of this." His voice was full of threat.

My mother backed off.

I left the table and abandoned my food then stormed outside. I didn't want to look at my father or my family. I wanted to hide my face. Moisture bubbled under my eyes and they burned as they touched my cheek. I finally made it outside and stood away from the windows, getting some privacy.

I hated crying. It was weak and pathetic. I quickly wiped the tears away, refusing to be anything but strong. Sometimes I felt like I was screaming as loud as I could but no one was listening. I was lucky I had a father who cared so much about me, but for once, I wanted him to trust me enough to take care of myself. He treated Roland that way. Why should I be treated differently?

The door opened again and I felt someone come near me. Judging by the cologne in the air, I knew it was my father.

I turned my back to him, not letting him see the redness around my eyes. I should have held my tongue and not gone head-to-head with him in the middle of a crowded room. It wasn't smart to corner him when we were on a family trip. Perhaps I was stupid after all.

My father stood behind me but didn't touch me. "Skye, I'm sorry I upset you."

"You didn't." I said it with a strong voice, hiding my vulnerability. "I just needed to get away from you."

"Then why are you crying?"

How did he know that? I decided not to answer.

He came closer to me then rested his hand on my shoulder. "Skye, I love you so much. Please know that everything I say comes from a good place."

"I know…"

He sighed then dropped his hand. "Pumpkin, look at me."

Since he already knew I was upset, I turned around and faced him head on.

He stared at the redness around my eyes. He took a deep breath, the self-loathing coming into his features.

"I'm sorry I made you cry. Please tell me what you're thinking."

"I'm just sick of you babying me, Dad. I can take care of myself but how will I prove that if you won't let me?"

"I know you can take care of yourself. I've always known that."

"It doesn't seem like it."

"You know what our problem is—both of us?"

I crossed my arms over my chest and listened.

"I'm too overprotective—I admit it. But you're too proud."

"Proud?"

"You will never ask for help even if you're drowning. That's the reason why I'm like this. You're so determined to do everything on your own that I fear you won't reach out to me or anyone else for that matter when you need to. And that scares the life out of me, Skye."

I processed his words then looked at the ground.

"Correct me if I'm wrong."

I knew he wasn't.

"Does that explain my behavior a little better?"

I nodded.

"Do you honestly see Zack as nonthreatening? Be honest, Skye."

He did threaten to hurt Cayson but I thought he was just being an ass. And he did hold down Trinity. And he did spend six months lying to me just to be with me. He was controlling when we were together, trying to get me to follow his rules. Perhaps he had psychopath written all over him. Maybe I was wrong about the whole thing. "No…"

My dad didn't gloat. There was no victory in his eyes. "Then I'm really glad Cayson came to me. But Skye, it should have been you."

"I know… I just…you've babied me my whole life and—"

"You're my one and only daughter. I can't begin to explain how much I love you. I understand you're going to get hurt. That's how life is. As much as it pains me, I accept that truth. But when it comes to stuff like this, serious stuff, I have to intervene."

"I know, Dad."

"I promise I'll be better from now on. If you ask me to back off and leave you alone, I promise I will. But I want a promise in return."

"What promise?" I asked.

"That you will come to me when you need help. You will not be proud and try to figure it out while you're drowning. You will not try to prove anything to me. Skye, you've already proven how amazing and self-sufficient you are. I don't need anything else."

I nodded.

"Can I have that promise? I know you'll mean it if you give it to me."

"I promise."

He breathed a sigh of relief. "Thank you."

"I'm sorry, Dad…about everything."

"I'm sorry too, Pumpkin." He came to me then held me close. "But I'm glad this happened. I feel like we've really covered new ground here. I feel a lot more comfortable knowing you'll make the right decisions even if I'm not around."

"And I'm glad you know I can take care of myself."

"You're just like your mother." He cupped the back of my head with his hand and held me close. "In every good way possible."

"That's a big compliment."

"It was meant as one."

He pulled away then stepped back. "Are you ready to head back inside?"

"Yeah. I want to finish the rest of my food."

He laughed. "That's my girl."

***

Cayson and I sat in front of the fire with cups of cocoa.

"How was your day?" he asked.

"It was okay. My dad and I got into a fight."

"It seems like that's all you ever do," he teased.

"Well, we are a lot alike."

He smirked. "And I know how you are…"

"We talked about the whole Zack thing."

"I'm sure that went well," he said sarcastically.

"He made a lot of good points…but I think we're better off because of it. He made me realize how proud I am."

"Wow…you finally admit it."

I gave him a hard look.

"Sorry," he said quickly.

"And he admitted he's too overprotective. We agreed to work on our shortcomings."

He nodded. "A compromise…I like it."

I sipped my hot cocoa then tried to get a few marshmallows into my mouth. The fire burned in front of us and snow fell outside. Everyone had gone to bed already. It was just he and I.

"No sex tonight," he said quietly. "It's a miracle we haven't gotten caught."

"It's our last night and it's so romantic. Let's just do it."

"No. I feel like I'm going to have a heart attack every time your father looks at me."

"He's not a mind reader," I snapped.

"He could be. Maybe he developed some technology that allows him to do that."

"My dad is smart...but not *that* smart."

"I'd rather not risk it."

"I'll sneak into your room anyway. And when I start doing stuff you like, you won't be able to get rid of me."

He glared at me. "You're such an evil enchantress."

I smirked. "I know."

We heard footsteps from the stairs and were joined by Theo and Thomas.

"Hey." Theo had a leftover slice of cold pizza in his hand.

"Hey," I said. "How was your day on the slopes?"

"I got sunburned," Theo said. "Can you believe it?"

"I told you to put on sunblock, man." Thomas sat on the couch then sunk into it.

"Well, I never listen to you for a reason," Theo said.

Then Silke joined us. "Why is everyone awake?"

"We're plotting to kill you," Theo said without looking at her.

"That's so ironic because I was planning to do the same to you." She held a pint of ice cream and started to eat directly out of it.

"So much for a romantic evening by the fire," Cayson said sarcastically.

"Go upstairs and screw like snow bunnies," Theo said. "What's more romantic than that?"

I gave Cayson a flirtatious look. "I couldn't agree more."

He ignored my comment and stared at the fire.

Slade came downstairs with Trinity. "It's a full house tonight."

"Why are you two together?" I asked.

"We aren't." Slade took eight steps away from Trinity. "It was just a coincidence."

"An unfortunate one." Trinity looked through the fridge until she found a leftover sandwich. Slade dug out his own then joined us in the living room.

"Why are we all huddled here?" Slade asked.

I shrugged. "Cayson and I wanted some alone time…but we clearly aren't going to get it."

"Like fucking in the middle of the night isn't alone time," Slade snapped.

I glared at him. "So much for keeping quiet about it."

"Hey, I didn't tell any of the old people," he argued. "They are the only ones that count. None of us give a shit."

Roland and Conrad came down the stairs next.

"You guys are talking so loud that I can't sleep." Roland plopped down on the armchair by the fire and started to rock it back and forth.

Conrad took a seat on one of the couches. "I'm so glad we're going home tomorrow."

"Why?" Trinity asked.

"I'm sick of seeing Mom and Dad," Conrad said. "Dad keeps talking about the company and what I need to be prepared for. And then Mom keeps bugging me about settling down with a nice girl who will give her grandkids. I'm only twenty-one. Give me a break…"

"I don't want to go home," I said. "I like seeing my parents."

"Me too," Cayson added.

"You guys are the worst suck ups ever," Silke said.

"I'm not sucking up," I said. "I really do like my parents."

She rolled her eyes. "Whatever."

"I want to order a beer and wings," Slade said. "And watch a game. All they have is cable here."

"It's nice to take a break from the rest of the world," I said.

"God, you're annoying," Slade said.

Trinity ate her sandwich. "I'm horrible at skiing so I'm not too upset to leave the resort. But I will miss my parents."

"Another suck up," Silke said.

We fell into comfortable silence by the fireplace. Cayson held me close to him and wrapped his arm around my shoulder. My hot cocoa was abandoned for his warmth. Theo fell asleep and started to snore. Silke pulled out her phone and was typing away. Roland started to snore when he dozed off. It was late so we should have gone to bed but nobody moved. Just being together was comfortable enough. We were together constantly, but there was a reason for that. We were family, allowed to be ourselves in front of one another and still be loved. It was something I took for granted once in a while. But when we took trips like this, knowing exactly where we belonged, I cherished it. A lot of people hardly had any family in the world. But I had a huge one. And even though they teased me relentlessly and often told me to shut up, I knew they loved me.

And they always would.

You Are All I'll Ever Need

Book Three Of The Forever and Ever Series

AVAILABLE DECEMBER 22TH

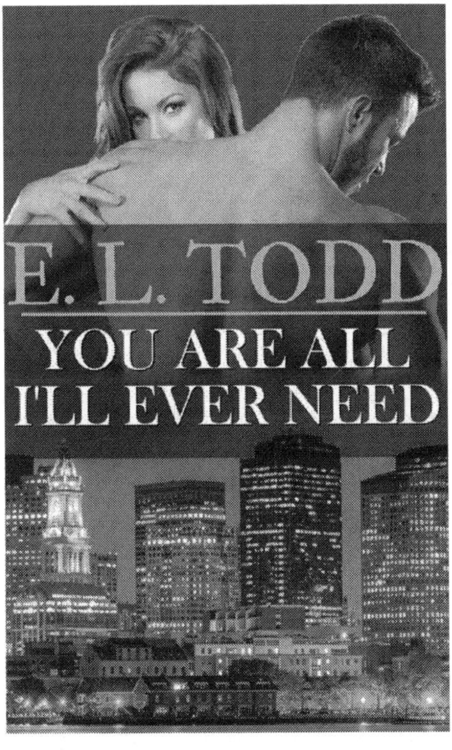

Dear Reader,

Thank you for reading If Loving You Is Wrong. I hope you enjoyed reading Skye and Cayson's story as much as I enjoyed writing it. If you could leave a short review on Amazon.com, iTunes, or BarnesandNoble.com, it would help me so much! Those reviews are the best kind of support you can give an author. Thank you!

Wishing you love,

E. L. Todd

Please Show Your Support

Like E. L. Todd on Facebook:

https://www.facebook.com/ELTodd42?ref=hl

Follow E. L. Todd on Twitter:

@E_L_Todd

Subscribe to E. L. Todd's Newsletter:

www.eltoddbooks.com

Other Works By

E. L. Todd

Alpha Series

Sadie
Elisa
Layla
Janet
Cassie

Hawaiian Crush Series

Connected By The Sea
Breaking Through The Waves
Connected By The Tide
Taking The Plunge
Riding The Surf
Laying in the Sand

Forever and Always Series

Only For You
Forever and Always
Edge of Love
Force of Love
Fight For Love
Lover's Roulette
Happily Ever After
The Wandering Caravan
Come What May

Again and Again
Lover's Road
Meant To Be
Here and Now
Until Forever
New Beginnings
Love Conquers All
Love Hurts
The Last Time
Sweet Sins
Lost in Time
Closing Time

Southern Love

Then Came Alexandra
Then Came Indecision
Then Came Absolution
Then Came Abby
Abby's Plight

59606716R00182

Made in the USA
Lexington, KY
10 January 2017